Oliver Swindler wanted to return to is idyllic roots in the small town where he was raised. Murder had other plans for him.

Peter Loewer's cinematic debut mystery, set in the mountains of Western North Carolina, delivers a great cast of characters!

—Jon Mayes, founder, "Advance Reading Copy,"
the literary blog about books, authors, and publishing

Rich folk are seeking refuge, but bring the ills of their world with them. Ordinary folk just want a familiar place that stays the same. Fernglade native Oliver Swindler, unhappy with life in the big city, just wants a quiet place to call home and a garden to cultivate, but is charged with solving a mystery in a process that will change all the things he's come to value in his community.

Peter Loewer excels at bringing this small town to life. Yes, this is a murder mystery; but beyond that, it's an excellent inspection of the social and political currents that affect the town's citizen's lives and Oliver's choices, placing the backdrop of the murder in as important a position as the social conflict itself.

The Last of the Swindlers is a vivid story of not just investigations, but shifting interpersonal relationships. It will prove thoroughly absorbing and satisfyingly complex to the end.

—Diane Donovan, Editor, *California Bookwatch*
Midwest Book Review

Pisgah Press was established in 2011 to publish and promote works of quality offering original ideas and insight into the human condition, the realm of knowledge, and the world around us.

Published by Pisgah Press, LLC
PO Box 9663, Asheville, NC 28815
www.pisgahpress.com

Cover design: Jean Jenkins

Library of Congress Cataloging-in-Publication Data
Loewer, Peter.
The Last of the Swindlers/Loewer

Library of Congress Control Number: 2020950755

ISBN: 978-1-942016557
Mystery/Fiction

First Edition
May 2021

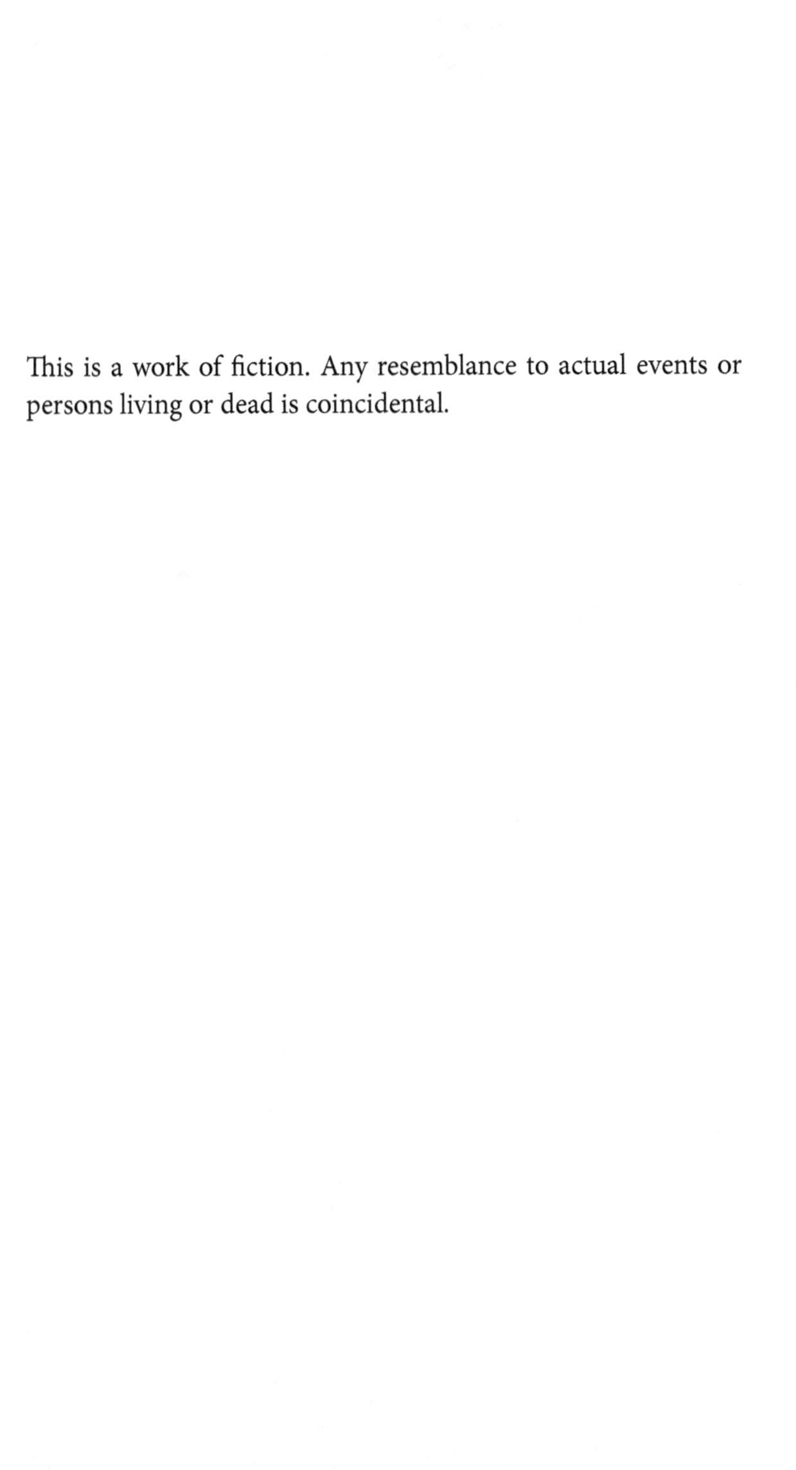

THE LAST
OF THE
SWINDLERS

by Peter Loewer

Dedication

To Jean: Talk about mysteries, the finest example of one is how I became so lucky as to have not only a great home and greater partner, but still, on occasion, actually find the quiet time to write, not for a living, but to keep the mind alive.

Acknowledgment

And a special thanks to Andy, one of those great men who find the time to do many wonderful things for his friends and still find the time to be a successful publisher.

Table of Contents

THE LAST
OF THE
SWINDLERS

Prologue
Fernglade, N.C. 1978

Shortly after two o'clock in the afternoon, a small straggly dog of indeterminate age and tangled fur sniffed his way from under a bank of rhododendrons, then trotted out onto a graveled driveway. After a moment's hesitation, he raised his right rear leg and sprayed the left rear tire of a luxurious limousine: a sparkling new, charcoal-gray, 1978 Lincoln Town Car with dark-tinted windows and a vanity license plate reading HEALER. He then turned to follow an invisible leader and began to leave the scene.

Inside the building overlooking the car, three men sat at a large oval table made of raw oak planks. The first, an extremely thin man with a wrinkled face and sharp eyes peering through golden pince-nez, opened a wicker picnic basket, withdrew a bottle and three glasses, and slowly, carefully removed the cork. His companions—one whose designer sunglasses complemented his expensive, well-tailored white suit, the other a man of almost noble bearing, who held a thick wooden cane topped with a golden head of Christ—watched him pour the wine.

The room was grand. Over the centered table a great crystal chandelier hung from the sixteen-foot ceiling. Heavy hewn-oak rafters crossed wide expanses of white plaster and drew the eye inexorably to a wall of floor-to-ceiling windows looking out on some of the lesser mountains of western North Carolina.

"I think," said the man in the white suit, polishing his wire-rimmed glasses with a silk handkerchief, "this is the beginning of a great period of expansion."

He lifted his glass in a stiff salute to the man with the cane.

"Thank you, Simon," said Reverend Stalker with an air of solemnity, "I do believe that all the signs point to our success in the time left ahead. Over the past few years, we've had false starts and disagreements, but today, the portents are all there to be read: a year from now we should be able to close yet another volume in the history of our little organization."

He waved his right hand in a broad gesture that drew attention to his diamond ring, large enough to cast glints of sunlight on the nearest wall. Their light sparkled briefly on the shadowed, empty bookcases at the far end of the room, where the wall was dominated by an oil portrait of himself dressed in flowing robes of white and holding an ornate red leather book decorated with a golden rose.

The three men sat quietly for a few moments when The Leader happened to look up at the chandelier.

"Martin, that fixture is not in the center of the room."

The man with the pince-nez put down his glass and raised his head. "Let me see," he said. He stood and eyed the chandelier and the dimensions of the room. "Leader, if it is off-center, it's only by a few inches."

"That may be, but as you know by past experience, we must strive for perfection. A miss is as good as a mile." He quoted the aphorism as though it had sprung from his own profound wisdom. "Call the electrician and have it corrected as soon as possible."

"It will cost quite a bit of money, even using the men available around here."

"That cannot be helped. Just see that it's done."

"Of course, Leader."

The Leader relaxed, sipped his wine, and drummed his fingers on the table. Then, looking at Martin, he asked, "How are things going at remodeling the school and the store?"

"The school will be finished by mid-September and the store is set to open no later than the height of leaf season in October."

"And the clinic?"

"We've had some trouble getting the more sophisticated medical equipment, but procurements seem to be moving ahead and I believe we'll be ready to take the first patients by the new year."

"Excellent," The Leader said, then paused for a few seconds before repeating, "Excellent."

His heavy eyelids rolled up like a tiny roll-top desk, and with them the entire eyeballs; for a moment his eyes were dead white. The irises reappeared as he said, "If we are ever going to succeed with our mission, this is the right time—fail now and we will forever fail." He paused, leaving his words heavy in the room, before continuing in a more businesslike voice. "And now shall we go? Mr. Black, if you would be so kind as to gather up the lunch leavings, we'll head back to Atlanta. I have a very important dinner tonight with some of our new sponsors."

The Leader carefully rose from his seat, and taking the cane that was now propped against the table, supported his elegant body on its shaft of ironwood and walked to the window. "There's a stray dog dirtying the car."

Slowly he opened the casement window and with great deliberation pulled a small silver revolver from his coat pocket. He took aim and shot the dog cleanly behind its ear.

"An empty house is better than a stray dog or a body from which life has departed," he said.

Only Simon noted the misquotation of Samuel Butler, but

knew better than to correct The Leader. "Let that be a lesson."

At the entrance hall he waited patiently for the front door to be opened, then led the small procession out into the bright, sunny afternoon.

The chauffeur backed over the dog, turned the wheels, and headed down the graveled drive.

Chapter 1

Black alligators of stripped-off truck retreads lined the tar-splattered shoulders of Interstate 40 as backlit clouds seemed ready to suck his car into a black hole. He was driving east through the tunnels some twenty miles from the Tennessee border.

Clever people say that when Bulwer-Lytton wrote, "It was a dark and stormy night," most writers knew that stories should never begin with references to weather. But for Oliver, coming home to the mountains of western North Carolina, it was hard to ignore a daily feature of everyone's life, and tonight was no exception.

Early that Thursday morning he'd awoken in a cheap motel outside of Harrisburg, Pennsylvania, with a humming TV warning of bad weather for the late spring day—a third strike to an already depressing awakening that had begun with the sight of the shabby, impersonal room and his awareness of his 55th birthday.

Now it was five o'clock, and ahead of him the evening clouds rolled over the mountains. The burned sugar-brown of winter was highlighted with a touch of green, though the promise of spring was no more comforting than the piercing songs that poured from the car's tinny radio, interspersed with loud pitches for big, beautiful deals on mobile homes.

Five miles down the road the rain pelted his car with such force he considered turning off at the next rest stop. Collected drops flowed over the top of the car and ran in split streams over the wiper blades, while flashes of lightning repeatedly lit the sky and thunder rolled across the mountains.

Finally he pulled over to the shoulder to sit out the worst of the storm and let the water cover the car in a single, transparent membrane. Being close to Asheville, a city large enough to support its own classical music FM station, he listened contentedly to Wagner and dreamed on.

At last the rain stopped. Tractor-trailers moved out to conquer the country, still carrying soft drinks from the East while Mayflower vans from the West transported the household goods of minor, but self-important, junior executives. Even with the air-conditioner on he could smell farts of sulfur dioxide from the eighteen-wheelers' exhausts.

With a tissue he wiped his glasses clear of fog, blew his nose, and with a last swipe patted his gray mustache and beard. He started the engine and carefully pulled out onto the highway. Crossing the French Broad River on the bridge at Riceville, he turned left onto the two-lane county road that paralleled the river from the small town of Trust south to Poverty Corner. Eight miles farther along he crossed the long viaduct spanning the valley before it hooked its way up to the mountain that sheltered Fernglade.

Some hundred feet below the bridge the South Toe River was a straight ribbon of water. He knew if he stopped the car and looked over the guardrails, he'd see part of the town—including his old family home with its once well-tended garden and the dark woods beyond.

At the end of the viaduct he turned right onto a graveled road, the back way into town that wound down the side of the hill. Just ahead, next to the driveway leading to the old Catholic monastery—itself a black phallic mound like a latter-day castle from a Walt Disney theme park—a large billboard of a backwoodsman in a raccoon hat pointed to his left with an oar while a voice balloon proclaimed "Welcome to the East Toe River—Canoe from the present to the past!"

He turned left onto Bridge Street just as a bolt of lightning arced over the car; an instant later a thwack of thunder jolted his toes as the smell of ozone knifed through the air vents. A half-block ahead an old battered truck with oversize tires backed into the one vacant spot on the street. He drove on.

It would soon be dark, and as he passed slowly down the main street, he saw a number of small businesses that spoke of a new prosperity. The old Red & White Market was now a self-consciously stylish mini-mall with three maroon awnings over bow-front windows featuring, in turn, a summer extension of an Atlanta art gallery, a book shop that, for a novelty, sold books other than religious tracts, and a card gallery that looked like it had more cards than balloons. Next door stood the remains of Cliff's Hardware, which Cliff had divided into a new tackle shop with an uninspired collection of themed T-shirts.

Neon signs buzzed on and off in the window of the only open restaurant. Here any change had been met head on with burly defeat; the names of two local beers were strangely garbled, as the black paint that had once separated the letters of the neon signs had long since chipped away. Above an immense jade plant, a sign reading "The Mountain Diner" also blinked, but its vibrant, strangely morbid blue light was diffused by a thin layer of moisture that streaked the window. Next to the restaurant, replacing the old A&P, a new supermarket announced itself as "Shield's: Feeding the River." Its sign, as large as an eighteen-wheeler, was embellished with a painted croissant for the apostrophe.

Directly across the street stood the funeral parlor, a grotesque production of newly restored backwoods Art Nouveau. Next door, the Olde English lettering that spelled out **The Fernglade Republican** was backlit by fluorescent lights, though its motto, "The News of the River," was blocked by a large poster board cut out in the shape of a turkey. It was too dark to read, but he knew it was inscribed with the names and weights of the feathered victims in the annual spring turkey-shooting contest.

The Fernglade Hotel, a fixture since his childhood, stood opposite the newspaper. Oliver stopped the car in the middle of the roadway, where he sat and looked from one to the other for a long moment. Then, snapping to himself, he drove a little farther down Main Street before turning onto Mill Road toward his old home.

The house was dark, and he decided not to go in quite yet. He had telephoned last night to no avail. Imogene, he was sure, was out: it was impolite not to answer one's phone, and more so to allow an answering machine to do so, however convenient they might be, and his sister was always polite.

He drove down to the street's dead end and parked for a few minutes, his mind lulled by the river's reflected lights from the backsides of buildings off Main Street and a few glimmers from homes hidden in the woods across the water. He had always enjoyed this view, almost from the edge of town; from childhood on it had given him a useful perspective on his place in it.

The front door key was, as expected, under the doormat. He entered the front hall and stood quietly in the gathering dark. He caught the smell of a lived-in home: a jumbled mix of old wallpaper, furniture polish, and cut flowers. A scented candle in the shape of a large orange, spiked onto a wrought-iron holder, stood next to his bronzed baby shoes and a silver-framed photograph of Uncle Walter, the founder of the Fernglade Bank.

Oliver's sensitive nose also found hints of mothballs, cedar from the upstairs closets, and fresh wax on the kitchen floor—all the familiar components of that subtle perfume that represented home, its formula as individual and complex as that of a Guerlain or Chanel.

The last light of day faded from the fan window over the front door. He reached for the light switch and the small crystal chandelier that hung from a polished brass chain blazed into light.

Nothing had changed. The wallpaper shepherds and shepherdesses still tended their flocks, the lambs gamboled over the French countryside with the same gusto they'd shown some fifty years before, the meadow still shone yellow-gold; only the rich forest green had faded to a softer shade. Two wall lamps of crystal and brass were bright and clean. The double doors on either side of the hall were closed, but they glowed with polish. The stairs were covered with crimson carpet held tight with bright brass rails.

He sat down on the second stair, leaning against the wall, and remembered.

Chapter Two

Oliver Swindler was his name. As he sat on the stairs of the house where he was born, he remembered wandering the woods with the warmth of summer on his back, fishing with worms or catching crayfish with bits of raw potato and, when older, family dinners listening to radios that mingled voices of Burns and Allen and Gabriel Heater. He remembered the death of his parents, and his older sister stepping in to take a job she never wanted. Like a deck of cards shuffled by a master hand, the memories rushed past, though he recognized no faces, only moments, incidents, sequences, details which, somehow, formed a bigger, more meaningful picture of his life.

He remembered trying his luck at art—but failing. He saw the people he worked with when selling real estate in Brooklyn. And all those years that began when, by unexpected serendipity, he found a job as a junior editor in a small Manhattan publishing house specializing in re-issued travel books and trendy little novels about fairies in the bottom of the garden.

There he had moved up the line in a predictable way until, by chance and luck, he signed on a best seller. *Trying Out: Everything an Actor Has to Do to Get the Part*, by a notorious Broadway director—

and such a man- and womanizer that his reputation alone sold the book—went through ten printings.

But by then he was unhappy with life in a big city and wanted nothing better than to come back home to the mountains. And, again by chance, or fate, or sheer coincidence, Imogene wrote that *The Republican* needed a new managing editor. She told him the job demanded a working knowledge of horticulture so there would be plenty of good copy for the people moving in—young couples, retirees, halfbacks bored with their Florida lives—who wanted to be part of the soil. She knew that, even when living in a Manhattan walk-up, Oliver was surrounded by pots of plants from ferns to palms and back again. She suggested he try for the job, offered him his old room in the family home, and now, just a few weeks later, here he was.

It was dark outside, and the house had turned chilly, so he went to the back of the hall and found the new digital thermostat, but the system light read "Off." He opened the front flap and with the light of a match read the instructions, pressing "Change" and "Start"; but nothing happened, not even a dull roar from the basement. Nothing, he thought, ever happened; the older he got the less faith he had in the mechanics of mankind.

Maybe the emergency switch was turned off. He went to the cellar door where a quick check proved it to be on. At that moment a sudden, brief squall came across the mountains with a flash of light and a whistling roar, and though the lights flickered they never dimmed.

He pushed open the swinging door to the kitchen, turned on the overhead light, and stepped into disaster. There were no dishes in the sink, and Imogene's polished linoleum floor reflected the light with the brilliance of the dawn, but everything else was chaos. Ladders were piled up against one wall; a canvas tarp sprawled in a monstrous heap, and brush buckets, gallons of paint, and rolls of wallpaper were everywhere. A piece of paper was tacked to one of the ladders: "Imogene, sorry to be late—I'll start tomorrow, Thursday – Ebert."

Of course! While Imogene was off somewhere the kitchen and bathrooms were to be repapered and all the woodwork in the house painted for another twenty or thirty years. Obviously neither had happened. And with his luck Ebert would show up early tomorrow morning, shorthanded as usual, and somebody would have to spend the day helping him out.

Oliver moved roller pans and rollers to reach the refrigerator—a pointless effort, he discovered, as it was bare. Perhaps, he thought, the best thing to do is eat in town and spend the next few nights at the hotel where at least it would be warm and dry. He went back to his car.

When daylight fades on Fernglade's Main Street, bright orange streetlights flicker on. Their eerie sodium glow bathes everything and everyone in unhealthy beams, underscoring the small veins in people's cheeks and noses. The paper had editorialized against their adoption, urging the town to keep the old-fashioned white variety, but lost out to the taxpayer's pocketbook. The new lights, however deplorable, were cheap.

Oliver pulled into the local garage, narrowly missing a hand-chalked sign advising Fernglade drivers to "Get Reddy For Winter—Check Your Antifreeze Now!!!" Getting out of the car he caught his heel in the trip-wire, setting off a continual clang of bells, then misjudged the distance and stepped in a pool of used oil with his left foot.

Forcing a smile, he opened the worn screen door and walked into the garage office. Inside, a kerosene heater with the wick turned too high stood next to a battered metal desk. The air was overly warm and thick with the smell of old oil and dry rubber.

Even by country standards Frank Wallace was a heavy man.

Just sitting still, the worn springs in his office chair made worrisome noises. A small bit of warped leather cushion bubbled around the edge of his bottom, but most of it was hidden by his bulk.

Frank was dressed in a black flannel shirt and dirty black-and-orange-checked hunting pants, gathered and stuffed into dirty black boots. A week's gray stubble covered his chins. He was leering through thick lenses at a large digital watch that rode atop the ridges of his left wrist.

"Ho, there, Frank!"

Frank looked up from the watch to an old electric clock on the far wall that spelled KEND_LL around its perimeter. The hands read 6:50. At the same time he was fiddling with the watch and kept pushing a tiny button on the rim of the case with his huge thumb. He muttered, then picked up a chewed cigar from an ashtray in the shape of a studded snow tire, coughed, then asked, "Know anything about these damn digital watches?"

"Not really, but I think you just adjust one of those two buttons on the side. Got an instruction sheet?"

"Nah, they never packed the damn thing. Got it for buying some Chink sneakers. Hey, you look familiar."

"I should. We went through high school together. I'm Oliver Swindler, Imogene's brother."

"Holy Shit! You sure are. Back to work at the swindle sheet, huh? Your sister told me the news."

"How the hell are you, Frank? And don't you think your antifreeze sign is out of season?"

"Nah, I'm just early. I'm fine. Nothing changes. You want gas or what?"

Though tempted to say "what," Oliver answered, "Gas—and I have to eat out tonight. Which should it be, the diner or the hotel?"

Frank screwed up his eyes in thought, chewed on the cigar, and said: "Hotel." With an effort he pulled himself up and walked out to fill the tank. Oliver idled around the familiar room, unchanged, it seemed, from decades before.

"$22.50. Everything else OK?"

"Fine, Frank. Start me a tab, will you? All right if I leave my car here for now?"

"Sure."

He picked up his duffel bag and walked across the street to the hotel.

Chapter Three

The Fernglade Hotel had begun life in the pre-Depression 1920s as a vaguely rococo wooden frame structure. Each of its three stories had a verandah that spanned the entire front of the building, with fire escapes at either end. Its current owners— out-of-towners, he had learned from Imogene—had gussied up the old clapboard with white vinyl siding embossed with a wood grain design, though they'd kept the gingerbread trim that graced every possible corner and angle. The massive mahogany double front doors featured etched glass panels depicting the founding of the town: on the left stood an angel handing a surveyor's transit to a tall gentleman in a top hat who, in turn, leaned against a boat rudder bearing the date 1895. Florid lettering etched into the glass panel of the right door read "The Fernglade, Your Hotel Away from Home!" In the lower right-hand corner were the initials "OS + L.M.–1938," which Oliver had carved in the glass using the diamond ring that Loretta Milford had received on her fourteenth birthday. Glowing white glass globes on either side of the doors attracted a few late-winter moths that flew a zig-zag dance until, dizzied or exhausted, they hit the glass and fell to the sidewalk.

Oliver opened the right-hand door and entered a short dark red hall of velvet walls and old gilt mirrors reflecting on a worn hardwood floor. At the far end stood a large desk flanked by two-foot-high bronze female nudes, each holding a lighted globe. There sat a balding man in his late fifties wearing gold-wire glasses, a rather threadbare plaid shirt, and an equally worn leather vest, set off by spanking-clean white trousers. He was reading a copy of *The National Enquirer*. A label on his vest read "Mitchell Ackermann."

"Is the dining room open?"

"Opened at six. Just find yourself a table."

"Could I get a room for a few nights?"

"No problem—plenty of rooms at this inn."

He pushed a big ledger across the desk, almost throwing the pen at Oliver, then read his upside-down signature.

"Oh, you're the new editor at the paper. Here's the key to Room 10." His voice said ask no more and expect no more.

Oliver entered the restaurant and sat down at an empty table removed from the bar. As if by magic Ackermann appeared, wiping his hands on a clean but wrinkled apron hastily thrown over his vest. He handed Oliver a menu and a rolled-up copy of *The Republican*, then smiled with worn teeth, patched with gold that glistened under the light from the four old chandeliers that lit the room.

"Good evening, Mr. Swindler," he said.

"How come you know me?" Oliver asked.

"Well, this is, after all, a small town," Ackermann chuckled. "Besides, with that beard you could only be a writer, an artist, or work for a small-town newspaper, and the first artists and writers of the summer season aren't due around here 'til June—they're still down in Atlanta living it up."

"Glad to meet you, Mr. Ackermann. How long have you been in our little town?"

"I've worked here about six months now. I was a jockey at an Atlanta ad agency but needed a change."

"You approve of Fernglade?"

"I do, I do ... though it still has a long way to go." He paused to adjust the silverware and flick an imaginary speck from the water glass while Oliver perused the menu.

"How's the meatloaf?"

"Excellent," he said as he reached in his apron pocket for an order pad. "Care for a drink first? And salad?"

"I'll have a glass of white wine on the rocks and oil and vinegar on the salad."

"Mashed or fried?"

"Mashed."

Ackermann turned on his heel and walked back to the kitchen.

Oliver glanced around the room. A number of newly acquired varnished and browned oil paintings set off by heavy and ornate frames hung on the dark red walls, most of them depicting cows, either with landscapes or without. All the furniture was imitation antique. The only things Oliver recognized from the hotel's past were the original brass chandeliers and the large mirror, with its green marble frame, that had backdropped the bar since it was built. Between the top of the mirror and the tin ceiling the management had added a row of deer antlers.

The mirror was too large to fit through the doors or windows, so the building had gone up around it. Most of the silver still held, but decades had turned parts of the glass into windows looking through to other worlds, places of ancient roads and rivers etched with spider webs of dark gray against a parched blanket of purple-brown rock.

The display of bottles in front of the mirror was also new; all were carefully stacked in pyramids on thick glass panes with polished edges. Behind each crystal Cheops sat a different colored light: green, blue, green, pink, and yellow, left to right. Twelve high-backed stools sat in front of the bar and six large tables filled the middle of the room. A jukebox of uncertain vintage silently glowed in the far corner; a wooden speaker in the shape of an eighth note, hanging between two sets of antlers, softly played elevator music.

Oliver saw only five others in the room. Two men in dark suits sat at the bar. Judging from the hunch of their shoulders, they had been there most of the afternoon and would probably still be in place far into the night.

A tall, balding man in his mid-forties shared a table with a young woman who was too beautifully dressed for either the hotel or the town. From the intensity of their conversation, Oliver judged they weren't married.

The last small table in the row was completely covered with piles of newspapers and a large notebook sticking out of an open briefcase. A good-looking woman in her mid-forties was busily cutting out coupons and arranging them in neat piles. An empty glass of wine sat at her elbow, and at her feet Oliver saw more newspapers, all copies of *The Fernglade Republican.*

From out of the shadows came a sixth guest, a very thin man wearing gold pince-nez.

Many of the people Oliver had met over the years apparently got most of their energy (and their heartaches) from alcohol, and he himself was never one to turn down an honest drink. But the rail-thin man, his face pockmarked as if armies of golf shoes had camped on his cheeks, was, Oliver thought, someone who should have said "No!" years ago.

The man's complexion was sallow, his nose and cheeks netted by tiny purple veins. Behind his nose-pinchers—the sort worn by slightly fey nobility while examining butterflies in the park—his yellow-rimmed eyes, not quite brown, appeared in sharp contrast to his closely-cropped salt-and-pepper hair. The glasses were tied to his jacket with a shiny black ribbon.

"Good day to you," he said, crossing past the bar, the glasses bobbing up and down on his nose. He stretched out his hand to Oliver. "Welcome to our little town. I thought I would not have the pleasure of meeting you until tomorrow morning when you signed in to the paper. However …" He gave Oliver the slightest of smiles. "My name is Simon Black, and I'm your—what should I say—your advertising manager—of sorts."

Oliver shook his hand as briefly as politeness would allow, and did nothing to suggest Black join him at the table. "I thought a woman ran the advertising. I sort of suspected the lady sitting with the coupons might be she?" he said, nodding in her direction

"No, no, no! Not at all! Adrian *sells* the advertising but I work with Greig—I trust you've met the publisher—in developing the grander concepts."

"I'm stunned to learn that a small town like this needs two high-powered folks in the ad department."

"Adrian's a good soldier, but in Fernglade, sophistication"— he pronounced the word with an accent on *phis*—"is what's needed, something to appeal to the city people and properly represent the inherent and innocent charm of the town. That's why they're all coming up here: They want clean air, good health, and charm."

"Having been born here, I haven't missed much of that charm," Oliver retorted. "I always saw a lot of people down on their luck. In my opinion, a lot of 'charm' is the result of not having enough money to make any improvements. And if enough city people come up here the charm will soon tarnish and the air become decidedly foul." He looked around vaguely. "But dinner is certainly more interesting than local history at this point, at least to me."

As if on cue, Black stepped away as Ackermann brought a heavy water tumbler half filled with Chablis, which he set on a disposable Coors coaster. He stopped to speak to the woman clipping coupons and returned to the bar.

She glanced up, flashed Oliver a dazzling smile, and walked

over to his table, still carrying clippings and her scissors. Her eyes were bright blue, hair a curly black with just a touch of gray. "So you're Oliver Swindler, the new editor. I'm Adrian Knapp."

Oliver half-rose and nodded for her to take a chair.

"Yes, I know, you're the new sales manager. The publisher Greig Davis mentioned you, but I guessed your identity when I saw you clipping those coupons. Shield's Supermarket, is it? I bet you talked him into that full-page ad, and if he doesn't get a respectable return, he'll figure the ad didn't work and, knowing him, he won't try again."

She set her handful of coupons on the table. "Tomorrow I'll hand these out at the paper and tell every employee to go out and use them." Almost as an afterthought she added, "How are you, Simon?"

Black hovered, but did not move or speak, though he continued to watch them with a predatory smile.

"Why," Oliver asked, "with a warm comfortable office across the street, are you sitting here?"

"It's turkey season," she answered. "All afternoon the mighty hunters bring their dead and bleeding birds into the front office to have them weighed. I was starting to feel like a turkey vulture myself, watching them," she added with a wry glance in Black's direction.

"Your dinner's coming, Oliver," said Black, as Ackermann approached with a tray. "And far be it from me to stand in the way of new friendships. I'll leave you two to broader horizons and clipped coupons." He walked quickly away.

"Anything for you?" Oliver asked Adrian as Ackerman set down his plate and silverware.

"Another glass of wine," she said, half to him and half to Ackermann. "And a cup of black coffee, and a pack of nuts from the bar."

Nodding toward the door as Black went out, she continued, "You know, Simon really looks like that evil Emperor—what's his name, in *Star Wars*, the one in the black cowl with the face like a commercial for California prunes." Seeing the bemused look on Oliver's face, she added, "I'm sorry, that was stupid. He could be a friend of yours."

"I never met him before tonight—and Greig never mentioned two people working in advertising. Anyway, speaking of new employees, how about lunch tomorrow? I'm meeting Greig in mid-morning to check out the paper and the staff."

"Great," she said as Ackermann brought her order. "But eat your dinner. I've still got a lot of coupons to cut. I'll be at the paper early tomorrow and look forward to seeing you. Here's a copy of last week's edition." She smiled then, almost conspiratorially, though with a twinkle in her eyes. "And a coupon. Make sure you use it."

It was a thirty-cent discount on an eight-ounce jar of instant coffee.

Oliver dug in to his meatloaf, suddenly surprised at how hungry he was, occasionally glancing across the room at Adrian, still diligently clipping. The two finished at almost the same moment, she her clipping, he his dinner. She packed up her papers in a neat pile, stuffed them in a shopping bag, got up and quickly slipped through the front door.

He sat quietly for another few minutes, thinking about the contrast between Adrian and Simon Black, when his attention was drawn to the two men at the bar, now sunk lower in their seats. He had enough personal experience to know that soon their cheeks would be flat against the wood.

They both appeared to be middle-aged, wearing suits that were a step down from Robert Hall, and from the number of empty glasses between them, would soon be unable to answer any questions they might be asked; but for now, though speaking in hushed terms, they were clearly heard by Oliver.

"Lou," slurred the one clenching a worn-out cigar in his teeth, "we gotta get out of this town. There ain't nothing here for either of us and I'm sick of promises of great things to come from Black or Ackermann. Jesus, while we still have the car and enough dough for gas, why not just vanish and head for 'lanna? Huh—?"

"Listen, Harry." He stopped to look around the room and quickly passed by Oliver, who appeared to be deep in his newspaper, and continued, "Black said he had a job for us and it's too late to leave here now. 'Sides, we got a clean room upstairs, let's finish the bottle and get a good night's sleep..." Steadily and inexorably his head slumped onto the table, his voice trailed off until it was too deep to be understood, and he slowly passed out.

If the hotel owners wanted to cash in on Fernglade's new sophistication, they should start with some of the clientele, thought Oliver. As he turned to look out the front windows, he was blinded by a dazzling bolt of lightning hitting somewhere nearby, immediately followed by a roar of thunder—and the lights went out all over the hotel.

Chapter Four

J ust hang in there, folks," said a disembodied voice from the lobby door. "This happens every time a big storm comes up the river. I'll light some lamps and we'll all be cozy as clams."

Oliver quickly rose and, stumbling a bit, stepped out to the lobby, where Ackermann was sitting at the front desk lighting a kerosene lamp.

"How was dinner?" he asked.

"Surprisingly good. Do you have any newspapers other than our local?"

Ackermann reached under the desk and pulled out ratty copies of *The New York Times*, the Charlotte *Observer*, both Atlanta papers, the *Journal* and the *Constitution*, and the *Asheville Citizen*. He pushed them across the counter.

"Thanks. Will the lights be off long?"

"Never can tell," said Ackermann with a gentle sigh as he began poking around in the same place he got the newspaper. "Weather's always a strange brew of the river and the mountains around us. Here's a flashlight to help you on your way."

Oliver walked up the two flights to Room 10. As he opened the door the hotel lights suddenly flashed on, illuminating his way into a 21st-century interpretation of early 1900s country kitsch.

The walls were papered in a tan and beige pattern—*Malibu Modern*, thought Oliver—and a shiny brass-framed lithograph of three gulls circling beach grass hung over a faux-bamboo bed, covered by a cocoa-brown chenille spread with dime-sized balls of fuzz threaded around the edges. The television was hidden in a cheap-looking imitation 17th-century cabinet, and the well-worn but beautiful American Orientals that had once covered the hardwood floors had been replaced with easy-care wall-to-wall carpeting, marked by plenty of signs that little care had ever been used. A basket of dried flowers mixed with potpourri sat on the bedside table, though it did nothing to scent the stale air.

With a touch of sadness, Oliver accepted that all the charm of the hotel of his childhood was gone. The Mission oak furniture, the needlepoint bedspreads, even the old prints like "September Morn" were gone, probably sold to local antique shops and now serving as conversation pieces in private homes and weekend getaways.

The small bathroom, with its ancient, inefficient water-wasting fixtures, had escaped the makeover. The new management, he thought, probably had found it too expensive to replace faucets or original porcelain tiles. An exception was the mirror: a square pane of new glass bolted to the wall with four scallop-shaped plastic clips had replaced the ornate framed one. Three long black human hairs were caught in the bottom right scallop shell. The overhead light was bare.

Unpacking his gear, Oliver set the small travel alarm for 7:00 a.m., took a quick look at the Atlanta edition of the *Times*, stripped to his underwear, climbed into bed, and prepared to read himself to sleep. Even in Manhattan he had rarely watched television, except the late-night movie channel; he wasn't about to change that habit here. He thought Reginald Farrer's *Among the Hills*, about climbing to 8,500 feet in the Maritime Alps in 1910 while looking for *Dianthus neglectus* and *Aquilegia alpine*, would beat magazine stories about nighttime flyovers by black helicopters chartered to the United Nations.

He could barely see the book, much less read the small print. He looked over and discovered that his bed lamp was a 20-watt bulb buried deep within a polished brass bullet-lamp. Resigning himself, he put Farrar aside and turned on the worn plastic radio. A station out of Tennessee airing a late-night talk show about flying saucers and interstellar messages in cornfields soon lulled him to sleep.

At 2:55 a.m. Oliver awoke with the dim light over his head glowing like a distant moon. He reached up to switch it off and the bed squeaked with such conviction that he made a mental note never to engage in illicit couplings in Room 10. Outside the night was deadly still.

A light shone through the slightly open transom and he heard muffled, angry voices from down the hall. They increased in pitch as he tried to make out the words. Suddenly a door opened and a woman's voice yelled: "You creep! You fucking creep! You bastard! If you think you can get away with this you're, you're fucking nuts—"

"For Christ's sake," said a man's voice in a hollow whisper, "keep your mouth shut."

"You want me to keep my mouth shut? You bloody jerk!"

The door slammed and a pair of high heels clicked along the vinyl floor, then pounded down the stairs. A few moments later he heard the front door, two stories below, bang with almost enough force to break the glass. Silence returned.

Oliver ran to the window, pulled back the paper shade and looked out, but the verandah blocked his view. He heard an engine start; a car roared down the street and slowly faded to nothing. The room was chilly, and he tiptoed back to the warm sheets, balled up the chenille spread, and promptly fell asleep.

The buzz of the alarm forced him to open his eyes to bright sunlight that seared the edges of the window blind. In the bathroom he trimmed his mustache, brushed his beard and teeth, combed his balding head, put on his suit and a clean white shirt, and tied his favorite paisley necktie. His boots were polished and nails were clean: he was set to start the day.

For breakfast he went to The Mountain Diner. Except for a new calendar hanging on the stainless steel wall, a number of tears in the upholstery—patched with black tape—and a bleeping electronic register instead of the clattering ornate till, the diner looked just as it had when as a teenager he and his friends stopped for cokes after a Friday night movie at the old Rialto.

Four men in National Park Service Ranger uniforms filled one booth. Three aged farmers sat talking in another. Frank Wallace was at the far end looking exactly as he did when on duty in the gas station; he was sharing the booth with another overweight man wearing camouflage and a heavily corked face and hands; three turkey calls hung around his neck. Other hunters, decked out in more traditional garb, sat around a table. The single waitress looked harried.

Oliver chose the middle of three empty counter stools. He ordered orange juice, toast, and coffee, then hid behind the morning newspaper from Asheville. But hiding wasn't necessary: aside from Wallace, he recognized no one, and no one recognized him.

Simon Black walked in for a takeout coffee. Spying Oliver, he wished him a good morning and asked about his comfort. Oliver nodded.

On his heels came a heavy gentleman with a gray beard. The cashier addressed him with deference as Dr. Hill. Two minutes later Adrian walked in for coffee, saw Oliver, and sat down on the stool at his right.

"Get a good night's sleep?"

"Fine. Well, first there was the storm, but it passed and everything quieted down. And how could I say otherwise on such a bright and beautiful day?"

"There are," she smiled, "better places for a good rest than that hotel."

"Truthfully, as I lay there cocooned from the night by a chenille bedspread, the only thing that ran through my mind was that old ad for cheap wine: 'What's the word? Thunderbird! What's the price? Thirty, twice!'"

She laughed and said: "I arrived in town ... gosh, five years ago, when they had the removal sale and started to remodel the hotel. You should have seen some of the furniture that went. It was all old and heavy—you know, solid stuff—some of it even Gustav Stickley, then everything was replaced by a warehouse full of the Twilight Zone. At least he left the dining room and bar alone." She paused, then asked, "Are you coming over to the paper this morning?"

"As soon as I have another cup of coffee. Oh, I'm also going over to the bank to open up an account. Know why he remodeled the hotel?"

"At first I thought it was money but then I realized the simple fact that like many people, he hasn't any taste. I don't think he made much on the sale. I know a little about antiques and old furniture and believe me, all the sharpies came up from Atlanta, beating out the local dealers, but still paying less than a quarter of what it was worth. Then a resort hotel some fifty miles from here went bankrupt and he hauled over what was left of the 1950s from East Tennessee."

The cash register beeped once, then again; two men left,

and immediately two more hunters walked in.

"It's busy here," said Oliver.

"You should see it during the summer when all the canoeists from Atlanta jump in to sober up for the morning. Well, cheerio, being Friday I have a few papers to drop off for waiting clients, so I'll see you in a little while over at the paper."

Oliver finished his coffee, paid his bill, and walked quickly down to the new bank building, a one-story steel structure faced with thin layers of red brick and white colonial trim and shutters. The landscaping consisted of juniper bushes and clumps of daffodils protected by a brick edging between the sidewalk and the new blacktop parking area. A large sign atop a white post read 𝕱𝖊𝖗𝖓𝖌𝖑𝖆𝖉𝖊 𝕹𝖆𝖙𝖎𝖔𝖓𝖆𝖑 𝕭𝖆𝖓𝖐 in "Olde-English" letters identical to those on the newspaper's window. Just below it a digital light display gave the current temperature as 52°F. Then it flashed and gave the time as 9:30, and immediately a set of speakers mounted in a fake dovecote on the peak of the roof gave forth a peal of tinny electronic chimes vaguely resembling a 19th-century church carillon.

Oliver pushed a polished brass handle and listened to the swooshing sound of the door as he stepped onto wall-to-wall carpet, the color of sea foam. Soft music came from hidden speakers, and to his left a folding partition displayed local paintings of red barns, gray barns, tumble-down barns, and barns used to cure tobacco, all with an emphasis on autumn leaves and tobacco-drying racks. Colonial brass chandeliers held imitation flickering-flame bulbs.

A uniformed guard with gold braid approached and asked if he could help with anything. Oliver explained his business and was led to an oversized desk with brass accessories hiding the bottom part of a pleasant-looking woman about his age. She glanced up, back down, then did a double take.

"Good morning, may I—for heaven's sake, it isn't, but you look exactly like—my God, Oliver Swindler."

"Loretta—how the hell are you?"

"Oliver, sit down!" She gestured to an imitation Chippendale chair with a satin seat.

He quickly explained about his new job and listened to updates about her family (he had to come over for dinner!). But her voice was just a touch too high and every few moments she looked around the room as if somebody was watching them.

"What ever happened to the rest of our class?" he asked.

"Most everyone moved away, like you did—not enough work around here. David Loring died last year and Bob Fisk was killed in Vietnam—you know he stayed in the Army twenty-five years, and was set to retire in sixty-eight, and then...Well, it was just sad. The Belter twins both married men from Charlotte. In fact, except for Clark Wechsler, you and I are all that's left from the old days. I think our total graduating class was only twelve kids. I'll look it up in the yearbook."

"What about you?"

She started tapping her pen on the blotter.

"Oh, nothing much," she said, with a slight tremor in her voice, "I married a boy from Burnsville, but we divorced a few years ago. Then with the help of our leader at the Starker Clinic, I married Jonathan Wheatley—he works for the Reverend in their tackle shop—oh, it's a long, long story, Oliver, and sometime when there's more time, I'll fill you in."

He couldn't help but notice how her eyes lit up at the mention of "our leader" at the Starker Clinic.

"What's Clark Wechsler up to now?"

"He's our local entrepreneur—controls a lot of real estate, chairman of the board of the bank, and runs the funeral parlor. Owns a big new house overlooking the river high up on Limbaugh's Bluff. Frankly, to me he's the same creepy kid he always was but—." She stopped abruptly and tapped her pen a bit harder, again glancing around the room. "Oh, I see your sister often—she's doing great."

He wondered why she was nervous—and whether it had to do with him. But he had to get to work.

"Loretta, I'm glad you're doing so well. We will have to catch up, but right now, well, I still haven't been over to the paper."

Murmuring "Of course, Oliver. I understand," she helped him fill out several forms and handed him his complimentary welcome pack.

"I never imagined a bank as a place to have friends—in Manhattan it's all business, all the time—but with you here it might feel like a friendly place after all. Well, I really must get over to the paper."

"Oliver, please stay in touch," and she shook his hand with what seemed to be nervous fingers. "I'm glad a friend has returned." She turned away and began clicking at her keyboard.

Oliver left the bank, marveling once again at the door's swooshing sound.

Chapter Five

The newspaper building was old, dating to the last century, and sometime during the late 1930s, in an effort to renew the paper's image, the front had been covered with asbestos shingles, now painted white. Two first-floor windows flanking the front door were trimmed in green. **The Fernglade Republican** arched across the left window; across the bottom, smaller letters spelled out "The News of the River," backed by a three-foot-high piece of white poster board in the shape of a turkey silhouette, partly covered by names and weights printed in heavy black marking pen and the heavier stenciled words, "The Republican Turkey Contest." Someone had hand-colored a few of the feathers. The right window was open to the office within, except for a snake plant in a pot that came from the 1950s. Oliver stepped up and opened the door.

The room held four desks, two on each side of a center aisle, the first on the right occupied by a thin young woman with long blond hair. A large green blotter held two pots of African violets and a pile of invoices. Three framed pictures of her children stood next to an old brass lamp with a glass shade.

The first desk on the left was covered with newspapers and in the center stood a large scale of the kind found in meat markets.

The pan was stained with dried blood, and a few turkey feathers blew about as he shut the door. There was a faint smell of ink in the air. Adrian sat at the desk behind the blonde, still cutting coupons and ads from this week's paper. The other desk was unattended but held an antique-looking Radio Shack computer with screen and keyboard.

"Morning," said the blonde. "May I help you?"

"Good morning. I'm Oliver Swindler, the new managing editor—and a day early, I'm afraid."

"This is Mary-Beth Hunsucker," Adrian said, standing quickly at her desk. "She takes care of subscriptions, billing, all the mail … and she makes pretty good coffee. She doesn't do windows or the johns."

"That's quite a lineup," he said and shook her hand.

"Oh!" she exclaimed. "Welcome. We've been eager for you to arrive, Mr. Swindler."

"Oliver. Nice to meet you, Mary-Beth. You sound like the indispensable employee."

"Adrian's kidding. I don't do all that—and in fact, I don't even keep cleaning out that weighing pan because as soon as it's washed out another hunter will be in to weigh his bird."

"Yeah," said Adrian, "and if you think that's bad, wait 'til they march in for November's Big Buck Contest. They stand out in the street, spread-eagle their legs over the body, and hold the antlers up to the sky. Then you take a pic for the sports page."

"I grew up with it," he said tensely. "In fact my father won the contest a couple of times. I know I'll be writing captions for every picture on the sports page—but I still don't like it."

"Mary-Beth, if the City Store calls about their Easter ad, please take a message and I'll get back later. Right now let me introduce Oliver to the rest of the building. Come on and follow me."

He followed Adrian down a short hall.

"Most of the staff is off on Fridays except Mary-Beth and me, but they all worked early this morning folding and packing papers for the post office. That's Greig's office," she said, opening a door on the right to a small room mostly filled by a huge handmade desk covered with framed photos, three phones, and backed by a large leather swivel chair facing three smaller chairs. Almost every inch of the dark paneled walls was covered with awards from the State Press Association, awards from the Lions, from the Kiwanis, from the Jaycees … in fact awards from the entire past century. What little space was left held four pairs of antlers mounted on wood panels.

She pointed to the next door. "That's the ladies room. And it's clean. The men's room is in the back."

"It always is," he said.

"That door ahead goes upstairs to the files, the break room, and the old photo lab."

They passed through an open doorway on the left and he stepped back a hundred years.

"All the old linotype presses are still here," she said. "When he bought the paper Greig switched to photo-offset, but he couldn't bring himself to sell the presses. That's an old Heidelberg Press in the corner. It a great machine; it printed just about every poster in this county, from 'Wanted' to 'Private Property' to 'No Hunting Allowed.'"

The room, running along the entire side of the building, was very large with nine-foot ceilings. Wooden walls were painted white with clean windows facing the side street. On the back wall more windows looked out on a mowed yard that gently sloped down to a bank overlooking the river; there some old lawn furniture sat beneath a huge sycamore tree that towered over the building.

Eight old-fashioned fluorescent lamps hung from short chains. Toward the tops of the walls mounted deer heads circled the entire room, and although there were a few large dust bunnies on the floor, every antler was free of grime and every artificial eye gleamed as though it had just been Windexed. The floor was stained with years of ink and burn marks from hot linotype. Three new flypapers hung from the center of the ceiling. Adrian looked at them with distaste.

"Sometimes we eat lunch out there," she said and pointed to the lawn. "That small door to the left is the men's room. The door to the right goes to the basement—nobody ever goes to the basement."

"Why? Past mistakes? Or is that where the bodies are buried?"

"No, just millions of old, damp newspapers. Five years ago, the river flooded and a great deal of water flowed into the building and soaked half the basement. Most of the foundation is solid rock, so no harm done to the walls—I mean, the building's sound as can be—and luckily most of the newspaper piles were left dry—and they were already on microfilm--but nobody could bring themselves to throw them out."

Just below the trophies were shelves that held piles of papers and boxes of envelopes, each with a partially folded sample sticking out. A large mechanical stapler stood in one corner. An elderly A. B. Dick press stood in another, and a shiny new sorter and folding machine took up the center of the floor. Around the walls the floor was stacked with more cardboard boxes or ancient file cabinets, many with open drawers and contents almost spilling out.

"If you ever get a chance to explore, those drawers are full of things from the old days: wooden type, metal cuts, wood cuts, and various samples of stationary produced over the years. There are programs from the various summer camps that date from the turn of the century."

They walked through another open doorway into the

adjoining room. A window looked onto the street and an old iron spiral staircase disappeared through the high ceiling. On the other side of the stairs was a closed garage door. Long deal tables with laminated tops lined two walls. Two banks of waist-high slanted benches ran down the center of the room.

"Those benches were once used for pasting up the pages of the paper and making the ads, but of course almost everything's been done on computers for years. Most papers do pagination these days using a paperless layout system; we still do a little manual layout, although a few of our most recent issues have been totally paginated. In a few weeks—or, depending on you, no more than a few months—we expect to abandon these layout tables. Our darkroom will soon suffer a similar fate.

"But I need to tell you, tradition says that any editor's first paper is delivered by that editor to the presses in Asheville—they do our printing for us. After that it's usually the handyman. Just for safety's sake he takes printed copies of each page over to the same place, even though the entire paper is uploaded direct to their prepress office. Unlike past editors, you'll no longer have to manually line photos or find pull-quotes. Everything now is incredibly easy to create—although with a dozen computers on the network, finding files can be a challenge. All in all, it's quite a fascinating change."

He followed her up the stairs. "Old Mr. Mullens told Greig that he knew it was time to sell the paper when he had trouble climbing these stairs to the editorial office. He was 90 at the time. He also said if you were as angry about an issue at the bottom as you were when leaving the top, you were probably right."

At the top of the stairs was a smaller room with a shuttered window. Centered, and dominating the room, was a round table encircled by six chairs. Hanging over it on a heavy chain was a single light with an immense milky white glass globe. A closed rolltop desk was in the left corner to the rear, its twin in the right corner. Wooden swivel chairs were pushed into each desk well. Between them, two long strips of 1" x 2"s, full of thumbtacks, were screwed to the left wall. They were numbered to hold twenty-four pieces of 8" x 10" notepaper. A 1950s-style electric clock hung over the door.

"Your desk is on the right, and that's the editorial john."

Another old and scarred office desk sat next to the open door. It was covered with piles of papers and notebooks, three phone books, a half-filled bag of potato chips that covered a phone, a fairly clean, fairly new computer keyboard attached to a tower below, plus two empty cans of diet soda. The wall above held a jumble of posters, pictures, and out-of-date calendars. A poster of Darth Vader stood next to another that featured *Citizen Kane* and a long banner that read: "Eschew Obfuscation."

"That belongs to our current intern. He calls himself 'Scoop.' He's not exactly neat but he doesn't drink—and he wants more than anything to work on a paper."

"I didn't think there was anything left like this in the world. I thought they had all sold out to designer furniture with Herman Miller clocks and virgin Naugahyde seats."

"I'll tell you all about Greig when there's more time. He's a decent guy—his wife is just as nice, although she can get the wind up on a few things. They both love the smell of newsprint and know what a newspaper really is. They've been great for me. True, the money isn't flowing in like wine, but everyone gets along. The Asheville and Atlanta papers have both tried many times to hire the typists away for more money but they'd rather stay here. And Fred Niven—he does most of the ads and will paste up whatever pages you can't finish—has been loyal, too."

Oliver opened his roll-top, where a computer monitor allowed him to view the finished and justified pages of a new edition that were being composed by two typing champions ("Typing Jewels of the Press Room," said Mary-Beth)—local ladies who before marriage were secretaries at the local bank, and who now composed all the copy for the paper on two Compugraphic Typing Machines not too far from where one of the smaller printing presses once stood. Next to the monitor was a brand-new IBM Selectric Typewriter.

"It's got the internal correction feature," said Mary-Beth with surprising enthusiasm, "so you don't have to paint over mistakes with white correction fluid and a brush! Plus it's got proportional spacing so you can get an idea of how a new editorial will fit in the space provided."

On an upper inside shelf were three new—or at least unused—books held by old-fashioned library bookends: *The Harper Dictionary of Foreign Terms*, *The Associated Press Style Book*, and *Manual for Writers & Editors*, plus a very worn but still-bound-with-duct-tape Merriam-Webster dictionary. A bent pica ruler lay on top of a small pile of paper clips next to an extremely dog-eared copy of *The New York Times Guide to Style*.

He turned on the overhead light and went for the current bound-paper file, setting it on the table. Opening it to the previous July 4th weekend, he saw a three-column picture of a car-and-motorcycle accident on I-40 and a front-page editorial on the menace of misguided motorcycles on the roads. The rest of the front page covered the problems between the local residents and the National Park Service. He knew that most of the summer people in the area came from Atlanta, with a few from Johnson City to the West or Raleigh to the East, seeking the so-called pleasantries of country life coupled with electricity and garbage collection.

The editorial page featured another swipe at roadside litter by a well-known syndicated columnist; two chatty feel-good columns by local women; and a photo of some misidentified wildflowers: even after decades in the city, Oliver still knew that Indian pipes were not Jack-in-the-pulpits.

Flipping through several other issues, he murmured—to himself as much as to Adrian, though she nodded her agreement—"Well, except for the flowers, most of the things that people buy a weekly paper for are either missing or relegated to the back pages. Those are the things they want—the barbecues and firemen's parades, church socials, weddings—they need to be up front. I can see why circulation's been slipping—and with it, sales."

They went carefully down the spiral stairs and into the composing room.

Although he had never actually worked on a paper, Oliver knew something about publishing. When he began as a junior editor, he learned to correct proofs using an X-Acto knife to move words about. He'd never pasted up an entire book, much less a newspaper; but he was confident that, familiar as he was with judging type and the traditional methods of paste-up, he would learn enough of the new methods to get along. Whatever they used, he would focus on content and leave the technology to the technologists.

They turned out the lights and went back to the front office. Mary-Beth was on the phone with a disgruntled subscriber about an article in last week's paper. He could hear the angry, four-letter expletives from five feet away. She was obviously adept at the creampuff technique, repeating "Oh, dear," "I'm so sorry," and "I just don't know what I can do," until at last the caller hung up. As soon as she put the phone down, it rang again. Adrian was already busy on another line.

With a gust of fresh air the front door opened, and a man who looked like an extra from a Rambo movie walked in. His face was covered with soot, and he was dressed in a camouflage pattern of brown, black, and olive drab. In one arm he cradled a shotgun, in the other a newly dead wild turkey, slowly congealing blood occasionally splatting on the linoleum. His mouth held a half-burnt rum crook cigar that wobbled as he talked.

"Where do ya want it?" he asked, pointing the bird's dangling feet toward Oliver.

"Put it on the scale," said Oliver. "What's your name?" he asked, pulling the cardboard out of the window.

"Fred Grover, Bristol, Virginia." He watched the scale carefully. "All right! Twenty-two pounds, six ounces, huh? Great! Hey, I'm the best, so far, right?"

As he added Grover's name and the weight with a black magic marker, Oliver said, "Yes, you are, Mr. Grover. The biggest tur—"

Adrian quickly cut him off. "It's the best so far," she said and flashed him a brilliant smile. "We'll announce the winner next week." As soon as the man left she added, "There's a bottle of cleaner and paper towels right there."

Mary-Beth looked up. "I think that bird is probably okay, but last year that same gentlemen loaded his bird with about a pound of lead shot. You've got to be on your toes with these guys…"

She exchanged a glance with Adrian, who was packing her purse and locking her desk drawers. Adrian picked up the sentence as if the two women had discussed the shortcomings of local men many times before.

"… and they usually have very short fuses. But turkeys are nothing. I already told you about the Big Buck Contest; you'll love going out in a cold December rain to measure rack sizes and count points on antlers. They bundle the animals either on their engines—so the bodies stay nice and warm—or in the backs of dirty trucks …"

"… and a lot of these guys don't even know how to properly field dress an animal," interjected Mary-Beth. "Their idea of removing internal organs is to make one long incision—"

"And run!" said Adrian. After a burst of shared laughter, she said to Oliver, "Let's get some lunch."

Chapter Six

I thought we'd drive over to Yancey County," she said. "There's a small roadhouse called Ralph's, rough looking but the food is good. Most of the time we eat at the paper, but I've got to get out once in a while and the diner or hotel are just not enough. My car's in the back."

Five minutes later they were looking down at the gently flowing Toe River flickering through the rusted side rails of the bridge. When they reached the other side a sign reading "Welcome to Yancey County" arched over the road.

The road formed a Y, the left branch changing from asphalt to pounded dirt that quickly disappeared under a canopy of trees. The right branch sloped up a gentle hill. A small, whiskey-barrel-shaped sign nailed to an aged white pine announced that Ralph's Mountain Tavern was just ahead on the left.

Adrian turned and slowed to follow a crudely cut-out wooden arrow that pointed to "Parking" behind a large, low-slung log cabin with a red roof. In the almost-full dirt lot one or two cars shared space with several dozen pickups, none of them new and all pretty well banged up.

The roadhouse building was literally on the road, so close that the front door was endangered by every passing car or truck; a number of torn hinges were mute testimony to past amputations.

Inside it was dark with a long and crowded bar on the left and scattered tables spread out on the right. The ceiling, when visible through layers of little stalactites of dust, was ancient patterned tin. With the unerring instinct of a night owl, Adrian threaded them to an empty table against the far wall, lit by an overhead 40-watt bulb in a red paper shade.

A pleasant-looking waitress with frizzed blonde hair held back by a red satin bow gave Adrian a wide grin and said that Ralph would want his standard ad for the Easter Week paper but would be closed that Sunday. She took their order for the special hamburger of the house and two bottles of Mountain House ale.

"How the heck did they decorate this place?" asked Oliver. "By reversing a vacuum cleaner and using it as a dust thrower?"

"Ralph's stock in trade is a combination of good food with a 'used' look to the decor … and do the city folk love it. He even sells T-shirts. Don't worry, nothing will fall on your food. And on the way out look over the bar. You'll see one of the original Anheuser Busch posters of Custer's Last Stand."

He glanced around the darkened room and noted that except for Adrian and the waitress, everyone was male, from mid-twenties to late eighties, all dressed in dungarees, plaid flannel shirts, and caps that in better light displayed logos from Agway, John Deere, International Harvester, and the NRA.

"This place wasn't here when I was a kid. What in heaven's name do all these men do for a living?" he asked quietly.

"The farmers and the lumberjacks—there's still a lot of forest to cut around here—are nothing new, but the rest are carpenters that work in the second-home industry. Some of them do beautiful cabinetry work. You should see what's happened around Asheville or Franklin, not to mention Georgia. And we can't forget members of local or state road crews: the new residents want weeds trimmed and potholes filled. It can be rough in here on a Friday or Saturday night, but you could bring your mother here for Christmas or a Sunday dinner and she'll have a great time."

"But not for Easter Sunday," he reminded her.

Food arrived—to Oliver's surprise, an excellent lunch—after which they ordered coffee and sat back to talk.

"How did you wind up with the newspaper?" he asked.

"Knocking from pillar to post. My mother lives in Statesville, so I'm familiar with the area, and after my divorce—"

"I thought so, you have that look."

"So do you—I had to earn a living and always had a gift for sales plus an ability to write good copy. There's obviously more to twenty-some-odd years but that's enough for today."

"What about Greig?"

"He and his wife Alice bought the paper about four years ago when Mr. Mullens wanted out. They've been waiting for a small weekly to buy for years. After trudging all over the country—you should hear some of the towns and papers they've visited—they found Fernglade, liked it, and saw the potential in the town. They bought a beautiful old house along the River Road.

"The paper's just breaking even right now. At first Greig acted as the editor, but that became difficult because of the time involved. He felt he couldn't do everything, then Mr. Mullens suggested a man who came down from Bristol, Virginia, and ran the editorial end for about three years. His name was David Mangini and he was good. Everything went like clockwork ... but then David moved to Florida and Ackermann suggested Black. And Black knew everything about running a paper—or so he said."

She paused, as if to decide precisely what to say. She was pleased, and pleasantly surprised, that instead of filling the silence, Oliver said nothing. After a long moment she continued.

"But while people can sometimes be conservative, the

folks who want to live in a bunker and make their own soap are not that common, and that's who Black was aiming for. So sales plummeted and Greig almost fired him—the only time I ever saw him really angry. He actually broke a hinge on his office door slamming it after Black—but Black came back like a roll of fake pennies. According to Greig the paper needed Black, so he rehired him as an advisor to the paper, knowing you were on your way. Apparently your sister had suggested you a few weeks before."

She savored a deep taste of beer and smiled at him. "And I know a lot about you because I met your sister when she came into the paper about hiring you."

"Damn, I suspected as much."

"And I know you'll like Scoop. He's a good kid, has a sharp way with words and an ethical outlook rare in kids his age."

"You seem to be happy working there."

"I am. I've never enjoyed a job quite as much as this one. It gets lonely at times, especially in the winter, but I always know that spring will come—and the turkey contest," she added with a grin.

He finished his beer and, looking around the room, saw that most of the others had left. The waitress came over to the table and he reached for the check.

"I've got it," said Adrian. "Greig told me to take you out on the paper. And now it's time for you to begin to settle in and time for me to start selling, an activity that continues most every day ... so I'll run you back to the paper and then I'm off to Spruce Pine."

Adrian dropped Oliver at the bridge. He walked up toward Main Street looking at what he remembered of his past. To the east up Bridge Street he could just see the remains of the old railroad station, its copper gutters now green with age. The railroad was still there, though one of its tracks had been ripped up due to a misreading of maps by the government and Conrail.

He could see in his mind's eye the signs that read "Atlanta" and "Fernglade," only now they would be weatherworn and hanging on rusted hooks or sitting in someone's private collection; only freight cars used the track going to and from upriver lumberyards.

The hardware store was now a canoe rental, and the old bank—where he'd had his first savings account at the age of ten—was now a camp supply outlet. The coal company offices, once black with dust, were now bright and new, selling gas heat and shiny tin-wear for hot air ducts; next door was a new electric company office whose window was filled with come-ons to the simplicity and economy of electric heat.

Oliver stepped into the newspaper office to let Mary-Beth know that he'd answer the phone while she went home to prepare supper for her husband.

"Oh," he added, "the furnace in my sister's house is out. Who should I call for service?"

"The—and don't laugh—the Faucett brothers. They came up from Birmingham about ten years ago and take care of most of the furnace problems in the town. Here's their number."

He took a pile of news releases up to the editorial offices to edit for next week.

At the top of the spiral staircase, he set the papers on his desk, walked over to the window and opened the shutters. The second floor looked out onto the verandah of the hotel; to the right he could see the railroad tracks atop an artificial embankment built out from the hill that rose above the town. A Southern Pacific train passed quietly, including a man on the caboose waving a red lantern down the line.

The mid-afternoon sun reflected on the shiny rails and on the trees that covered the hills rising beyond. Topping the hill above was a giant antenna that brought civilization by cable to the valley; it stood out like a prophet of mechanical doom against the blue sky. It was, he soon found out, a joint venture between

Mitchell Ackermann and an old high school classmate of Oliver's, Clark Wechsler.

Ensconced at his rolltop, Oliver called his sister's house but got no answer. As the phone rang and rang, he looked up at the *Star Wars* poster and said to himself, though out loud, "Darth Vader has got to go."

"The hell he will!" returned an even louder voice from the stairwell. "He's the spirit of the County Board of Supervisors and deserves a place of honor."

A tall young man stepped up from below, crushed a diet soda can in one huge fist, tossed it into the wastebasket, bounded over to the desk by the door, pulled out the chair with his left foot, and finally reached for Oliver's hand to give it a hearty shake. It was all done with an economy of motion that rivaled the Harlem Globetrotters. He spoke at a similar pace.

"Hi, I'm Scoop. Real name is Phillip Wicker but I like Scoop better, even if it is a little bit clichéd. I'm your star reporter and I don't always want to be a newspaper man since I'm really a writer," he paused momentarily to let go of Oliver's hand and sat down with a thud, "but until my ship arrives, this is all good practice. Someday I'll let you read my novel. I've got a degree and I know how to spell. You're my new editor, Oliver Swindler, and am I glad because Black isn't a nice guy, being an absolute jerk, first class fuck-up, plus he has cereal breath."

"Glad to meet you," Oliver smiled, "especially if you're as valuable as you say."

"I am. I go to all these Town Board meetings and county government meetings and more meetings and more meetings, then I review restaurants and drive the back roads in rain and sleet while you sit home and philosophize about the freedom of the press."

"What's up for next week?" Oliver asked. "In your opinion?"

"There's a local bowling tournament but that's being covered by Bob Rydel—he's one of your fleet of three high school sports reporters and he knows how to take pictures. Then turkey season is coming to an end and you get to give the winner a check and pose for a picture with Greig. And then the hospital fund drive starts, but I'll cover that. I guess the biggest items are the public hearing on the River Management Plan being held in Asheville— it's not that far away and a lot of folks around here think the Park Service is in league with the U.N., the U.N. being represented with black helicopters, so there's big interest in government planning. Then the local Planning Board's donnybrook over the coming of the Heavenly Cheeseburgers restaurant chain," he shuffled through the mass of papers on his desk. "Unfortunately it looks like they're both next Thursday night."

The young man paused for a breath, and Oliver quickly asked, "Heavenly Cheeseburgers? Forgive me, but I've lived in Manhattan most of the past twenty-five years. What are Heavenly Cheeseburgers?"

"It's a restaurant that gives you cheeseburgers made with a lot of different cheeses—something we all need to keep our livers in shape. Now the river stuff is always loud: the same approvers and a-ginners show up at every meeting, and I've covered so many that I pretty well know the scorecard. But since you're from a big city, you must be familiar with the arguments over fast food outlets and growth, so I'd say the burger hearing is right for you."

"Must you smoke?"

"I don't drink and I know smoking's bad, and I work my butt off ... so lay off. Right?

"Right," Oliver muttered. He was the boss, but only in name as yet. "Can you give me a succinct statement on each issue?"

"Sure." He leaned back in his chair at a precarious angle. "The Feds are making this river one of the first national parks in the state where land control is handled through local zoning regulations with the minimum of land purchase using public monies. A lot of locals are for it, arguing that money and new business will be coming in and the park service can help in policing the visitors. But almost as many people are upset that property values will fall—they cite the messes at other national parks—and small towns will lose local control, and they're most upset because the final word in any condemnations of land will be in the hands of whoever happens to be the Secretary of the Interior."

Scoop didn't wait for Oliver's reaction but continued his freight-train delivery. "Finally, the people from the government are arrogant and never seem to be able to answer a straight question with a direct answer. Okay?"

"Yes." Oliver paused, then asked, "What do they all think of Heavenly Cheeseburgers?"

"This one's got everyone upset. The Chamber of Commerce and most of the businessfolk are for it. Even the holier-than-thou friends of Black seem to be in favor of letting the restaurant in."

"And who are they?"

"This self-styled preacher from Atlanta who runs some kind of an AA rehab joint up on Stalker Mountain—he's right out of stories about cults and all the stuff that goes with it. I ask you—why would anybody start anything to do with alcoholics and set up shop just outside of Fernglade, then start a school for the families in the Stalker Mountain Community? Most of the people up there are more interested in largemouth bass and the price of kids' clothes.

"As for Black, he's a member of this sort of AA group that bought the old Ferrell estate up in the woods at the edge of town. They're friends of Greig and rather strange, if you ask me. Their leader has an incredible ego. For some reason he has a lot of followers who live up there in dorms, and according to a few people I know, a lot of friends in Atlanta and New York. In fact, they brought some hot-shot lawyer up from Atlanta to 'manage the business' or something. Why would they need a big-city lawyer for a little mountain rehab center? I ask you."

After a momentary pause to see if Scoop had more to say, or if, perhaps, he would ever pause for breath, Oliver asked, "So I gather there's more to this than meets the eye."

"Yeah, but this isn't the place to talk about it. Anyway, the only major group of entrepreneurs against are the real estate people because they think they can make more money selling summer homes to upscale Atlantans and feel that within a short time the Feds will claim most of the old buildings as historical so the only place left to sell for development is raw land and there's not too much of that fit for building—at least according to the present zoning laws and until a new sewage plant is installed."

"What's the paper's editorial stand?"

"Greig is guarded about commercial development along the river; says he wants to keep an open mind. He and his wife are dead set against the burger chain, but Black has a powerful influence on Greig so I really don't know."

"So if I should write an editorial—"

"Make it about glorious summer days ahead or geese flying south or something—at least until these latest meetings are over."

"Cereal breath?" asked Oliver.

"Black's idea of a snack is to fill a bowl with Quaker Puffed Rice, then squirt out a lot of honey by squeezing one of those plastic honey-bear containers all over it. It's pretty disgusting."

"So," said Oliver, "I attend the Planning Board on Thursday night. Where do you go now?"

"No place special—just came in to say hello. Nothing doing now until Monday morning. I get here about seven o'clock."

"Glad to know you, Scoop. I guess there's no need for me to worry; it sounds like you've got things under control." He give the kid a warm smile. "Oh, is there a number where you can be reached, just in case something comes up?"

"Sure, I got a room over in Mars Hill. Here's the number. If I'm not there someone will take a message."

"Why don't you stay here?"

"Mars Hill may not be the best place in the world but at least it's alive most of the time and for what it's worth, a college town. This place is frankly dull. One of the only reasons I stay around here is to have a job. But I think Greig will eventually open a Mars Hill office and I'd like to work out of there. Anyhow, it's good to meet you, Oliver," he said and with one movement rose from the chair, stepped quickly over to the hole in the floor and disappeared down the spiral stairs.

Oliver thought for a moment about what looked like all sorts of deep, still waters in the town and what might be some of the resulting events, but suddenly gardening came to mind. It was early spring in the mountains and the paper was already behind in having a garden column. What would it be? Something catchy, he told himself. *Got it. We'll call the column "The Wild Gardener."* Remembering that nobody ever minded a double entendre, especially a mild one, a picture rose in his mind of one of the glories of a mountain spring, *Lindera benzoin.* And immediately he had both a column title and a byline: "Spicebush."

He rolled a sheet of paper in the minty-green Selectric and, with a manila folder at his right hand—now labeled "Spicebush"— he began to tap out his first column about the wonderful part of the world that western North Carolinians lived in. Then he cut a few news releases from three paragraphs to one, inserting correct punctuation, fixed some typos, and felt as if he had accomplished something, however small, in his new role as Editor of *The Fernglade Republican.* He then made a call to the Faucett brothers, but their line was busy.

Downstairs in the office Mary-Beth was talking to Adrian about an ad in what Adrian hoped would be an upcoming advertising supplement. Adrian turned to Oliver with a handful of material—including photos of caskets and close-ups of lining materials. He looked over her shoulder at an article on handling bereavement.

"You've got to be kidding," he said. "This is a special?"

"It's 'Death as a Way of Life.' It's supposed to tell the reader how to go about getting funeral services and in general to deal with death and all the rest of the problems surrounding funerals—and sell ads. I heard about it at the State Press Association Dinner."

"How many funeral houses are there in this part of the state?" he asked.

"I think about five."

"Would they all take ads?"

"Unfortunately not all of them," she answered with a snap in her voice.

"Then who pays for the supplement?"

"Well, I would hope to get some other ads."

"Adrian, who besides people directly connected to the industry is going to advertise in a supplement devoted to the cause of death?"

"Not too many," she said, chagrin and a touch of contempt in her tone. "Florists, maybe. Caterers, if there were any." She stifled a giggle. "Hairdressers that specialize in blue tints?"

"And while this paper isn't raking it in, is it out of the red?"

"I told you we're under pressure from that other paper but yes, the paper is doing okay."

"Was this Greig's idea?"

"No, and it wasn't mine either, damn it."

"Who," he persisted, noticing that Mary-Beth had suddenly become very busy.

"It was Simon. I knew it wasn't a good idea ... but he often can't help but give in to him."

"I'm sorry," he said.

"You should be. You haven't known me long but I should think you'd see that I wouldn't fall for this funeral stuff. This is the kind of ad best served up by a big-city daily, well, like the Asheville paper."

"You think Greig would give it up?" he asked.

"If you asked him, maybe ... and offer him a good substitute."

"How about a special on hunting along the Toe River or around western North Carolina? I'm sure we have plenty of photos dealing with deer and turkey, not to mention great fishing; that kind of subject matter would appeal to all sorts of suppliers."

He turned to Mary-Beth. "Any calls for me? I mean for the editor?"

"No calls for you as you, but as editor there were three. The DA's office called; seems the state police raided an old farmhouse in Burnsville and found a pornographic film ring in full—or should I say, lack of regalia—and he'd like some coverage."

"I assume some of the actors will, too. What's the timetable?"

She consulted some notes.

"They were arraigned before a local justice of the peace and sent to the county jail on $2,000 bail. Charges were second-degree obscenity which is a misdemeanor. Eleven people and a horse were involved. The case is going to a county grand jury next Tuesday."

"I'll make a note to call next week."

"And the Dalai Lama is visiting a monastery located above the village of Bear Valley, specifically a tax-free religious organization that runs a big hotel up there on five hundred acres."

"The real Dalai Lama?"

"In the flesh. But you've got to hurry. They said he'll only be there for lunch, then he's off to other Tibetan centers in Buffalo, Boston, Miami, and Colorado. Here's their number. Ask for Dick

Andrews."

"Before you say anything," interjected Adrian with a grin, "remember: they've been pushing that 'one-world' idea for generations."

"One other thing, Oliver: Professor Miles Felter from the community college called. He's giving a series of lectures on early settlers in the mountains and wondered if you would call him about doing a feature on his class. Here's his number."

Oliver sighed, as much with pleasure at having actual responsibilities as with chagrin over the likely tedium of some of his tasks.

"Thank you Mary-Beth," he said before climbing the stairway again.

"Felter, here," said a cultured voice full of self-importance.

"Mr. Felter—"

"Professor Felter."

"Right. Professor Felter. This is Oliver Swindler, editor of *The Fernglade Republican*. You called earlier?"

"Yes, I did." He paused. "Now, Swindler, what I—"

"Mr. Swindler." Two could play that game. "You want my paper to cover something you're doing, I understand. Something important, I presume?"

He could hear controlled irritation coupled with barely modulated arrogance in the other's voice.

"Certainly it's important. I'm actively involved with organizing a series of scholarly get-togethers for members of the county who maintain an interest in their familial roots. In essence, people with an active respect for history. I have planned a series of lectures on several important aspects of county history. I'm especially interested in locating those who are second or third generation in the area, and I know that many of them read your local paper."

"How do you propose wording the press release to make sure the newcomers stay away?"

"Well, I wouldn't go so far as to limit the lectures in such a cavalier fashion."

"Then you will open them to anyone who applies."

"Certainly."

"Could you type me a short release, double spaced, and drop it off or mail it to us?"

"I'll see if I have the time."

"I need it by next Wednesday, Professor. Thank you for letting us know about your project. Have a good day."

"Good day."

The phone went dead, and Oliver smiled. No doubt their paths would cross again, and it was just as well to maintain chilly politeness instead of cordial animosity—especially if the arrogant gentleman was his sister's friend. Just for fun, he called the number for the Lama. The lines of Ogden Nash flitted through his mind: "The one-L lama, he's a priest. The two-L llama, he's a beast."

"Peace," said a young girl's voice. "This is the Haven."

From the way she said it he knew there was a capital H. "Is Dick Andrews there?"

"Just a moment," and, as expected, the phone turned to taped music; instead of modern melodies, it was a Tibetan chant.

"Dick here, who's this?"

"Oliver Swindler from *The Republican*."

"Oh, Swindler. I've got a great story here. The Dalai Lama is visiting today, in fact he's conducting prayers right now"—there was the sound of a hundred or so sandals slapping on a dais and a gong rang, the same pitch used to introduce Oliver's favorite J. Arthur Rank pictures—"and he's going to deliver a discourse on the nature of reincarnation. Confidentially, we had hoped to get Shirley MacLaine here but she couldn't make it—oh, it's all so beautiful. You know, peace and love, love and peace—"

"—all over the land."

"Yes. We're having five different private ceremonies, each with different flavors of tea and various kinds of bean cakes, then solemn meditations. We will pray for the people of his former country. You know according to Tibetan teachings, there will be only fourteen Dalai Lamas, and this gentleman is the last."

"But he's leaving shortly?"

"Oh, yes. Though most people think he has his own private plane, he must use the same airlines that we all use and as I understand, he sits in coach and has to check his own bags as well."

"Well, it would take me an hour to get there. Would he wait?"

"Oh, heavens no! He has to get to Asheville for a flight. He's divine. As such his mission can never be relegated to time. He comes, he goes."

"Well, Dick, it's impossible for today. Could you let me know when he might arrive again? Now I understand you're a tax-exempt religious organization?"

Suddenly, the voice became icy. "The Constitution guarantees religious freedom. We are legally exempt."

"I'll make a note of it," Oliver said, and quickly hung up, wondering at the defensive note in Andrews's voice.

When he descended again to the front office, he asked about the professor.

"He ... well, he can be charming, but oh so arrogant," said Adrian. "He believes—really—that he's the spiritual heir to all the kings of England."

"A perfect delight," added Mary-Beth, "but keep him at arm's length. A very long arm, you know?"

The three of them left the paper and walked across Main Street to the hotel. A ruckus in front of the National Park Service office stopped them momentarily. Five people marched up and down the sidewalk carrying hand-lettered signs that proclaimed: THE PARK SERVICE GIVES RATTLERS A BAD NAME! FEDS GO HOME, and various other forms of empty venom.

"Don't bother to get your camera," Adrian said, grabbing his elbow. "Scoop has plenty of stock footage on the picketing and it's always the same people anyway."

"That doesn't mean they shouldn't have coverage."

"No, you're right. Frankly I think I agree with them. We have enough government here anyhow. But it gets tiresome after a while."

The bar was empty but for a local who greeted Mary-Beth and immediately turned back to his drink. The trio sat down at a table and Black came over for the order. There was almost a domino effect to the wrinkles on his face when he opened his mouth and said: "Good day to you all."

Almost before they could get settled in, Black returned with a sour for Adrian, a fuzzy navel for Mary-Beth, and wine for Oliver. As soon as he was back behind the bar polishing glasses, Oliver leaned close and asked, "Why is he so creepy, and why doesn't he like us?"

"Well for one thing, how would you like to wait on tables when you're an advisor to a newspaper instead of being the editor?" asked Adrian.

"I never tip him," said Mary-Beth.

"There's a group in this town," continued Adrian, "that likes to run things. They're a double old-boy network, worse than in most small towns, and this bunch is especially mean and greedy. I think Clark Wechsler is the ringleader; at least he seems the smartest of the three. I wouldn't trust any of them as far as you can throw a cotton ball against a hurricane."

"Hear, hear," said Mary-Beth.

"Scoop can tell you a lot more," continued Adrian. "The Heavenly Cheeseburgers chain didn't show up out of the blue or find this spot by throwing darts at a road map."

"I remember Clark Wechsler from school days," said Oliver. "Besides making money off of pet funerals, he was the kind of kid who never got in trouble with the teachers. If he blew a spitball through a soda straw he looked like sweetness personified before it hit the poor kid in the front row. And if he ever was caught, his parents would descend on the school like a pair of praying mantises, ready to bite off the teacher's head. Or the principal's, for that matter."

"Tell him," said Mary-Beth, "about Alice, Mr. Davis's wife."

"Must I?"

"You must."

"Alice is a pain in the butt. She's not very nice. She puts on airs and openly wishes she was back in a big city. Snobby is the word. Unfortunately for us—"

"—but fortunately for her—" interrupted Mary-Beth.

"—she's loved by our publisher," continued Adrian. "And when I say she's trouble, I'm being kind. Greig tries to make up projects for her and sends her off to the city to do research fairly often—"

"—not often enough—"

"—and lets her design the whole paper. So my advice is to give her a wide berth and, if you want to make changes, make them nice and slowly."

"He probably won't have that much trouble," said Mary-Beth, "because he's a man."

"You're right. She'll keep quiet whenever Oliver's around."

"How was she with Black?"

"Explosive," said Adrian. Mary-Beth vigorously nodded her head and grinned. "They were constantly at each other's throats.

Black's ego was even larger than Alice's. They literally screamed at each other all the time."

"Frankly," said Mary-Beth, "I thought there was a little bit too much screaming."

"I knew," he said, "that this set-up was all too perfect. But to change the subject, how about dinner?"

"I'm off for home because after a week of paper work, I'm due for socializing with mom," said Mary-Beth, "See you on Monday."

"And I promised my mother I'd come over for dinner tonight long before you showed up. Unless you want to come home and meet my mother?"

Oliver couldn't quite tell if Adrian's smile was inviting or ironic. He decided to assume the latter.

"I'd love to but not tonight. I'll just go back to my lonely hotel room and read back issues of *TV Guide*."

Chapter Seven

Oliver left the hotel and walked slowly back to the newspaper office to call Scoop. Finding the door to Davis's office open with light flooding the hallway, he knocked on the side of the doorjamb.

"Come in," boomed a voice. Oliver saw a large man, not fat, just big, turned and stretched out a massive hand across the desk in greeting. "Oliver, sit down. I hadn't planned on seeing you until tomorrow, but I'm here, by chance, so let's get acquainted."

Greig Davis, Oliver noted, had the largest nose he'd seen outside of a circus. It propped up a pair of heavy bifocals, the stems disappearing under a tousled fringe of graying brown hair. But his eyes were kind and he exuded a feeling of trust.

"First," he said, "I wanted to invite you over for dinner this weekend but Alice just learned of a death in her family and left for Atlanta on the ten o'clock bus. Maybe we could meet at the hotel later tonight or tomorrow and talk about schedules and such. That way you could take the rest of the evening off to settle in.

"There's really no problem with the paper," he continued. "I went over and checked the unused news from last week and there's plenty of stuff to fill out an issue, and Jerry is up to date on doing ads for Easter. You'll need an editorial, and of course, perhaps a short note of introduction to the readers, but that could all wait 'til Monday morning."

"Thank you. You OK with my using 'Greig'?"

"Certainly. Everyone does. After all, we're going to run this paper together."

"Well, I think I will get out for the day," said Oliver. "But before I go, I'd like to get a little more information on—I suppose you'd call him my predecessor. What do I need to know about Simon Black?"

Davis bridged his fingers and settled back in his chair.

"When Mullens ran the paper he never noticed that circulation was not keeping up with the increased costs of doing business. As long as his subscriber rolls stayed fairly constant he was happy. Besides, the paper was paid off and his wants were small.

"After Alice and I picked it up we knew something had to be done. Especially about the advertising. Within our second week we lost the local supermarket account when the owner went to direct mailing. That was a big loss. Alice and I worked ten-hour days every day except Sunday to figure out what to do, and do it.

"The next problem was covering all the local activities and taking more pictures. For example, when graduation came around, I had the idea of running an individual photo of every child who graduated in this and neighboring counties. But I was warned that using family-provided pictures would lead to disaster—this was before we were fully computerized, so I don't think you realize— you can't even imagine—how much time it would take just to crop the photos, much less retouch them, get them in shape for reproduction. Some were out of focus, or had three people in them, the boys' hair wasn't combed, not like real head shots..." He sighed, though almost, it seemed to Oliver, with pleasure at recalling the days of chaos.

"I couldn't do it alone. Alice was already doing all the layout—

luckily we had Adrian almost from the start—and she sold ads—my God, did she sell. So I asked Mullens for some advice and he told me to hire a man named David Mangini, and he was a wonder. He ran this place like a well-ordered machine, made appointments for photos, used a good camera, shot most of them outside by the river. In the end, it became a great edition. But, unfortunately, he was called home about a year ago with family problems.

"So, I ran an ad in the paper for an experienced editor and Simon Black walked in. He was an ex-advertising man and promoter, first from New York then from Atlanta, and knew all the angles—plus he was one fast talker: the original and one-and-only snake-oil salesman. And he really didn't walk in unannounced. Clark Wechsler—who you probably remember, he says he knows you from high school days, and who's been an occasional business partner of mine—told me the man was too good for any other job, and luckily, I listened.

"Things started out in a reasonable way. Some of his ideas were very, very good. The problem is, Black has little sense of responsibility, and we continually lost money because advertisers had been promised the Holy Grail and got a rusty tin can. Remember, Oliver, one price for everyone and never guarantee placement of an ad. Adrian can ask for it and if it's a good customer perhaps we can go along, but never, never guarantee."

Oliver nodded, though inwardly he doubted there were many times that Adrian didn't get what she asked for.

"After a few months Black began to get the Pulitzer Complex. That's an affliction that every newspaperman or woman gets at least once, I suspect, though eventually most of them get it out of their systems. So, instead of dealing with local priorities he set his sights on the big news picture and tried to become the John Chancellor of Fernglade. Frankly, people didn't buy it. Nobody wanted to read about political decisions in Washington. People who work hard every day in an area like this want a little peace of mind, especially in the paper they read for obits and who's getting married next week. They have enough trouble reasoning out some of the actions of their own local politicians—and that's not a put-down. Since I've been here I've spent hours trying to figure out many of the actions of our own Board of Supervisors. Anyway, it didn't take them long for our readers to react. For the first time in years subscriptions went down, both new and renewals. And you should have read the letters to the editor. When I approached Black he said it was his responsibility to educate the readers. I agreed but only to a point, and that point was falling circulation.

"Finally—and I would appreciate your keeping this to yourself—he and my wife did not get along. Alice is not always the easiest person to live with, and she can get on a person's nerves. But the fighting between them became intolerable. And not only did he cause trouble with her, he inspired disruption among the entire staff.

"One thing led to another, and in the end I had to ask him to leave. But my good friend the Reverend Starker convinced me to hire Black as an advisor to help in various business decisions that are often out of my reach. Now we have weekly conferences—but let me say up front that if Black suggests something you're not in entire agreement with, I'll try and back you the entire way."

Oliver couldn't miss the word "try" but said nothing.

"When Black left here," continued Davis, "he went back to work for Mitch Ackermann. Why he waits tables is beyond me, but sometimes I think he takes a perverse delight in doing it." He stretched behind his desk, then sat forward again. "That's the story. It's hard to believe it's been less than a year."

"I appreciate that information, Greig. I had to ask. I find him extremely strange."

"That's okay. Ignore him and all will be well. Listen, why don't we get together for dinner tomorrow evening? It'll be more relaxed, we can get to know each other better. How about eight o'clock, at the hotel?"

"That sounds good, Greig." Oliver got up, thanked Davis for his time and the rather useful background information, and went back upstairs.

The man who answered the phone at Scoop's rooming house said he'd take a message but that the kid probably wouldn't be in until late. After checking the paper for sources of entertainment on a Friday night in the mountains, Oliver settled for the big time and drove the thirty-some miles to the new Asheville Mall, where he bought a few shirts, a new tape recorder, and finally stopped for a Chinese dinner at an Asian food buffet. Then he drove back home.

It was about nine-thirty when he crossed the bridge to Fernglade, where he was stopped just before the town line by a uniformed North Carolina State Trooper in a patrol car with a flashing light.

"May I please see your driver's license, sir?"

"Certainly, Officer. What's up?" he asked, noting the nameplate on the trooper's pocket was Hindshaw. He probed his memory while the man scanned his license, then it came to him.

"You're Lionel Hindshaw, aren't you. Mary Hindshaw's kid. You were the little boy that found the bear cub and brought it home to Sunday church when I was in my senior year."

"I surely did," he said and looked more closely at Oliver's license. "And you're Oliver Swindler. Why, you wrote a short story about me and the bear and it appeared in *Reader's Digest*. How are you?"

"Fine, fine. I'm moving back to town now and I've taken the job as editor of the newspaper."

"That's good news," he said and handed the license and cards back. "Don't forget to get your license and registration changed."

"I won't, Lionel. By the way, why did you stop me?"

"I guess it's okay to talk to you. In fact some publicity might just help. It's your car. There are drugs entering the county and they usually come up the back way. And the pushers don't drive around in big fancy cars; that only attracts attention. They pick cars like VWs. We've stopped a lot of garbage on this bridge. Problem is the people who live around here refuse to believe what's going on. They think everything's perfect, just like the old days. If a kid gets hooked on coke or painkillers, they pretend it's just growing pains showing up, usually until it's too late and the kid's been picked up and winds up in court. It wouldn't hurt, Mr. Swindler, for the local paper to report some of this."

"Any leads to people involved?"

"This has to be kept confidential—no kidding--but I do have suspicions about that guy who runs the hotel and his crew. He or somebody like him could be bringing the stuff into town. I'd suggest you check with the sheriff."

"I will, Lionel. Oh, didn't you marry a local girl? I believe my sister said something a while back...?"

"Yes, but we're divorced. I'm living in the barracks now."

"Sorry to hear that," said Oliver. "Well, good luck to you."

"And good night to you." Hindshaw walked back to his car, Oliver's parking lights reflected by the well-polished leather of his tall black boots.

Dim lights were shining through the hotel's basement windows, and two old pickup trucks were by the back door. Oliver parked his car and walked around to the front.

The lobby was empty, though music was playing from the restaurant. He walked into the dining room; no-one was there except Ackermann and Black, sitting at the far end of the bar, deep in a muffled conversation. The colored lights around the bottles reflected in the giant mirror reminded Oliver of the inane, yet somehow charming, lighting in the Disney movies he'd seen as a child.

They hadn't heard him enter, and when Black saw him he did a quick double-take. For an instant he would have credited them with anything from planning to shoot the governor to stealing the Statue of Liberty's torch, but in microseconds a look of innocence beatified both their faces.

"Swindler, good evening," said Ackermann. "How about a drink to take off the evening's chill?"

"Nothing, thanks. I heard the music so I thought I'd look in. There's not much going on in town; the streets are pretty empty and I was curious who might still be up and around. I'll just say good night. I think I'll walk over to my sister's house to see if she's back from Atlanta. Night, gentlemen."

By now the sky was black, and what little cloud cover there was seemed to float just high enough over Fernglade to reflect the amber streetlights on the damp pavements. As he walked he could suddenly hear a great deal of traffic, much of it coming from the direction of Mill Street. Another state trooper passed by, lights flashing and siren wailing.

Suddenly, a thought flew into his brain, warning him to take it slow and easy, to walk with a measured pace and keep out of sight as long as he could. He approached his old homestead from across the street and stood behind a clump of bushes to take in the scene before him.

All the downstairs lights of the house were shining brightly, and lights flashed atop two sheriff's cars in the driveway. Behind them was an ambulance and a new Pontiac sedan with MD plates, and two more state trooper cars out in the street.

With the patience and care of an experienced woods-walker, Oliver crossed the street down by the river, came up the other side and crept up to the back of his house, then crouched down behind the row of trimmed boxwoods under the kitchen window.

"Check over here," said a voice.

"Right, Sheriff," said another.

"Is she dead, Doc?" asked a third.

"No doubt about it," answered another man.

Slowly, Oliver looked over the windowsill.

The kitchen door was wide open and every light in the room was on. The floor from the old gas stove to the refrigerator was littered with broken china, shards of white and blue. A small teapot in a complex pattern of gold and green was broken in half, the handle side near the kitchen table's left leg, the spout near the right. Starting from a broken bowl, granulated sugar swirled and sparkle across the Mondrian pattern of red and brown squares of shiny quarry tile.

The wooden wall lamp that Oliver had made in shop class hung by its cord from the wall socket over the table; a large and wicked instrument, its handle smeared with blood, just balanced in the crack between the table edge and the extra leaf. A bright, cheerful wallpaper of tiny teapots, coffee grinders, and pendulum clocks was now spattered with dots and lines of what, he realized, had to be drying blood. Uniformed men were everywhere, and Oliver had avoided looking at the one man among them in street clothes. He finally forced his eyes in that direction.

A doctor—Oliver presumed that's who he was—was just covering a woman's face with a coroner's blanket. His sister's face.

Oliver sank to his knees, his breathing hard, his hands in the dirt, the right hand suddenly gripping some familiar object.

"Who's out there?" somebody cried out. "There's somebody out in the bushes ... near that window over there."

In an instant flashlights were shining in Oliver's face and strong hands grabbed his shoulders.

"Bring him in to the kitchen." The sheriff walked over.

"Who are you?"

"I'm Oliver Swindler. I was born in this house and my sister—that's my sister on the stretcher. This is her house. What's happened to her?"

"It would seem your sister's been ... it looks like there's been foul play, Mr. Swindler."

Without ceremony, the sheriff removed the shroud from the body long enough for Oliver to know beyond doubt it was Imogene. A state of shock froze him in place.

"What's that in his hand?" asked the sheriff.

"Looks like a bloody knife," said the deputy.

Putting on a rubber glove, the deputy took the knife from Oliver's clenched hand.

"It's a knife of some kind and it's covered with fresh blood."

"This yours?" said the sheriff.

"No," said Oliver, "it was in the dirt under the window. I fell on it, and just ... grabbed it."

"I'm sorry, Oliver. There was nothing we could do to save her. It was ... pretty much instantaneous," said the man who looked like the doctor. "You don't recognize me, but I'm Dr. Selfert. Haven't seen you in a dog's age."

"You know him?" asked the sheriff.

"Sure, that's Oliver. That's his sister over there. And from what I've seen of her body, he had nothing to do with killing her. There's too much blood."

"What in God's name happened to her?" asked Oliver.

"I won't know everything until I do a better examination but from what I found I'd say she was—there's no polite way of telling you this—she was slashed so many times it looks as though a maniac was loose in this room. If it's any consolation, many of the cuts were so deep that she must have died immediately."

"But who would do something like this?" Oliver stammered,

before realizing how silly it must sound to the men in that kitchen. He had read enough big-city crime stories and seen enough nightly television to have witnessed violent scenes like this before, but before he was always removed from personal involvement; the bodies had been anonymous.

"Sorry you had to find out his way, Mr. Swindler," said the sheriff, sounding less blunt now. "Are you able to answer a few questions for me?"

"I guess so," he said, his voice still shaky, and followed the sheriff out into the hall.

"Why are you here?"

"I arrived in town yesterday afternoon—I've been hired as the new editor of the paper ... the *Republican*—I'm supposed to start tomorrow. So I came right home last night, and when I drove up the house was dark. I thought my sister was in Atlanta with a garden club she belongs to and would be back sometime today. I came in—I used a key that she hides on the front porch and let myself in." *You're babbling*, he told himself. *Calm down. Speak slowly*. He took a deep breath.

"The house was cold—the furnace isn't working—and I didn't want to cook dinner and eat alone, and then it began to storm again. So I went over to the hotel and got a room there."

Electronic flashes continued to go off as men walked about the kitchen with cameras, tape measures and chalk. From the kitchen a deputy's voice floated into the hall, loud enough for Oliver to hear.

"It looks like she was alone all right. The broken china on the floor is all clean ... must have fallen out of the cabinet when she grabbed for the door."

"Listen, Mr. Swindler, I know this'll sound, well, kind of strange, but did your sister have any enemies, you know, people that you might suspect of ...?" The sheriff's voice trailed off.

"Of course not, at least nobody who would do a thing like this. You aware of any crazies running around the county?"

"No," answered the sheriff, "but of course I'll continue to check. Any other relatives?"

"We have two other sisters: Florence lives in Spruce Pine and our other sister Linda is in Atlanta. But no other close relatives that I know of."

"Spruce Pine isn't that far away," said the sheriff.

"Let me call her?" Oliver asked.

"In a few minutes, Mr. Swindler. Just answer a few more questions first, and then you can call her and go back to the hotel."

Dr. Selfert stepped into the doorway. "I'm going now, Sheriff. I'll do a P.M. tonight and call you later."

"Any idea of how long she's been dead, Doc?"

"Knowing that the house has been cold for a day or two makes it easier. I'd say sometime late this morning, before noon."

"Thanks," said the sheriff and turned back to Oliver. "We'll be here quite a while, and I've got to check the rest of the house. Right now there isn't a sign of who the intruder was. I suggest you stay at the hotel again tonight."

Oliver stood there a moment then asked: "Could I at least wash up a little?" On the sheriff's nod he walked down the hall to the powder room; while he scrubbed his hands, they rolled the stainless steel stretcher out to the ambulance on its silent, black rubber tires. He came out to watch them load the body—*Imogene's body*—into the ambulance; felt a shudder as the edge of the plastic blanket caught in the thorns of a barberry bush, one of many that lined either side of the path to the street. A deputy tugged the blanket into place, and Oliver turned back to the kitchen.

Another deputy was just handing the sheriff a plastic bag containing the knife Oliver had picked up.

"Ever seen anything like this before?" the sheriff asked.

"As a matter of fact, it's a Japanese eel-skinning knife. Years ago I was a fisherman—of sorts—and that knife was one I used to use. I think it's been out in the garage, probably ever since I moved away."

"Ugly looking thing. I'll have more questions for you later."

"Could I call my sister now?"

"Hey, have you guys checked out the front where the phone is? Okay, Mr. Swindler, you can use the phone to call your sister."

Imogene kept the phone in the living room. Even with all the lights on, the hall seemed dark and foreboding. He reached for the bridge lamp, his arm remembering where it should be. He flipped through the address book—also exactly where he expected it to be—and quickly found and dialed Florence's number.

"Oliver," she said, "how good to hear your voice! Where are you?"

"I'm at Imogene's, Florence. But I have some very sad news."

"What? Is Imogene okay?"

"No. She's not. There's no good way to put this, Florence, but Imogene's dead. She was murdered sometime today."

"Oh, my God!"

Oliver let his sister sob, loudly at first, then, after a moment, more gently, and soon her voice was calm. Slowly and deliberately he told her everything he knew.

"Who could have done this?" Florence sounded as bewildered as Oliver had been with the sheriff.

"It looks like a madman. Nobody sane could do what's been done here." He paused. "Would you call Linda?"

"Of course. Oliver, take care of yourself. And if you learn anything call me."

"I will. Of course."

It was Thursday night, and they agreed to meet Saturday at the Fernglade funeral home "to make arrangements."

"Good night, Florence."

After a moment's thought he called the paper, where the answering machine kicked in. He waited until Scoop's extension came up, then asked Scoop to call back with a number where Oliver could reach him.

He went back to the still hectic kitchen to tell the sheriff he was leaving. His last thought as he walked out the door was how pointless it would be to call the Faucett Brothers now.

There was a bright quarter moon in the sky. Clouds were quickly creeping in from the west, and by the time he reached the street filtered moonlight washed over the lawn and was reflected in the windows of the police cars. He turned to the left and quietly strolled down to the bank overlooking the river. A cold breeze blew off the water. The ripples reflected the moon countless times.

He pivoted and walked back to Main Street and then to the hotel, heading straight for the bar; except for one man at the far end the room was empty. Oliver pulled up a stool. Ackermann was polishing glasses.

"What'll you have, Swindler?"

"A double scotch, please."

Oliver looked at his reflection from behind the bar, almost blinded by the colored lights shining on the bottles. Even though he had not seen Imogene until his recent return, they talked on the phone ever month or so. To have her throat cut in her own kitchen seemed to him the ultimate violation.

He was glad he was staying in the hotel instead of at the house and its scene of horror. He lost himself in the old cracked mirror, following the clouded spider webs from one edge to the other. He didn't remember how many drinks Ackermann set in front of him before he finally went upstairs.

In his room he took off both jacket and shoes. Then he

looked around and even in his nervous state noticed that his book on rock gardening and the Maritime Alps was sitting on top of the radio. He had left it that morning between the radio and the travel clock. The rates in this hotel did not include room service of any kind: You got clean sheets once a week and made up your own bed, so nobody should have been in here. Obviously his room had been searched. He carefully checked his duffle; nothing was quite where he had left it. Whoever had conducted the search had been careful—but not careful enough.

He tuned the radio to some quasi-jazz music from Asheville and lay back on the bed to think for a moment. Then he heard a noise in the hall, a shuffling of feet that stopped by his door before it slowly passed by. A door down the hall opened and then closed.

He would have bet it was Room 11, though he was too tired to care enough to check. Nevertheless, before climbing into bed, still wearing the rest of his clothes, Oliver propped the one chair in the room under the doorknob: he wasn't taking any chances.

Whatever the threat, implied or real, he needed to sleep; his head was pounding from one eye to the other.

Saturday

Chapter Eight

The morning sunlight was strong, but the moisture in the air diffused it, making it somehow dingy rather than bright. It had been a long time since he had such a headache like the agony of last night, and it took some time for Oliver to pull his nervous system together. Now he felt only a slight roll of pain, so dressing was only a minor problem. His shirt smelled of cigarette smoke and an excess of alcohol. Lights continued to flash both within and over the top of his eyelids, and he turned on the Asheville news station for the nine o'clock news.

An announcer from the International School of Having No Accent said in fake-sorrowful voice, "One of the county's well-known citizens was found stabbed to death in Fernglade yesterday afternoon. Lifelong resident Imogene Swindler was known and loved by all. More on the local news report."

The national news from the wire services was depressing: a man who killed his wife in a mobile home park outside Phoenix over an argument about bingo winnings, a toxic chemical spill in Ohio, and, following a frantic-sounding advertisement for an interstate hardware chain, the latest failure of the most recent Middle East peace talks. Oliver tuned out through more dribble, more ads, a "lighthearted" story about a German shorthair pointer with a Columbus hat that sailed across the Mississippi River in a scale model of the Niña, and a brief local weather report. Finally, following a poorly created jingle that equally poorly sang the praises of Clark Wechsler's bank, he sat up to listen when the local announcer returned.

"Violence struck in Fernglade yesterday. The horrors usually associated with the big city visited one of the rustic towns along the Toe River where Imogene Swindler, born 62 years ago in the family home that sits just above the river, was brutally attacked and stabbed to death. According to our sources, the knife used is like those fishermen use for skinning eels. We have Sheriff Will Phibert on the line right now. What can you tell us, Sheriff? Any idea of who did this?"

"Not at this time."

"Are there any suspects?"

"There are always suspects."

"Well, can you tell us anything about the crime?"

"There's little to tell: an unmarried woman was brutally murdered in a small town. I have no other statement to make at this time."

"Thank you, Sheriff. That, ladies and gentlemen, was Sheriff Phibert reporting on the horrible crime in Fernglade discovered yesterday. We'll have more news following these messa—"

Oliver turned the radio off abruptly. He finished dressing, went downstairs to the bar and asked Black for a cup of coffee.

"Please accept my condolences over the death of your sister, Swindler," he said. Oliver felt that Black always put a certain edge into the pronunciation of "Swindler" that turned it from a name into a profession.

A pile of Saturday's Asheville papers sat on the edge of the bar with the headline in 80-point type: **MURDER IN FERNGLADE!** He scanned the story on page three and one paragraph stood out:

<pre>
    Miss Swindler was found by a neighbor's
son who had come over to cut her lawn on
Thursday afternoon. She had not been seen
since Tuesday so the lad walked into the
kitchen after calling out and found her cut-
up body in an untidy heap, partially wrapped
in an oilcloth from the kitchen table, her
right cheek next to an overturned cup of
cold coffee that had mingled with her blood.
The weapon was an antique eel-skinning knife
found sticking in the kitchen table.
</pre>

Oliver noted that the unnamed reporter had quite a flair, especially in his ability to write a complex sentence without breaking it into short cuts to fit the public's short attention span.

Black brought the coffee just as Sheriff Phibert walked into the room.

"Mind if I sit down?" asked Phibert.

"No, I expected to see you this morning. Want some coffee?"

"Sure, thanks."

Black walked off to the kitchen and was back with the coffee before the sheriff could hang his hat on the coat stand in the corner. Phibert settled his large frame into the chair, lit a cigar—nearly singeing his poorly-clipped moustache—and placed his hat on the table.

"Sorry to bother you again, Mr. Swindler, but I have to ask more questions. You haven't been in town for twenty-some years and the day after you come home, your sister's found murdered."

"I understand, Sheriff. This isn't easy to talk about yet. My sister was a good person and deserved better than this. Any idea how long she was dead? And was that eel-knife the weapon used?"

"Doctor Selfert is sticking to his original assumptions. He officially pronounced her death due to multiple stab wounds in the chest and heart. The tears in the flesh matched the serrated edge of the skinning knife. The time of death was sometime mid-Friday morning, probably between ten o'clock and noon. The doctor said there were many more cuts than needed to cause her death. Well, you saw how brutal it was. I tracked down the Woman's Club and they all arrived back from their trip in the morning. The trip organizer said your sister stepped off the bus at her corner about nine-thirty." He paused, then looked directly at Oliver. "So I have to ask you about your movements that day.

Oliver stared back at him. "Well, Sheriff, I left the hotel about eight, had breakfast at the diner, then went straight to the newspaper, had a tour, met the staff. Then I had lunch with Adrian Knapp, we came back to the paper and met my young reporter, Phillip Wicker. That kid Scoop. So if Imogene was killed before noon, I was with people all morning. Practically all day. I took phone calls in the office, then Adrian and I had cocktails, and then I met Greig Davis, and after that I drove down to Asheville and back. But listen, Sheriff, didn't Doctor Selfert say I couldn't have done it, there was so much blood? He said the murderer had to be covered with ... I mean, I presume you can count me out?"

"Well, yeah, according to the doc it's pretty clear it couldn't have been you. But I still have some questions for you. You're the new editor at the paper, right? What did you do before coming back to Fernglade?"

"I was an editor for a small publisher in Manhattan. And Sheriff, look, this is my sister we're talking about. I'm glad to give you any help I can. But my work history ...?"

"It's just important to know your background, Mr. Swindler. It's nothing personal at all. I'm just doing my job."

Oliver smiled despite himself, for the first time since the night before. "I heard you on the radio this morning and remembered Imogene talking about you a couple of elections ago, she said she thought you were 'a gallant broom ready to sweep the town clean.'"

"I don't know about 'gallant,' but I try to keep the town clean," he answered and took a puff on the cigar. "Just because we're small-town here doesn't mean we can't cope with violent death. During the summer when the population swells they all bring Atlanta ideas up to the mountains. It's just very unusual to have a murder of this violence without bringing in an obvious suspect within a few hours."

"Trust me, my sister had no enemies, at least not the type that would engage in this kind of behavior. Not for revenge or hate. Oh, sure, I imagine that over the years, Imogene had crossed some paths but the most obvious way for those enraged to retaliate would be unsigned letters or gossip behind muffled mouths at a church social or a tea party, not a frontal assault in a kitchen."

"I agree," said Phibert.

"I assume your men searched the rest of the house?"

"Every room, even the attic—and that's some big house. They were at it 'til early in the morning. No sign of a prowler anywhere. Her bedroom desk was neat and tidy; an open checkbook on the blotter and a short handwritten news story about her Woman's Club outing to Atlanta. Nothing of interest there. The back door lock was smashed with a hammer or like tool—but the interesting point is that the door was unlocked. There's no sign that the wood was banged or pushed in anyway."

"So someone wanted it to look like a break-in."

"Precisely."

"What about the knife?"

Phibert paused for a sip of coffee, then looked at his cigar. "Well, you pointed out the kind of knife it is. It's an eel-skinning knife, very old and worn. The blade has been carefully honed over many seasons so the maker's name is long gone. The handle's a very hard wood, also very worn. Apparently, the knife had been wiped clean before it became a murder weapon. There were no fingerprints, new or old, before the entire shaft was covered with your sister's blood—and you then picked it up."

"Would you have any objection to my looking around the house?" Oliver asked. "If you're finished with it as the"—he hesitated—"'scene of the crime'? I haven't seen it for many years but I might spot something that others have missed, something just out of place, or ...."

"We're done with it as a crime scene all right. If you hadn't offered I was about to ask you to do that. Just one thing: Don't touch anything, and, if you do find something, you're to let me know—so none of this 'keep-it-secret-for-the-big-story' kind of crap. I'm going back to Spruce Pine now. I'll be in the office all day," he said handing Oliver his card, "and my home phone is on the back. You call me if anything turns up."

After he grabbed his hat he turned for a moment.

"You know, just like most places in this great land there are drug problems here, too. I have suspicions but not enough to talk about, but you're in a position where you just might hear something. So keep me in mind, all right?"

Oliver nodded.

It was now a little after ten, time to lose himself in the operations of the news grind. He walked to the office and immediately noticed that the weighing pan was clean. Either the turkey season was over or the mighty hunters were still abed.

"Morning, Oliver," said Mary-Beth, her eyes glistening. "I don't quite know what to say. Are you all right? We all knew your sister and just can't believe what happened. If there's anything I can do—?"

"As a matter of fact, there is. If Adrian comes in would you tell her I'll call her tonight or tomorrow morning? I'm going upstairs to call my sister—our other sister—and see how she is this morning. I'll stop on my way down."

Florence, her voice still shaky, told him that Linda was already on her way from Atlanta, driving up, and would stay with her, but they would all plan to meet in the afternoon at the funeral parlor. He stared at the walls of his new office for twenty minutes or so, his thoughts hopping from childhood to yesterday, all the visions in his mind's eye superimposed over an indelible image of Imogene's body crumpled on the kitchen floor. Finally he roused himself. It was nearly noon, and he was already hungry, so he left the paper, stopped at the supermarket to buy a sandwich, a candy bar, and two bottles of beer from the deli counter, and slowly, almost hesitantly, walked over to the house.

It was crisp for the time of year, but the day showed signs of warming up. Maybe after he looked around the house a walk into the woods and down along the river would be in order. Something about the knife was simmering in the back of his mind, and he suspected he might find the answer back above the spot where the old willow trees hung over the river's edge.

Mill Road was short. He remembered his father explaining how the original town planners wanted to keep Main Street straight, but Mill Road followed the curve of the land. Stairs had once led down from the bluff to the old mill and the long-gone boat landing on Wechsler's Creek. Facing the creek, the old State Bank Building—now the library—stood on one corner, and the dilapidated Hanley mansion on the other. Along Mill Road were three houses, two on the right and the Swindler house on the left. His grandfather had purchased two lots when he'd built the house so there would always be plenty of room for a garden and lawn.

Behind the house the land was level for about a hundred feet, then sloped gently down to the creek, its twenty-foot width crossed by an ancient but well-cared-for iron foot bridge—also built by his grandfather. On the other shore the land rose quickly again, then for half a mile rose to a point some 1,300 feet high;

from the other side of the creek, the woods spread for miles.

A gravel driveway led to a two-car garage slightly to the rear of the house. A flagstone path ran from the street, paralleling the driveway up to the front door. There were no sidewalks. He saw no life in either of the houses across the way. The boy who had found the body lived in the second house, but he knew they were a fairly new family in town. The first house was boarded up and he remembered that Imogene had mentioned in a letter that the last of the Rahn family had died and the estate was now in litigation.

Oliver walked up the path and saw the bit of black plastic still stuck to a barberry spine. His key was for the front door. He opened it, walked into the hall and noticed the wallpaper seemed to have lost more than color since the other night—the shepherd and the gamboling flocks now looked slightly menacing.

There wasn't a sound except a faint rumble as a freight train slowly ran through the town, its vibration carrying through the living rock that every basement had for its walls. He walked down the hall into the kitchen. The place where Imogene's body had fallen was outlined in yellow chalk. It looked as though nothing had been touched.

He turned back and climbed the stairs to his old room, where he found everything as before and, as he expected, clean and ready for his anticipated arrival. The bed was covered with a newly washed spread, and the old mahogany and embroidered ribbon luggage rack that his mother brought back from a trip to England was standing at the foot of the bed.

His heart quickened as he opened the closet door and stretched his arm to reach the back of the hat shelf, where his fingers touched the old cigar box filled with the treasures of his childhood. He knew the sheriff had missed this as soon as he opened the top. For there, in a jumble with a Captain Midnight code ring, three Indian-head pennies, beer-bottle caps, a 10-X magnifying glass, a brachiopod fossil, and two arrowheads found down on the river flats, was the twin of the knife that had killed his sister, its wooden handle scratched with the letters: *To Oliver from Luther—1939*.

He raised the bottom sash of the double-hung window and carefully removed a small square of wood that hid the rope-and-iron counterweights. He put the knife inside, replaced the wood block, then closed the window tightly and turned the old brass lock.

He left the house through the kitchen door, passed the latticed gazebo and the armillary sphere sundial, crossed the bridge, and stopped in a small clearing surrounded by ancient lilac trees—and not visible from the house. There sat three wooden beehives and two bee-skeps made with ropes of twisted straw just as they were in the old days. He remembered that Luther had been warned years ago by the county agriculture department to give up the bee-skeps, known to harbor a mite that often infected the bees, but he had ignored the request. Bees were flying in and out of all of them, a steady stream in each direction, already gathering honey from early-blooming shrubs and wildflowers. Affixed to each hive was a strip of black cloth about four inches long and an inch wide.

Someone was observing the old country custom of "telling the bees" that the house mistress was dead—the friend of bird, beast, and bee. Oliver knew who it was and who would be blamed for Imogene's death. And that meant someone else knew about Luther, and how he had kept these bees for over forty years.

Years before, when Imogene decided to keep bees, she'd made a deal with Luther that if he cared for them and sold the honey, they would split the surplus. Luther was handy. He built the hives using lumber that he picked up here and there, and winnowed straw from abandoned fields with an old Dutch scythe that he sharpened with a piece of Indian flint. He never took money unless he worked for it and would never harm a living creature without cause.

Oliver went back to the house for his bag lunch, then headed back past the hives and on into the woods that covered the hills around Fernglade.

It was just past one o'clock. The woods were warming up and the carpet of last fall's leaves still covered the path that wound between giant lichen-covered rocks. Above his head the sun flickered in and out through branches of beech, oak, and pine.

He stopped to eat next to a huge rock that had probably witnessed the end of the last ice age, a piece of granite now bedecked with newly emerging ferns and marked, just above where it met the woodsy soil, with deeply incised lines that Luther had told him were left long, long ago by the Indians to mark a trail. Except for a few far-off crow caws there wasn't a sound.

Most of Oliver's childhood memories were shaded with thoughts of Luther Dyer Blankenship. A few years older than Oliver, he came from an old farming family that tilled the rocky soil in the valley up toward Freemont, just beyond Fernglade. Most of the villagers thought Luther, the youngest boy, was mad, as he always had a wild streak. Even his older siblings, married and on their own, wanted little to do with him.

He was still a child when his parents lost their farm in a fire. They both died not long afterward, and Luther ran off into the woods that carpeted the hills behind Oliver's house. There he built a small but serviceable shack with a tin roof, and lived on the land. It was the Depression, long before Child Welfare Services insisted on helping such "helpless" youth. Hardly helpless, he knew how to hunt, fish, and farm, and what wild fruit to eat, and he liked being alone. He earned a few dollars as a handyman, and Imogene hired him whenever she could. With a roof over his head and few other needs, he liked living alone in the woods.

It was hard to measure Luther's intelligence, as he had no formal schooling, but Oliver recalled coming home from grade school every day and teaching the older boy to read using his collection of Tom Swift books and a treasured pile of comics.

Oliver particularly remembered one afternoon in very early spring, the opening of trout season when he was fifteen. Days of rain had riled the waters, and he had lost his footing on the slick river bottom and began to move forward in the current. He caught an overhanging branch, but the water was too deep and too rough, and suddenly the rocks beneath his feet began to move. There was nowhere for him to turn when suddenly Luther appeared with a rope tied from a tree to his waist. He plunged into the water and made it fast about Oliver's waist, then pulled him up and over the edge and onto the shore.

The Swindler family had their faults, but pride was not among them. Luther became almost one of the family and continued to teach Oliver the things about nature that were mostly forgotten by other people. Every spring he set up an eel rack in the river, then cleaned and smoked whatever he caught before selling some at the local market. He had two old knives that he treasured: one he gave to Oliver before he left home, and the other had just killed Oliver's sister.

Oliver continued the climb following the well-worn track that Luther had made over the years. It was difficult to believe that a small town with a railroad track, a newspaper, even a supermarket was only about a mile away. The only sound was the rustle of his feet in the leaves and an occasional blue jay squawking at heaven knows what deep in the forest. He doubted if anyone came up here except on trail-bikes in the summer and snowmobiles in winter. The users of the river never went far away from the water, and the locals lived the modern life.

The path wound its way between two large rocks, their weathered surfaces studded with small pockets of moss, a few stunted ferns, and bits of shiny mica, a mineral that at one time was mined in the vicinity, especially over towards Micaville.

An almost perfectly round stone, about the size of a half-dollar, so heavily studded with mica chips that it looked like silvery gold, caught his eye. He picked it up and put it in his pocket.

Just before two o'clock he reached Luther's little house. Weathered, hand-hewn clapboard surrounded the two front windows, each with old glass that waved reflections as you passed. The plot of English lettuce in the small front garden was untouched by frost, so he knew Luther had covered them the night before. He also knew he was being watched.

"Luther!" he called, "It's me, Oliver!"

Silence.

"Luther, I know Imogene's dead and I know you had nothing to do with it. Trust me. I'm alone."

He heard a slight rustle in the witch hazel grove to the left of where he stood and turned toward it. Luther stepped into the clearing.

"Oliver? Is it really you?"

"Yes, and now everything will be okay. Nobody followed me. Come over. Let's sit down on the bench."

"I'll get wine, Oliver. We'll have a drink."

He went into the shack and came out with two clean glasses that would probably fetch a good price as antiques and an ancient green glass bottle with a porcelain stopper. They sat down.

Oliver hadn't seen him since he'd left Fernglade a few years after the war. Luther had been in his thirties then and was now almost sixty, but the only change was his gray hair and a few fine lines in his face; he acted as though the intervening years had never happened.

Luther poured thick red wine into the glasses that sparkled in the sun.

"How are you, Oliver?"

"Fine, Luther. And you?"

"Good, Oliver. It's been a good winter up here. And should be a great summer—lots of honey—but your sister's dead."

"I know, I saw the hives and knew you were telling the bees. Do you know who did it?"

Luther thought for a moment. "I went down yesterday morning, early 'cause your sister wanted me to move some furniture down from the attic. She said you would need a desk to work at. When I got there the back door was open and your sister was on the floor. She was dead. I checked. And there was my knife, my skinning knife, stuck in the table. I didn't do it Oliver, she was a good friend."

"I know, Luther. But how did your knife get there?"

"I don't know, Oliver. I lost it about a month ago. I went to the big supermarket to see if they wanted some honey. They usually took some. Then I went by the gas station and that Frank Wallace came out and yelled at me; told me to get out of there; called me Crazy Luther. He tossed a soda can at me. When I moved to let it pass by, my knife fell out of my belt. He ran at me, and I didn't want trouble, Oliver, so I ran away. But I saw he picked it up."

"Why didn't you take it from him?"

"I never thought about it until I got back home. Then it was too late. And like I said, I didn't want trouble. Don't let them take me, Oliver. I couldn't stand that."

"Don't worry, Luther. I'll look out for you. But I've got to tell them where the knife came from." He felt a pang of guilt, but he had promised the sheriff. "Nobody knows where this place is, do they?"

"No, Oliver. Most everyone that knew is dead or gone. Just you, I reckon. And your sister. Not anybody else, I imagine."

"Well, you stay here for now. Don't come down to the

village for anything."

Somehow Oliver had to explain to Phibert that Luther was blameless—although he knew that the mourning cloths on the hives would be bound to raise suspicions.

He left Luther sitting on the bench and started down the path to town. By the time he reached the beehives he felt a prickling at the back of his neck, the kind of feeling you get when there's trouble at the end of a dark alley. He stopped and looked around but saw nothing.

Chapter Nine

He had planned to meet his sisters at the Funeral Home about four o'clock. Seeing he had some time to spare, he drove out of town, toward the western part of the county. Everywhere he went there were signs of a new prosperity. Second homes dotted the land, as well as a lot of newer double-wide mobile homes on neat, well-cared-for squares of lawn. Traffic, too, was up a great deal in the towns and villages. Thirty years before you were lucky to see five cars a day except on weekends in the summer, at least on this side. Not anymore.

As he drove he thought of Imogene. She had never married and Oliver had always wondered if her spinsterhood was rooted in something now lost in the past. Although best described as plain, she had the kind of temperament that would turn an angry wasp aside. Some suspected that she simply didn't want the disruption that would come with sharing her life with anyone, as she liked everything to be just so, but other friends joked that the reason a man had never crossed the threshold was her name. It was pronounced "EYE-mo-gene," though no one at first meeting ever said it correctly. Family legend had it that their father mispronounced it three times at the child's christening, much to the embarrassment of Mrs. Swindler, who wished to give her first-born daughter all the advantages of life—though a name that would never be forgotten was not part of the plan.

Her childhood was happy because Imogene seemed to be content with her lot. She was always on the honor roll and served on the student council throughout high school. Although she had only a few beaux, it was rumored that when she attended the university to earn her a teaching degree, there had been a hint of romance … but to this day neither Oliver or anyone else knew any particulars. She had come home from college in the depths of the Great Depression to teach and live a quiet life.

And that life was blameless. Her former students and gardening friends adored her, and even after enduring the mind-dumbing years of attending high school—years that included her classes—the same students, long after they has spread across the country and the world, sent cards at Christmas. The Woman's Club of Fernglade elected her president year after year (despite the bylaws' time limit on any elected offices), and the ambulance corps owed much of its success in enrolling new members to Imogene's persistence in writing articles for the local papers and running the meetings—she was always elected to the governing board in one capacity or another—with dignity and dispatch.

Her diplomatic skill could soothe the hurt feelings of even the most proper members, even on the night that Georgie Banks and Bobbie Millard brought a whoopie cushion to the ambulance corps's tenth anniversary celebration.

Oliver turned back to town and parked behind the hotel. It was raining gently, and the last of the winter leaves still blew against the street and sidewalk, but he didn't mind the walk to the funeral home.

The "show parlor" was the kind of room usually found at coffin wholesalers, but with Clark Wechsler it was clearly an important part of his business. A sign in a polished brass stand directed visitors to the office, where his sisters sat together on an Empire couch covered in mauve velvet just outside Clark's private office.

Oliver hung his wet and worn duffle coat on a brass rack that stood between the door and a small gilt table on which stood a twisted red glass vase stuffed with artificial pink flamingo flowers. Above it hung an expensive, but not particularly good, painting of Botticelli's *Three Graces* tapestry. Clark's taste hadn't changed for the better in all these years.

After the expected, and unavoidable, tearful reunion, they wiped their eyes and Oliver pulled over a flimsy-looking, faux-bamboo chair with a striped satin seat. Carefully he sat down and faced his sisters. Florence clutched her handbag in careworn hands; Linda lit a cigarette with a tiny silver lighter decorated with the dancing Shiva.

At fifty-two Florence was petite, though Oliver noticed she had put on weight since he last saw her. She wore a size-5 shoe, favored frilly blouses, and still carried white gloves to church. Her hair was of that neutral, nondescript color that women called "honey-colored" but reminded Oliver of the vaguely beige hue of the lacquered maple floor of a basketball court. Her only child had been killed in an automobile accident and her husband, a used-car dealer in Burnsville, had died just a year ago. Florence, according to Imogene, had also been thinking about coming back to Fernglade. She was an adopted child, taken in by Oliver's parents when she was only two years old.

Linda, fifty-eight, was only slightly taller, but she had a slim build, more like Oliver than their sisters. Her sharp features were not unattractive, and were topped with still-black hair, though whether natural or not Oliver could not tell. She favored the kind of dress that most women of her age considered in bad taste. She had divorced her first husband, an energetic real-estate promoter, had no children, and now, according to letters from Imogene, lived in Atlanta at an armed truce with her second husband, who dealt in rare books. She and Florence had often been at odds throughout their lives; Oliver sensed that nothing had changed.

After a short silence that seemed interminable, Oliver burst out. "God! If I had only been here a week earlier, I probably could have helped her."

"I don't think so," said Florence quietly. "Whoever did this to Imogene wanted to do it. When you called yesterday I couldn't believe it was happening to us. But the more I see of the new world around us I'm not surprised at anything anymore. My whole life seems sometimes to be a *National Enquirer* story. It just seems so sad that it takes this kind of thing to get us together after … how many years, Oliver?"

"The last time I saw you and Carl was…" Oliver paused a moment … "that time I came to Asheville on the way from Chicago to New York. That's at least twelve years ago. I'm sorry I didn't make more of an effort to keep in touch … but at least I write at holidays."

"Not to me you don't," snapped Linda.

"I send you a card every birthday."

"Hush up, both of you," said Florence with a sidelong glance at her sister. To Oliver she continued, "Imogene had called me about your coming back to live in the old house and working at *The Republican*. She was so happy about it."

"I had everything set in my mind about moving into my old room and walking to work every morning—"

"You can still stay in the house," said Florence. "We all know about Imogene's will. Everything, I believe, is divided between us except for a few small provisions. I for one have no wish to sell the house right away, and there should be enough money in her savings for upkeep and taxes."

"Well what about me?" asked Linda. "Maybe Edward and I could use the money."

"Linda, our sister was just slaughtered. For God's sake forget about money for a while." Florence reached into her purse for another tissue, wiped her eyes, and softly said, "You told me two months ago that his book business was doing quite well and you were comfortable for the first time in years."

"Nobody ever has too much money," snapped Linda. "Edward hasn't been well of late. I don't wish to be unkind, but there are some fine pieces of furniture in that house and a lot of mementos that are mine by rights."

"Oh, my God!" cried Florence.

"Don't worry about the house and money," Oliver said, suddenly thrown back into the familiar, but unwelcome, role of peacemaker between his squabbling sisters. He looked Linda directly in the eye. "I'll find a place to live in town for a while while I settle into the new job. We don't need to plunge into planning an auction and making real estate arrangements. Imogene just died and already we're arguing the way we did when we were kids."

"You can have all the time you need," remarked Florence, glaring again at her sister.

Linda lit a fresh cigarette as the main office door opened and Clark Wechsler walked into the waiting room, slightly out of breath. He was about to hang up his dripping raincoat until he noticed Oliver's on the rack. He quickly draped his own over his left arm, then turned with a theatrical gesture to the siblings.

"Florence, Oliver, Linda," he cried in his most unctuous manner. "What tragic circumstances to bring us all together again." He then went into his private office, hung up his coat, came back to the outer room and pulled up another fragile-looking chair across from them.

Clark had long since mastered the exact amount of time

to allot to discussions of "the arrangements" of minister, music, and refreshments. In this case, for a family he'd known his whole life, and whose religious preferences and financial status he knew as well, he spent precisely fifteen minutes on the fundamentals—including which coffin, at what price, would be appropriate "for such an esteemed friend."

"Imogene will be in the Pine Room," he said. "It's one of the largest, and I'm sure there will be many, many mourners. She was so involved in so many things for so many years...."

He paused dramatically before continuing, sounding slightly more businesslike. "Of course it will have to be a closed-coffin affair. And because of the notoriety, we anticipate that a number of people will show up only out of morbid interest. I thought Sunday and Monday would allow enough time for her friends to pay their respects but not too much opportunity for the overly curious to stop by. Then the internment on Tuesday, when a lot of those folks would be at work, followed by tea and punch before driving to the cemetery.

"As you know, of course, Imogene was always prepared for everything and anything." He reached into his breast pocket, pulled out three envelopes and passed them to the three siblings. "Just last year she brought by a well-written obituary. I made copies for each of you, and, of course, Oliver, if you want to edit it.... And I took the liberty of adding that in lieu of flowers contributions in Imogene's memory could be made to the Library Fund, if that's all right with all of you. She was so devoted to the library."

With polite nods they all agreed and almost in unison thanked Clark for his considerations.

"And of course there's no need for payment until afterwards. I certainly can trust your family."

His unctuous smile and feeble attempt at humor grated on Oliver. After exchanging a few anecdotes about Imogene, the conversation, without warning, turned in a new direction.

"You've become quite a businessman, Clark," said Linda. "I don't know how you can run a lunchroom, a funeral parlor, and oversee the bank, and still have such a ruddy glow."

Wechsler, at 56, did indeed have a ruddy glow, though Oliver suspected it was due more to martinis at lunch than healthy walks in the woods.

"I've just been lucky, I suppose," he answered with a slight chuckle, adjusting his silk tie with manicured fingers. "And if there's ever a case of food poisoning at the lunchroom," he added, "well, I send the customer's family over here."

Linda stifled a laugh but looked at him indulgently. Florence, who had never regretted declining Clark's marriage proposal thirty years before, gave him a disapproving look and clucked her tongue. "It's most likely because your competition has not seen fit to move up from Atlanta to take advantage of the summer tourists."

"Well that's changing now," he said, "Why, the Zoning Board is about to clear the way for one of those fast food chains called Heavenly Burgers to be built right on Main Street. On the lot where the old Hanley house sits."

"That is a shame," said Florence. Though her husband had sold cars, she had never caught the entrepreneurial spirit of eager businessmen.

"Now, now, Florence, progress is timely. We must never stand in its way. All of this new blood coming to town is good for everybody. In fact, after you've all settled in I really want to talk to you about a business proposition … not now, of course," he added in his most consoling undertaker's voice. "Later, when it's more convenient for us all."

Florence pursed her lips and watched him with distaste; he quickly removed the toothpick he had pulled from his handkerchief pocket. Linda looked to Oliver as if she was silently calculating how much the old house might bring—especially if Clark Wechsler had his eye on it.

Having spent exactly the calculated half hour with the grieving family, Clark adjusted his tone like a car shifting gears. No longer the unctuous funeral director or the businesslike tradesman, he suddenly became an old family friend.

"And now after all these years, Oliver is back home again," he said with a broad smile that showed his perfectly capped teeth. He stood and added, "We'll have to have lunch one of these days."

He crossed to the coat rack and gathered everyone's wraps; then, with an almost balletic movement, he handed them to the bereaved family and, without breaking stride, escorted them to the front door.

"I'll have my assistants greet any mourners until you officially get here tomorrow afternoon," he said with just the right inflection to sound like a command.

The three stepped out into the rain and wind.

"We should've gone in and looked at Imogene," said Linda.

"She would understand why we didn't," Oliver said. "By the way, the house is all right, it's just the kitchen that—"

"Don't worry, we thought of that. We can call a maintenance service after clearing it with the sheriff."

"Shall we go home and have some coffee?" asked Linda, "then we can make plans to eat out somewhere."

"I don't want any coffee this late in the day," said Florence, opening the door of her car, "but I'd like to take a look at the house."

Florence drove carefully, and as they turned the corner Oliver said, "Imagine the Hanley house being torn down and replaced with a fast food restaurant. It will be a big change for the town. I wonder what Clark wants to talk about?"

"Whatever it is," said Florence, "he wants it badly. He was

never subtle and I smell money. I wonder who bought the old Hanley place. I'll just bet he owns it."

Florence drove up the driveway. "Did anyone look at Imogene's car?" she asked.

"I'll open the front door," he said, "then I can check the garage."

He turned on the hall lights and stood by for the sisters to enter. Linda opened the double doors to the living room while Florence started down the hall to the kitchen. She pushed open the door and almost immediately let out a piercing scream.

"My God, Florence," he hollered. "What's the matter?"

"There's a dead body in the middle of the kitchen floor!"

Oliver and Linda rushed to the kitchen door. Linda began loudly, dramatically sobbing, while Florence held the doorframe for support, motionless as if stricken. Oliver pulled her upright and spoke authoritatively. "Florence, take Linda into the front room and I'll call the sheriff."

Surprised by his own calm, he made the call without hesitation. Phibert was in his office and said he'd be there within thirty minutes—and nothing was to be touched. As soon as he hung up the phone, Oliver retreated to the kitchen, knelt down and touched the victim's left temple, taking care not to disturb the body. It wasn't life-warm but not too cold either.

Stuck to the sole of the right shoe he noticed a small piece of lichen or rock tripe, a primitive plant that grows all over the rocks in the local mountains.

If, thought Oliver, *Luther didn't kill my sister, and I know he didn't, then why would he do this—he wouldn't. But it had to be someone who knows about the knife and the hives, with the straw rope pointing a definite finger of blame. But I doubt if anybody involved, except me and Luther, knows about lichens … which must mean Luther was here this morning and knows about this murder.* He picked off the tiny plant and pocketed it.

He went outside and looked across the street. The neighbor's house was still deserted. Even in the summer, few people came down this road, clearly marked "Dead End." As narrow as it was, it took a bit of doing to turn a standard car around, but even if the murderer had taken a chance, no-one was around to see.

Back inside he checked on his sisters. Florence had calmed down, though tears were silently running down her cheeks, but Linda was still shaking.

"Oliver, do you think you could find me something to drink? I think there's some whisky in the cabinet over the refrigerator," said Florence.

Oliver poured out three glasses of scotch.

While the women sat side by side on the sofa, nursing their shock yet not comforting one another, each in her own small world, Oliver sat on the front hall stairs. Tightly holding his glass, he could imagine the wallpaper shepherds assuming evil leers and attacking the shepherdesses one by one, then turning to slaughter the sheep.

Though it was only twenty minutes since his call, it seemed forever before the sheriff pulled up in front of the house with at least ten men in tow. Like a stampede they raced to the kitchen to look at the dead man.

He lay on his stomach, his right cheek against the floor. Turning the body over, they found that both hands had been severed at the wrists, but there was little blood from those wounds. In addition, his teeth and jaw had been smashed—and strangely, many of the scattered teeth had old-fashioned gold fillings.

He was dressed in well-worn jeans, more brown from dirt than blue, a stained and ripped nylon jacket over a flannel shirt, and old work shoes with patched leather laces. They were fairly clean, though small bits of earth and grass clung to the bottom edges of each heel. From his shoes and the marks on the floor it was clear the body had been moved to this spot.

The man appeared to be a hard-used middle-age. Around his throat was a long hank of twisted straw just like that used to make Luther's hives. From the bloated look of the face, he had been strangled.

Oliver left the sheriff's men to their work and joined his sisters in the living room. There Sheriff Phibert found them some half hour later. The women answered a few brief questions and agreed to go straight back to Florence's house. They would meet at the funeral parlor again on Sunday.

Phibert turned to Oliver. "Know who he is?"

"I've no idea."

"Found something caught in his belt, though."

"What?"

"A torn piece of gray leather, looks like a glove, man's I think. And he wasn't killed here but dragged from the driveway across the lawn; you can see the tracks in the grass."

"It would be easy to do anything on this street now: The people across the way seem to be gone and anyone visiting the library on the corner would park along Main Street. But why bring a body here?"

Phibert lit a cigar.

"I don't know," he said between puffs, "but I've got to detain your friend Luther. My great-uncle once kept bees so I know what that straw cord is used for, and it's not a typical hardware item."

"Who told you about Luther's bees?"

"We got a tip."

"And you don't think that's suspicious?"

"Sure I do. But when the papers get hold of this and blow up a story about a crazy old hermit involved with two murders, I've got to act."

"Don't forget, Sheriff, I'm one of 'the papers.' You don't think I'm going to blow this story up, do you? After all, it is my sister, and my home, and my friend that we're talking about." Oliver's voice carried only a hint of the irritation he felt.

"Don't worry, I'll look out for Luther. But I have to do something, just for the present. Anyway, our jail isn't exactly a big city prison. Some folks even think it's a mite old-fashioned. Know where I can find him?"

"You're sure there's no other way?"

Phibert shook his head.

"Did you question Frank Wallace about what Luther said about how he took the knife?"

"Wallace? He denied the whole thing. Just as you'd expect, of course. Now, Luther might be right and Wallace wrong, but I've got to bring in your friend.

"And what about that piece of leather?"

"Well, I'll tell you, I've attended quite a few funerals and been a pallbearer often enough to recognize mourner's gloves, the kind they give you at a funeral parlor if you don't have your own. Of course I'll question Wechsler. Now where do I find Luther?"

"I'll go up and get him."

"I'd like to seal the house for a few days. Can you continue to stay at the hotel?"

Oliver had no desire to stay in a house where there'd been two murders in as many days. "That's what I'm already planning to do, Sheriff."

At the sheriff's bidding, Oliver went out the front door, walked carefully across the lawn, and up the path through the woods to Luther's shack.

Luther came quietly, as Oliver knew he would, especially after explaining about the second murder and that somebody was trying to make it look like he had been involved. As the sheriff escorted him into his car and drove away, Oliver offered Luther a reassuring nod.

Oliver walked to the garage and looked at Imogene's car. It was a dark red Pontiac, a sporty two-door Sunbird, with only some 12,000 miles on the odometer. The keys, as he expected, were hanging over the end of the turn signal; he put them in his pocket and went back to his hotel room, hoping for a nap.

At precisely eight o'clock Oliver entered the dining room and found Greig Davis sitting at a corner table drinking a martini; other diners, many somewhat dressed up, filled the tables around him. Black was not on duty; the service was carried out by two local women working as waitresses and a high-school kid who had been drafted as a busboy.

Davis waved him over. He seemed delighted to talk, but Oliver found that the murders, his sisters, Luther's detainment, and an impending funeral were pounding on his mind. He had little appetite, but he picked at a salad and drank two glasses of wine while Davis chatted away about the town and the paper.

"I think it would be a good idea to have some kind of an office over in Mars Hill," said Davis, "because Alice and I think the Asheville paper would consider us out of the game if we let them cover it. College life, a college town, we don't look upon this part of the state as small time even if they do ... and if we want to increase circulation, we have to get readers from that side. And the only way to get them to read is to continue to report all the local news—their news—and keep it on a more personal level than other papers do."

Oliver was burning to ask about the rehab center on Stalker Mountain and its connection with Black but thought it might be a good idea to wait. He sighed, as much from boredom as from fatigue.

"Oliver, you must be exhausted," said Davis, belatedly attending to his editor's personal troubles. Oliver wondered if

Alice customarily handled "the niceties."

"What you've gone through must be ... I'm going to take my leave and let you go up to bed." He offered what Oliver presumed was meant to be a sympathetic smile, picked up his raincoat from the back of his chair, shook hands, and strode out of the hotel.

Oliver went back to the front desk, wondering just how many people were staying at the inn. The mail slots over Ackermann's now-cold chair were always empty, and there were lots of keys hanging on the board.

In his room he took a long, hot shower and fell exhausted onto the chenille bedspread. After all, he thought, just how much living can you pack into twenty-four hours?

Chapter Ten

He remembered thinking about gardening and listening to a fly buzzing against the window pane before dropping off to sleep. An ancient English saying floated in and out of his dream thoughts:

"When elum leaves are as big as a farden,
It's time to plant kidney beans in the garden."

He vaguely, subconsciously, wondered what a farden was, but it started to rain, both on his dream garden and in reality, and he jumped up in bed as the window shook with a gigantic clap of thunder. The river valley gets almost tropical at times, and often a violent "goose-grinder" of a storm seems to arise from spontaneous generation. A clear night sky will quickly blanket itself with thickened clouds and a rising wind sends shivers down through the trees; only the oldest and strongest will be able to resist the force that literally bends them to the ground. The clock read 1:20.

Raindrops pelted the window and the white cord with its embroidered ring that hung from the window shade whipped about and beat upon the heavy paper like a small drum. Flash after flash of lightning lit the room like a photographer using an old-fashioned giant flashbulb.

Oliver pulled the blanket over his ear and tried to ride out the din. His fear of thunderstorms had begun as a child when one summer night, in the middle of a particularly violent round of lightning, a ball-of-fire came through the open window of the living room and floated across the room, through the hall into the kitchen, where it collided with the metal stove and set the wall behind on fire. The following summer, while sitting on a friend's veranda with his back to the field and woods beyond, an unexpected bolt of lightning hit a tree less than two yards away and knocked him out of his seat. In a sense, Oliver had been in shock ever since.

He could hear nothing but thunder and ringing in his ears. Sleep was impossible; after ten minutes of the roaring wind and lashing rain the storm seemed to be getting worse rather than letting up. He began counting out loud the seconds between a lightning flash and the accompanying thunder: one thousand, two thousand, three thousand, remembering that sound travels about two thousand feet per second. Suddenly there wasn't even time to count one second: a bolt of lightning and a wall of sound simultaneously hit the gabled roof, and the smell of ozone pierced the air.

This wasn't funny, he thought. Any place out in the hall is better than being close to the window. He got up, quickly put on his pants, and reached for a sweater from the duffle. He didn't bother with socks or even tie his shoes but let the laces drag across the vinyl floor.

Once in the darkened hall with his room door closed behind him, the only evidence of lightning was the syncopated flashes from the transoms over the doors of the rooms. The wind made a susurrus sound, but even the thunder was muted here.

The one hall light was a brass wall sconce with a single dim bulb. He didn't want to see anybody—he didn't want anyone to see him—so he went to the edge of the stairs to sit silently in the dark stairwell until the storm blew over. And there, in the dark and relative quiet, ignoring the heavens raging overhead, he drifted off to an ungentle sleep.

Then he heard shouting. A door opened and high heels clicked down the hall.

Before he could move or cry out he was kicked in the thigh and a rather heavy woman was flailing about on his lap, one hand gripping the stair rail and the other punching him in the shoulder.

"Let me go! What the hell are you doing there and who the hell are you," she demanded, through a flood of tears.

"Sorry," he answered. "No harm intended. I've just been sitting here riding out the storm."

"Well dammit, buddy, there's better places than this to sit!"

He helped her up and her bag fell out of his lap to land on the third step. As she stood, now in the light, he recognized Mrs. Hill, the chiropractor's wife. Although a big woman, she was very attractive. About forty, she was dressed in slacks and a blouse and had a light coat still hanging over one shoulder.

"You know I could have gone down those stairs," she said, the tears still streaming down her cheeks.

"I'm really sorry—let me help you," he said as he picked up her bag.

He walked her down both flights to the first floor. She took her bag from his hand, slung it over one shoulder, and stamped down the hall and opened the door to the storm, not bothering to close it behind her. Lightning still streaked across the sky as a gust of wind blew dust bunnies across the hotel rug. He walked over and closed the door, turned, and stepping on his laces went back to his room.

When he reached the top of the stairs, lightning flashed through the transoms at the end of the hall; at the same instant he saw the open crack of a quickly closing door just down from his own room on the right. It was the room that Mrs. Hill had just left, he was sure of it; and he remembered the other night when heavy high heels had made the same kind of clattering exit. He wrote a mental note to find out just who had that room.

His clock now read 2:10. He took off his shoes, turned off the light and lay back on the bed. Occasional pulses of light still flickered across the ceiling, though the thunder was now only a faraway murmur. But try as he might, there would be no more sleep that night.

After twenty minutes or so he decided to go over to the paper, thinking it would be more comfortable than sitting in this room and counting the seconds until dawn. He dressed and, with some stealth, crept downstairs through the entrance hall and out onto a glistening street. He was surprised to find the door unlocked. Lightning still flashed in the east, but the sky was beginning to clear and stars were shining along the rim of the hills to the west.

Oliver unlocked the front door of the newspaper office. Orange light from the street lamps guided him to the pressroom, and he easily found the spiral staircase. In his office he considered looking through a few of the old bound volumes. Adrian said the older papers were in the front office; he went back down the stairs and, as he passed the presses, he noticed that the door to the basement was ajar.

Oliver had several vices, but only one that nobody knew about: he was a sucker for horror films. His eyes refused to turn away, so he stealthily tiptoed across the room and opened the door—both relieved and surprised that the hinges didn't give a warning squeak. At the top of the stairs was a long, dirty white string fastened to the railing through a screw eye, clearly tied to a light chain somewhere below. He pulled it, and the basement came into view.

At the bottom of the stairs he found himself in a large room that apparently spanned the entire building. Four light bulbs hung from cobweb-covered but solid-looking rafters and formed small pools of light that faded quickly into dark. The scene would rival the Collyer Brothers, history's worst hoarders: there were walls of newspapers in every direction with three-foot pathways between.

The stacks reached from floor to ceiling, creating an ordered maze. Each stack was piled with a sense of purpose: five copies with the fold to the center of the room, then five reversed, five upon five, up to the ceiling. Here and there a piece of yellow paper, in sharp contrast to the brown of the newsprint, was stuck between copies: 1932, 1933, 1934, and, as he advanced farther away from the door, 1906, 1905, 1904, unending, it seemed.

The visible part of the floor was solid rock, here and there embellished with a circle of dirt. He walked down the various pathways, overwhelmed by the sense of history that surrounded him. Somewhere in the 1920s he noticed a gap in the piles, a space about two feet wide that led up to a low door made of wooden planks, not much wider than the aisle.

Oliver could easily distinguish the cleaner papers above the flood marks from the darker ones some fourteen inches from the floor. Even the door was water-stained at the bottom, but the strap hinges were unrusted and, to his surprise, well-oiled. The door had a handle but no lock. And hanging on the doorjamb were a half-filled red enamel kerosene lamp and a pack of matches in a metal case.

He lit the lamp and opened the door. It revealed a tunnel carved or blasted out of living rock. Some twenty feet along it opened into a rock chamber about fifteen feet square.

Here in the bowels of Fernglade five passenger tunnels met, like winding intestines leading from a central stomach, the tunnels clearly labeled, although the wood of three signs was ancient in the faded black lettering of an early-19th-century style. By the light of the lantern he read: *Newspaper* (the one he just left and a fairly recent signpost); *Funeral Home* (also fairly new); *Hotel, River,* and *Bank.* In his mind's eye he could see the men fifty years before, hurrying from tunnel to tunnel, pushing carts loaded with prohibition liquor fresh out of stills in the Carolina mountains, wheeled to a dock close to an opening in the bluff that runs along the river, there to be loaded onto small skiffs, barges, and motorboats. The tunnels, he realized, had been here for decades, perhaps centuries; the town was very old, he knew.

He wondered who, besides Greig Davis, knew about the cellar and tunnels. Many on the paper's staff, current and retired, not to mention Clark Wechsler—and Black and Ackermann. Who else?

The stain mark of the flood was clearly visible on the walls and the lower levels of papers. He took an issue from the top of the 1947 stack and leafed through it. "The danger within," read a headline, warning of infiltrators from liberated Eastern Europe who might try post-war sabotage for the Communists. He read the screed with fascination, then took up another edition, and another, always careful to handle the old newsprint delicately. An hour passed, and another.

An early March issue reported on "The February 28 massacre, an anti-government uprising in Taiwan that was violently suppressed by the Kuomintang-led Republic of China government." Oliver vaguely remembered the incident from his youth, though at the time he'd been more interested in earning a living and finding willing girls to date than caring about a few thousand deaths in far-off China. He was fascinated to read that "The number of Taiwanese deaths from the massacre was estimated to be between 5,000 and 28,000 and marked the beginning of the White Terror, in which tens of thousands of Taiwanese were imprisoned, killed, or simply disappeared."

After a time he reached 1946, and found himself equally fascinated by the post-war report. Slowly, vaguely, he realized that glimmers of daylight were seeping into the basement; he returned the papers to their proper places and climbed back up to the office. He was surprised to see that was past 6:00 a.m.; he'd never imagined that 30-year-old newsprint could be so interesting.

Churches and businesses both opened early on a Fernglade Sunday, and Oliver wanted to avoid making unexpected noises in the quiet vault, especially if Black or Wechsler were listening. He tightly shut the basement door, went out through the front office, and walked casually down Main, trying to look like an early riser out for a morning stroll. He needn't have worried: the type of people who might have noticed him obviously slept well.

Rain continued to fall; for a time it seemed the river itself was rearing its watery self and rising up to drown both the high and the mighty. He bought a copy of the Asheville *Citizen* at the drug store and, wrapping it well in a large shopping bag, walked quickly back to the hotel, hoping that tomorrow would find a bright sun and sparkling streets. With a tinge of nostalgia, he remembered life in the big city, where you could wander the streets day and night, meet honest folk and endless crooks and politicians, find open bookstores at all hours, and see horror movies galore. He recalled seeing Edward Hopper's painting, *Nighthawks*, at the Art Institute in Chicago; how well it captured his own sense of solitude within the world.

Ackermann was at the desk when he came through the door. "Hello there, Swindler," he said. "Out early, I see. How you doing this morning? Do please again accept my sympathy over the death of your sister. Anybody find out who the other body at your house was?"

To Oliver it sounded like the beginning of a routine from an old Abbott and Costello comedy. If he hadn't lived it he would have laughed.

"No, they haven't. And I'm sorry about my sister, too."

With a rueful smile, he glanced casually over Ackerman's shoulder and saw a piece of lettered tape under the mail slot marked room 11; it read "Simon Black."

He was loath to have breakfast in the hotel dining room or, for that matter, at the diner. At the supermarket he picked up doughnuts and a quart of orange juice, knowing he could make coffee at the paper. Back at the office he put water on to heat. Adrian had never given him her telephone number, but it was, as expected, in the Rolodex file on Mary-Beth's desk.

"Hello!" She sounded more lively than he expected for that time of the morning.

"Adrian. How are you today?" he asked.

"Oliver—I'm fine. Had a good visit with my mother and I just woke up. Where are you?"

"At the paper, eating some doughnuts and making coffee."

"You could come over for a decent breakfast."

"Where?"

"I've got an apartment over the real estate agency on Main Street. Next to the drug store." She gave him the street number of the separate entrance.

"Fine, be there in a snap!"

He shut off the coffee, locked the office door and, with the first spring in his step for a number of days, walked the blocks to Karisoff Reality, Inc.

Adrian's apartment was an efficiency but smart with modern but comfortable furniture. A vase of fresh flowers sat in the middle of the dining table where dishes were set for two. She was dressed in a smart pair of slacks with a white satin blouse and a red cardigan sweater.

"As soon as we finish eating, I've got to tell you something about last night and this morning."

"Talk while I fix eggs. Fried or scrambled?" she asked.

"Scrambled. Are they restaurant eggs?"

"What are restaurant eggs?"

"Eggs with two yolks. They're laid by special hens just for commercial use."

"You've got to be kidding," Adrian laughed.

"Sure, but I remember my father telling city people about them and they believed it."

She whipped up a golden froth and poured it into the hot frying pan.

"During that storm last night, I couldn't sleep and went out in the hall. I started to doze sitting on the stairs and the chiropractor's wife, Jane Hill, fell over me. She'd just left Black's room in tears and didn't see me. I apologized and helped her downstairs but she stomped off. Then when I saw Ackermann this morning, I remembered that the day I arrived, he said I'd probably be staying at a rooming house when I settled in. So I wondered, what made him think I wouldn't be living at home with my sister?"

"I don't know——especially since Imogene had told everyone you would."

"Well, it made me wonder. Then later I still couldn't sleep so I went over to the paper, and I wound up in the basement—"

"For God's sake why?"

"Curiosity. The door was ajar. And down in the basement I found a series of tunnels connecting the paper, the funeral parlor, the old bank building, the hotel, and another that said to the river. Then this morning I checked the Asheville paper and there's not a word about the second body in Imogene's kitchen."

"A what? Another body? Who was it?

"I've no idea. Neither did the sheriff."

"Surely you're making this up!"

"No way. Not after what happened to Imogene. I'm not that crazy ... or insensitive. As a matter of fact the sheriff was immediately notified about the body—it was my sister Florence who discovered it, and I called the sheriff myself."

"For heaven's sake, Oliver. And the tunnels?

"I'll show you the tunnels tomorrow. But, meanwhile, Adrian, don't mention any of this to anyone. All right?"

"It won't be easy, but okay."

"As soon as we finish here I've got to get over to the funeral home. Imogene had a lot of friends and I'm sure some of them will want to stop in before church. I feel I should be on hand."

Adrian spooned the eggs onto the plates and produced perfectly browned toast.

"I find it hard to believe what's happened since you got here."

"Same here."

They ate in silence, and when they finished he could only murmur, "I really appreciate this—your saving me from doughnuts and bad coffee. But I really need to ..." His voice trailed off. He thought with little pleasure of sitting with his sisters to greet whoever might show up hoping for a view of the murder victim. Well, they'd be disappointed by the closed casket, he told himself with satisfaction.

He hadn't been to a funeral home for years; it was a surprise to find a world where the population, always aspiring to raise their social status, had instead gone kitschy in a big way. After handing his coat to an overdressed attendant and slipping into the Pine Room, Oliver noticed his sisters already fussing over flowers and quietly grumbling that it would be impossible to have a luncheon for the mourners after the interment on Tuesday. He reassured them that everyone would understand, but, just like forty years before, it was the sniping itself that animated them, not whatever nonissue they might be arguing about.

The coffin lay on a flower-bedecked catafalque, its frame

hidden by a pastel-blue satin cover with fringed edges, centered below a stained glass window framed in baroque gold and featuring a white dove with an emerald laurel wreath in its beak flying against a sapphire sky. White torchères at head and foot reflected a pink glow against a pine-paneled wall.

The room was thirty feet square, its floor covered with wall-to-wall carpet that would have been more at home in Radio City Music Hall. A few folding chairs leaned against the walls flanking the double doors. Bunches of gladiolus—flowers Imogene had detested—and other, more scented flowers filled gilded vases on tripod. In the center of the ceiling a dome rose into the roof above, lit by hidden pink lights, surrounding an overdone fake-crystal chandelier. Gilded angels—they would have served as cupids in a less reputable establishment—floated and swayed from invisible plastic wires. Oliver sought out the source of their motion and soon saw that currents of heat were produced by sixteen lights coated with a solution that, he supposed, was designed to make them glow like prisms. To Oliver they looked as if they'd been dipped in orange motor oil.

Florence, like him, looked about with distaste, her mouth pursed; Linda, he thought, approved of the tacky display.

People came and went, though Oliver recognized few of them. Passing years had changed those he remembered, but most belonged to faces he had never seen before.

Soon the clock read 4:00, and all they had had to eat was coffee and tea along with some cookies served by one of Wechsler's assistants in a small anteroom. Oliver was growing frustrated, hungry, and increasingly testy. Nearly another hour passed before Clark came in and suggested that they go out for some dinner and be back at seven. As they left a cold drizzle started to fall.

They drove together to a Japanese restaurant in Spruce Pine. Conversation over dinner was almost nonexistent, as each of the four was consumed by their own thoughts. As soon as they returned to the funeral home, Clark motioned Oliver into his office.

"Oliver, may we talk in private for a moment?"

"Just give me a chance to get my sisters settled."

Five minutes later he knocked at Clark Wechsler's door.

"Oliver, please have a seat. I think these are comfortable," he said, pointing to two club chairs upholstered with embroidered gold circles on green satin.

The office was in better taste then the rest of his business—but only slightly. Stuffed into the room were a huge desk with lion's heads at the corners and golden claw feet that sank into thick maroon wall-to-wall carpet. Clark sat in a heavily carved Jacobean chair that Oliver knew, without even looking, had a red velvet cushion with gold tassels at each corner. The window behind him was framed by floor-to-ceiling drapes of gold brocade, tied back with gold bows. The paneled walls were hung with heavy gold baroque frames, each lit by individual picture lights and containing scenes of Paris in an imitation Bernard Buffet style. The desk held a fake French phone, a polished brass desk set, and a large mahogany box that, Oliver assumed, contained a Victorian Tantalus and cut crystal bottles. The blotter was crimson and unstained—Clark, he knew, used a ballpoint pen for any business signatures. Elevator music whispered out of two small speakers mounted in the suspended ceiling. Oliver marveled that the floor could support everything. But this was clearly Clark Wechsler's concept of how a big-time entrepreneur dealt with business—a nouveau riche man's idea of how Old Money lived and worked. There wasn't a book in sight.

Suddenly Oliver became aware of a very well-dressed gentleman sitting next to the desk. In his Armani suit, even under normal circumstances, the man would not be easy to miss, but surrounded by such frou-frou he stood out.

"Oliver, I want you to meet a wonderful man, a friend of mine who strikes to the deepest part of my heart with his love and the beneficence he carries in his soul. This gentleman is my conscience and my provider. Some folks call him The Leader, being The Very Reverend Thomas Jefferson Stalker, the director of the Stalker Mountain Clinic. He's here to consult me about some problems at his association, but when he heard of Imogene's death and of your being back home—so to speak—in Fernglade, he wanted to meet you."

Oliver stood to shake hands with Stalker, and though he continued to smile, the man's name triggered an unpleasant memory from childhood. Charlie Stalker had been the town rapscallion some forty years back; he earned a meager living making very bad moonshine, not worth the jug it was purchased in. In fact, Stalker's hooch was tainted with juglone, an active component of walnut tree sap. When drinking Charlie's liquor, buyers sometimes felt they might have been poisoned. Oliver could not stop himself from wondering if the coincidence of names indicated a similarity of character as well.

"Mr. Swindler," said Stalker, "it's truly a pleasure to make your acquaintance. Let me say that I'm deeply grieved by your loss, and I hope when things calm down, I would like to invite you to come out to our little clinic and let me show you around. That's a promise, you hear?"

"You're most gracious, Reverend Stalker. As soon as time allows, I'll be glad to come out to see you."

"It's so difficult," Wechsler said—using, Oliver noticed, his most unctuous funeral director voice—"at a time like this when we've lost a loved one, but discretion must be exercised. I hesitated to bother you at this tragic time but things are moving at such a hectic pace and pressures of business are mounting so quickly, that I had to act. But first, Oliver–how impolite of me–would you care for a glass of sherry?"

Clark opened the tantalus with a tiny brass key and removed one of the bottles and three small glasses, and before Oliver could say anything, poured a small amount of revoltingly sweet wine. He handed his guests glasses and took the third for himself.

"Cheers!" he said and drank his with a gulp.

"Well, now, the problem is land. And, Oliver, the reason Reverend Stalker is here also concerns the land. You know the town is growing, and opportunity is now knocking with all the power of Fate. A decision must be made by next Thursday night, a decision to bring new business to our little hamlet."

"Heavenly Cheeseburgers?" said Oliver and sipped, letting the cloying liquor barely wet his lips.

"Precisely," said Wechsler, pulling a silk handkerchief from his breast pocket and wiped his dampening brow. "The chain is prepared to put in a Class A style of restaurant—that means real food in a real colonial setting. Steaks, chops, and even fish in addition to burgers and such—and they're prepared to design the building to be in keeping with the historic look of Fernglade."

"What," asked Oliver, "is a Class B?"

"Smaller and selling only, ah, fast foods. No style, no class."

"What's that to do with me?"

"Before she died, Imogene had agreed to sell the family home and lot to me so I could make sure the restaurant became a reality. You see, Oliver, they won't put in the restaurant without parking, and the old Hanley mansion is the only place in town it can be built that adjoins your beautiful—may I say perfect?—your perfect bit of property."

"Excuse me, but that was Imogene's home her entire life. She wouldn't sell. Where would she have gone?"

"Oliver, I can assure you that that, too, was taken care of. Your grandfather had the foresight to purchase a double lot, as you know. So while the extra lot will provide parking for the restaurant, the other, where the house now stands, we're developing into a condominium. A true place of beauty, an ideal retreat—yet still convenient to Main Street on the very site of the house. We had agreed to give your sister the best unit in the building: a ground-floor garden apartment, no stairs to climb, real plaster walls, beautiful carpeting ..."

"Elegant and lovely, like Miss Imogene," said the reverend.

"And what if my sisters and I don't want to sell?" Oliver said bluntly.

"I think," said Clark Wechsler, "a lot depends on who inherits the house and land, Oliver. But your sisters are too upset right now to talk about business, which is why the Reverend and I wanted to see you. There is some urgency, and as you know, time and tide wait for no man—we hoped that you might speak to them on behalf of our plans."

"And, let me guess, Clark: you own the Hanley place."

"Certainly, Oliver. I helped the last of the family to enter a wonderful nursing home in Florida. She was ever so grateful."

Oliver took a last sip of the sherry to gain a moment to choose the right words—and hold off the vultures for an additional minute. At last he asked, carefully knitting his brows, "You mentioned a decision by, uh, Thursday, I think you said. When do you need an answer?"

"By Thursday afternoon, at the latest." His voice dropped to suggest a tone of insider confidentiality. "The attorney for Heavenly Cheeseburgers will want to meet with the Planning Board that evening."

"And how much money are we talking about?"

"Oh, somewhere in the neighborhood of, say, half a million."

Oliver looked at the rug.

"Who's the building contractor?" he asked.

"Well, Ackermann, of course. You know Ackermann from the hotel and I are going into partnership—not to mention my good friend here, the Reverend. Nothing official, now, so don't, ha-ha, print it, after all everything hinges on you and your sisters— but if all works out, we'll form a corporation and act as our own subcontractors."

"Again, what happens if we don't choose to sell?"

"I really don't know, Oliver." Wechsler paused to scratch his thumbnail in the blotter. "But it certainly won't be good for the town or the people in it. This means lots of jobs and progress for everyone. I mean this is going to be an important place someday soon." He sliced his nail back and forth, delving a small but noticeable slit in the paper. "The newspaper, for example, will grow. All of these visitors will want to find out what's happening, and many will buy second homes—why, some even first homes— there'll be more places to eat, new shops, why there's no end." His nail went through to the polished surface of the desk.

"Thanks for the sherry. I'll get back to you as soon as I can. And very nice to meet you, Reverend Stalker."

He wandered back to his sisters in a kind of furious fog.

At nine they left the funeral home. Florence asked if he wanted to come back to her house for the night, as it was only twenty miles each way, but he declined. Someone, he said, should be at the funeral home by ten in the morning.

"But," he said, "we must talk."

"Well," said Linda, "let's go somewhere for a drink. How about the hotel?"

"No, not there," Oliver said. No doubt Ackermann and Wechsler were there right now, planning their new tomorrow that must include a few smart places to have sophisticated drinks and smarmy small talk.

"I'll follow you to Spruce Pine, Florence. You two start, I'll be there shortly."

He walked back to the hotel where a huge refrigerated truck was backed up to the delivery entrance, partially blocking the exit to the parking lot. A car larger than his VW would never have gotten out.

Sitting at Florence's round kitchen table, after enjoying her homemade deep-chocolate cake and a second cup of decaffeinated coffee, Oliver told them about Clark Wechsler's offer.

"$500,000," said Linda. "That's half a million dollars for that old house and a couple acres of land. But that's marvelous. And that doesn't count all the antiques, silver, and most of the china. After all, only that Chinese willow-ware was broken."

"I don't know, I just feel funny about selling so soon after Imogene's murder," said Florence. "What do you think, Oliver?"

"Anything we get is more than I ever thought about, but it is our old home we're talking about."

"Oh, fiddlesticks," said Linda, "You'll adjust."

"To begin with," he said, "the original offer apparently included a condominium apartment for Imogene, so there should be additional money for that. And I think Clark needs the land more than we need the money. If he doesn't get the property, the whole deal's off," he ruminated. A longtime member of the Sierra Club, who hated nuclear power, supported the EPA, owned a well-thumbed first edition of *Silent Spring*, opposed the use of DDT, Oliver—to his surprise and chagrin—found himself succumbing almost without hesitation to the enticements of unbridled greed. "I'd say more like $200,000 each."

He had no IRA, no pension, no reason, up to now, to listen to financial advisors. But suddenly he could see being part of the establishment. For the moment, he completely forgot there were already two deaths to explain.

"Then if it's agreed," said Florence, "why don't you call him, Linda, you're the oldest." Her voice trailed off.

"Does either of you know what's in her will?" asked Oliver.

"Yes," said Florence. "Outside of a few bequests to relatives, books to the local library, and so forth, the balance of the estate is to be divided equally among the three of us. But I think we need a lawyer. I'll call Albert in the morning," she paused, "though ... I'm not sure I want to sell."

"Florence," cried Linda, "don't be silly. Of course you want to sell! You'll never have to worry about anything again."

"I don't know. I'm not worried now. I have everything I need and enough to help the two of you if you were ever in trouble."

"Oh, for—" said Linda.

"Oh, go ahead. What's the use," said Florence as she got up to put the dishes in the sink.

"I'll see you tomorrow at ten," Oliver said, rising quickly. He bent to kiss his sisters on their foreheads before scurrying out to the VW for the drive back to Fernglade.

The meat truck was gone and the lot was empty. "Not too many guests this time of year," he said to the small white-faced statue of the jockey outside the hotel's back door.

Monday

Chapter Eleven

Oliver woke up Monday morning feeling as though he were drowning in depression. He dressed mechanically, slipped quietly down to his car and drove ten miles west to stop at a country diner near the reservoir where nobody knew him to offer sympathy or gossip.

First he called Florence and told her that, as much as he was expected at the Funeral Home, there was no way the paper would be put together without his being there both to work and to learn. He strove to keep his voice friendly while making it clear he could not join his sisters that day. Florence said, quite serenely, that she understood perfectly well, and so would Linda, but would he please stop at Wechsler's whenever his work was done.

At precisely nine he walked into the office and asked the ever-smiling Mary-Beth if Jerry Nickle was in the back.

"Yes," said Mary-Beth. "When he found out it's a slim paper he got here early to catch up on the ads, and get an early finish to this issue."

"Any calls for me? I mean for the editor?"

"No. Not a one."

Oliver sat at his desk in a daydream when suddenly he heard a sound like something kicking metal at the bottom of the stairs.

"Who's there?"

Silence. He thought he heard the creak of the back door in the production room, but by the time he got there the room was empty. The back door was open.

He went to the front office.

"Mary-Beth, is that back door in the production room supposed to be open?"

"No. We always keep it closed to keep the summer visitors from wandering in."

He walked back. The door was now closed and the spring catch was set to lock automatically. Everything was quiet but he was sure someone had been standing at the foot of the stairs.

Thinking it might be a good idea to check further, he entered the darkroom. Its original wooden floor was visible through jagged rips in worn linoleum; the old stained wallpaper was covered with dated pin-up photos. A large plywood worktable was covered with rolls of tape, a half-empty bottle of Windex, tiny brushes along with small jars of touch-up paint, a plastic bottle of developer hooked to an evil-looking length of rubber hose, and a half-eaten doughnut balanced atop a paper cup of black coffee.

Jerry Nickel was busy at what appeared to be a brand-new computerized camera, one of the best Oliver had ever seen. He looked about Oliver's age, though slightly overweight, with a graying, rather scraggly beard. A fringe of hair stood out all around from a navy watch cap.

Scoop, looking over the morning's digital output, introduced them. Oliver chose three photos: the principal of the high school astride an arrogant donkey surrounded by a cheering section of PTA mothers; six of the leading ladies of the hospital guild; and a sharp image of three deputy sheriffs in mufti, still wearing their deputy hats, sitting in Model T Fords ready to lead the fire department's parade.

"Jerry, let's make the donkey and the ladies both two-columns, and the cars a four-column. We can run the ladies on the editorial page and the other two will help take the edge off the obligatory front-page murder story."

"Right," said Jerry. "I'll have everything done by lunchtime. And Oliver, when you start putting the paper together you'll notice that page nine is set aside; there's a new mini-plaza opening up in Spruce Pine next week with balloons, lights, celebrities—well, what passes for celebrities around here—and the Chamber of Commerce took out a full-page ad. I'll work on it this afternoon and have it done by the morning."

Oliver nodded his assent and left. As he passed through the front office, Davis said good morning and smiled in the direction of the turkey scale. Another mighty hunter, looking like a refugee from Paunch City, was placing his feathered trophy in the enamel pan with such an expectant expression that Oliver almost hoped he'd win.

Mary-Beth adjusted the flaccid heap of blood-spattered tan and brown feathers and quietly said: "Sorry, this will be number three on the list. The winner is still over twenty-two pounds."

"Shit!" the mighty hunter exclaimed in a high tenor voice, and swinging his bullet-free bandolier in the air, walked out the office door leaving the bird behind.

"Hey, mister," called Mary-Beth, "don't you want your turkey?"

"Hell, no. You keep it, baby!"

"Another true sportsman, Mary-Beth," said Oliver.

"They aren't all bad, but this year it seems only the dregs showed up."

In the middle of the afternoon Oliver went down to ask the owner if the paper had any policies on granting favors.

"When I want a favor," said Davis, "I'll ask for it and it

will usually revolve around giving some extra publicity to one organization or another that either I or my wife are members of or have a fondness for. That's it."

Oliver went back upstairs.

By five o'clock most of the paper was put together. Oliver's editorial on the early days of spring included a mention of Oklahoma because its state tree was the redbud and they would soon be in bloom around here. He also tossed in a few words on the beauties of Berlioz's *Summer Nights*. He read the column one last time and, thinking it utterly dull, admitted it was still better than those from the previous two or three years.

With a sigh he sat down and dashed off another, on the incalculable value of the home-town paper. He quickly found a beautiful picture of the river from old unused photos to put on the editorial page and moved the hospital ladies to the coming events and society columns.

At five-fifteen, Adrian came through with an invitation to visit the Chinese Restaurant in Spruce Pine. Scoop and Jerry had already invited him to watch them bowl against the team from Shield's Supermarket. Oliver hated bowling; he instantly agreed to Adrian's invitation.

"Oliver, come with me to run an errand first?"

"Sure. Where to?"

"An antique shop that I visit occasionally. Harriet called me today about some unusual jewelry she's run across and I don't want to miss it. Then we can eat. If you don't want Chinese, there's a restaurant over near Burnsville that's pretty good."

"First, let me call Florence. She wanted me there this afternoon, but let me see if she can do without me, as long as I pledge to be there bright and early in the morning."

Florence, he thought, sounded relieved that he would not be there.

Adrian drove them down Main Street, across the bridge over Wechsler's Creek at the upper end of town, then along a back-country road to Burnsville. It was starting to get dark and the sky looked like a watercolor wash of sapphire brushed by a master. Most of the traffic they passed was heading the other way as people left jobs in town.

They followed Miller's Creek Road until they reached an out-of-business fast-food drive-in, then turned right up another country lane. It was dark as they turned into a driveway lined with rhododendrons that wound past a big white country house with brightly lit carriage lamps on either side of the front door and a sign that said, OPEN!

A flagstone path lined with more bushes led from the parking area and zig-zagged through a garden lit by small sunken fixtures, then past a concrete Buddha contemplating a small reflecting pool in lieu of a navel, and finally to a side door. Adrian rang the bell.

"C'mon in," boomed a voice. They squeezed themselves along a two-foot-wide aisle that led straight through from the front door to the back of what had apparently once been a front parlor. The walls were covered from floor to ceiling; no hint of the original surface was visible. The ceiling itself held a collection of Victorian glass lamps hung at different levels, fringed with crystal balls, prisms, or mixed glass beads, all brightly lighted to dazzle the eye with a bewildering brew of color. They passed a combination hat rack and gilt mirror on their left, a tangled mix of antlers and right-angled deer hoofs, each wrapped with green felt. A lamp on the right seemed to be constructed out of an array of brass balls and colored crystal. Finally, in the very back of the room, they encountered a stuffed brown bear dressed in a purple lace peignoir and a feathered hat, circa 1890. To its right stood a stately woman whom Adrian greeted with warmth.

"Harriet, how's everything?"

"Fine, Hon," she said. "Follow me in here, all this stuff even gets to me from time to time." She led the two into a kitchen—surprisingly uncluttered—with tiled walls and a large table on which stood the biggest begonia Oliver had ever seen. Its stems were wired with white fairy lights sparkling against a magnificent floor-to-ceiling window of stained glass depicting Fate weaving the warp and woof of Destiny, gently lit from behind.

While not quite as overwhelming as the stuffed bear, Harriet was still an impressive woman—*une femme formidable*, thought Oliver with a secret smile. She wore black slacks, a brown cable-stitch sweater, heavy rhinestone glasses, and had her long gray hair pinned back and up by a variety of silver and black ivory combs. An enormous pendant, a yellow enameled chicken emerging from a red-white-and-blue rhinestone egg, rested precariously on her ample bosom and sparkled with her every move.

"Harriet, this is Oliver Swindler, the new editor of *The Fernglade Republican*. Oliver, meet Harriet Talmage."

"Hell, I knew your sister very well." Harriet held out a surprisingly elegant, petite, and bejeweled hand, and shook Oliver's vigorously. "She collected china and bought a lot from me. Why, she was in here last week and got a beautiful Victorian teapot, lovely thing all gold and green. Nice to finally meet you."

"How's the rooster?" asked Adrian.

"Great. My nephew stayed here last week and complained the whole time about that bird's crowing at dawn … but outside of that he's a marvelous pet."

"What's unusual about the rooster?" asked Oliver.

"It hasn't any claws," said Adrian. "They fell off after being frozen on a bitterly cold night last winter and Harriet gave it a home."

"Right here," said Harriet as she led the way to a combination greenhouse and jungle room off the kitchen. There sat the rooster in a bamboo cage suspended over a partly covered hot tub that in turn was surrounded by large and ageless philodendrons. "He's okay until he tries to stand on one leg."

"Harriet has chameleons," said Adrian, "who live in the plants, and are they cute."

"Yes, they are," said Harriet, "but during the winter they live under the hot tub 'til spring. You kids have dinner?"

"Why, no," said Adrian.

"Well, come on and eat with me. There's plenty—I've got chicken and mushrooms in a sauce made of ginger, plenty of spiced rice, and I just made an angel food cake this afternoon."

"How about it, Oliver?" asked Adrian.

He could smell the food, an aroma he couldn't resist—and being called a kid again was the topping on the cake.

"I'll set up the table," said Harriet, "and you two can wander about the shop until I call. Your jewelry is on the top of the piano in the far room."

They wandered back through the long, crowded jumble, down a hall where countless oil paintings in gilded frames almost hid a busy violet and green wallpaper, and on to the nine-foot-high room at the back of the house.

Here furniture ruled. Victorian couches and chairs were in every corner, many of them newly upholstered in vibrant fabrics. Over a particularly blatant loveseat hung a more recent oil painting of a Nissen hut in the middle of a barren plain surrounded by English tanks and various pieces of battle gear.

The bowed windows were of old glass, one pair looking out on the now pitch-black road, the other into the rest of the garden.

"This is one mixed bag," Oliver murmured, thumbing through a collection of mostly erotic French postcards in a fret-worked basket of bone that rested atop a pile of old, bound *Popular Mechanics* magazines. The magazines sat on a large mat of tightly-woven straw interspersed with strings of parti-colored beads that portrayed the pyramids of Egypt.

"True, but most of it is beautifully crafted, and when she has things restored she uses the best materials. And look at this pin," Adrian said as she approached the piano. She picked up something large and round that scintillated in the light of a huge brass chandelier.

The pin, about two inches in diameter, comprised narrow concentric circles of marcasite alternating with carved and polished jet, all surrounding a cut amethyst that glowed in the center.

"Where will you ever wear that?" Oliver asked.

"Hopefully," she answered, "on a long white satin evening gown while dancing at a glamorous party along the Riviera."

"Wish I could be there," he said and meant it.

"No reason why you shouldn't be. Oh, Oliver, look at this." She folded her fingers over the pin and walked to a low marble and mahogany coffee table that held a silver tea service with a surface of such complexity, that, he thought, even Victoria herself would cry. "Boy, would I love to serve tea in this."

At first he thought the cat at his feet was a stuffed toy but when it dashed under a chair, he jumped.

"That's Max, a truly cosmopolitan cat," said Adrian.

"Any more livestock?" he asked, thinking of the rooster.

"A beautiful Dalmatian that only needs an active fire truck to complete the picture."

They exchanged a smile that, to Oliver's jaded sensibility coupled with Adrian's refreshing candor, suggested possibilities he had not pursued for longer than he cared to admit. He found himself gazing at her still though she had turned away toward other strange or intriguing objects in the eclectic collection. He was startled when Harriet called them for dinner.

The table was now set for three with crystal wine and

water glasses, beautiful unmatched plates, and gleaming silver, all surrounding a three-tiered epergne filled with freshly picked white daffodils from the garden.

"Sit down, kids, soup's on."

Dinner was the best he had in, literally, years. After an hour Harriet removed the plates and brought out the cake, its ivory-white frosting covered with candied violets. Over coffee they talked some more.

"Harriet, how well did you know my sister?"

"I considered her a good friend. When my husband Max died—it was unexpected, and such a shock—Imogene was one of the first people who came to help out. Emotional support, answering phone calls ... and practical help, too. She made it so much easier to cope. And she loved to talk about you, Oliver— lately she was so happy you were coming home again to live in the old house. That's why she redid the kitchen. And she planned on doing the bathrooms over next."

"In other words, at no time in your knowledge did she mention selling the property and moving?"

"You sound like Perry Mason, Oliver," Harriet said, half-seriously. "But sell it? Never! She was adamant, said it would only sell over her dea—oops, sorry—I mean she wouldn't sell at any price. She told me that if they put that fast-food restaurant on that corner, it would be her duty to spread thumbtacks on their parking lot ... and she'd call the State Board of Health over every dirty wrapper that touched the ground."

"Well, that certainly is interesting. I've been told that Imogene was delighted to sell and eventually move into a condo unit when it was built on the property. When's the last time you saw her?"

"About two weeks ago. Now come on, I know a lot can change in two weeks, but at that time, she was not budging one inch. And she didn't like Clark Wechsler, either. She thought he was a fool as a kid and was still a fool—and a mean one, to boot."

"Oliver, this is starting to sound a bit strange, isn't it?" asked Adrian.

"I think," he said, "it's time to tell it to the sheriff."

"Will Phibert?" asked Harriet. "He's a good man. Known 'im forever. My younger brother dated his mother for a while back in high school—way before she married Mark Phibert. Will was a nice kid. Popular, too—all the parties endorse him every election."

They sat silent for a few minutes; none of them could escape the import of Harriet's opinion on Imogene's devotion to her house.

At last Adrian spoke. "Harriet, of course I want the pin. You know my taste too well."

"I knew you would, Hon. Wear it in health and I'll send you a bill at the end of the month."

Oliver nearly leaped out of his chair when he realized the two women were already standing. Despite the somewhat slovenly habits acquired over recent years, he had been raised with manners—especially toward an older hostess and a very attractive young colleague.

As Adrian dropped the pin into her purse after admiring it one more time, Oliver reached for the older woman's hand. "Thanks for the wonderful evening, Harriet. It was delightful to meet you."

Oliver and Adrian were both quiet and thoughtful as she drove back to Fernglade. As she let him off at the front of the hotel, he took her hand in his, then quickly let go.

"You know, a fellow could get spoiled by this curb service."

"The fellow is welcome anytime," she said with a smile.

"I'll call you tomorrow," he said and walked into the hotel.

It was only about eight-thirty, early for New York, but latish for a town like Fernglade. He found Ackerman at his usual post at the front desk and checked to see if there were any messages.

"Not a one," said Ackermann.

Oliver went upstairs and, with no interest in what was on television, buried himself in Charles Darwin's log about sailing around the world. It was a fascinating story, Oliver found, the great naturalist writing of his own experiences on the expedition, eventually published as *The Voyage of the Beagle*.

Chapter Twelve

Tuesday morning Oliver's travel alarm went off at 7:00 a.m., and he woke to another gray and drizzly day in the mountains. He felt the way he had years ago in the Army when forced to rise at ungodly hours, knowing he might have to trudge through the snow to crypto-school, or share a bathroom with twenty other men smelling of Old Spice, or march off into the cold dawn seeking the Army's elusive unicorn—military intelligence.

He sat on the edge of the bed and struggled to put on socks. The left side of his brain wanted to go forward and get the day over while the right knew life would be better if allowed to go back to sleep (or was it the other way around?). He put on one of his new white shirts and his rarely used dark-brown suit, clipped his moustache and beard, patted both cheeks with Lagerfeld cologne, and headed down through the empty lobby into the rain.

The diner was full as usual, its stainless-steel walls and ceiling as bright as the chromium caps on a Soviet soldier's teeth. He ordered a large breakfast from a charming young girl, knowing that if the body didn't sweat with effort today, the mind would. He had a second cup of coffee with one of the two copies of yesterday's *New York Times* that were almost hidden in the rack by the front door.

At exactly eight o'clock he entered the paper's strangely empty quarters and headed up the stairs to find Scoop drinking a diet soda through a straw, a cigarette and a gnawed pencil sharing the opposite the corner of his mouth, as he tapped away at his computer keyboard.

"Good morning," the young man grunted.

"Morning," Oliver replied and sat down in front of press releases and reader mail that had arrived at the paper's postbox late Monday, sorting them into two piles: double-spaced pages in pile one and all the rest in the other. Among the submissions were notices of **"Extremely important!!!"** social activities for this week's paper. Then he looked through the second, registering dislike for most organizations there; individuals could be forgiven for not knowing the ropes about press releases, but the so-called pros should be ... pros, dammit. As he struggled with a ranting, poorly written letter to the editor, his phone rang.

"Morning, Swindler," said the sheriff. "Phibert here. Tried your room and Ackermann saw you walking out so I assumed you might already be at the paper. Thought you'd want to know that we still don't have any idea who the man in your kitchen was There was no identification, of course, and obviously the hands were removed because of fingerprints, but the doctor said something interesting about that. He said the amputation was very skillfully done. Same thing with the jaw smashed up: there's little hope of matching dental records, but the fact that it was smashed suggests some kind of connection to somebody in the case; we just have to find it. One thing that was curious was the sort of backwoods clothing; he wasn't dressed like a fellow from town. That got Doc curious, that and the general rough state of the body, and he found something very interesting. This guy had giardiasis."

"What's that, a social disease?"

"No, it's a parasitic condition of the blood. It's pretty rare, he said. You pick it up when you drink water from ponds or lakes that have beaverdams. Beavers carry it, apparently. And the doc said it's pretty localized: just a few mountain communities in the Southern Appalachians, including this part of western North Carolina. It's a pretty definite sign that the man was a hill person from somewhere in the area."

"Well," said Oliver skeptically, "I guess that narrows it down. What about the piece of glove?"

"I asked Wechsler about it and he said it was from a supply of gloves from his funeral home, all right. There's a code stamped on the inside edge. He says he's got no idea how it got there. Says he was in the office when the murder occurred.

"I did get ahold of the neighbors across the street; they locked up the house and took their kid to his grandmother out of town. Obviously, I'm not finding any witnesses. As you said, who comes down that street without any reason?"

"How's Luther?"

"Not happy, but he's all right. I'm sorry about keeping him, Swindler, but the DA said I could hold him on suspicion, since he admits it's his knife. That way I can keep him here until the publicity cools. I told him you'd be over for a visit by tomorrow. Oh, and if we get a late frost warning, you'll need to cover over his garden. I told him you would."

Oliver thanked Phibert for the update. Lowering his voice so Scoop could not hear, he told the sheriff about Clark Wechsler's offer to buy his sister's land.

"That could be some motive for murder," said Phibert, "if your sister didn't want to sell."

"As a matter of fact, I have it on good authority that she didn't. And I'm not sure that I do, either, at this point."

They were both silent for a moment, then Oliver said, "So you have no other clues about who did it?"

"No, not a one, Swindler. The knife had no prints on it, other than yours when you picked it up. The kitchen, too. It looks like the painters had cleaned it up pretty good, getting it prepped. The only new prints were Miss Imogene's, from when she got home, and a few of yours. Nobody was noticed in the neighborhood."

Oliver wondered momentarily how many people get away with murder. There were obvious suspects and a clear motive in Imogene's killing, but none that he could think of in the case of the unidentified man. Without motive, suspects, or even identification, it would be doubly hard to solve.

"Thanks, Sheriff," he said, returning to the moment. "I'll call you tomorrow morning for an official statement for the paper—let's hope there'll be more information. And again thanks for keeping me posted."

He started to sort through the mail again but noticed that it was already nine-fifty. He turned to his companion. "Scoop, everything's in good shape for the front page, correct?"

"It's all under control, Oliver. Don't worry about it."

"Good. Thanks. I've got to go to the funeral home by ten. I'll be back when I can."

"No problem. In fact, this is one of the few times I can remember that we could get a paper together ready to go out on time without even breathing hard. And, I've gotta tell you, the one thing that Greig gets upset about is not getting the paper out on time. He hates it when we're late—like it always was with Black. You should try to head down to Asheville no later than three, three-thirty. They charge by the hour for the press, and they start counting at four. On the dot."

"Why don't we print it here?" Oliver asked.

"Money. The paper's printed on a Webb offset press, and Greig couldn't afford to buy one, much less find room for one. The closest place with a Webb is down in Asheville, so the pages you bring will be photographed with their camera and used for plates."

"And the editor usually takes it down?"

"According to tradition, the new editor takes his first issue down. After that it's all by computer except large flats are hand-delivered by Jerry Nickel or whoever's handy. Don't forget, the last day of turkey season is tomorrow and you get to award the prize in the morning."

Oliver had little reason to dwell on the funeral. The Pine Room had opened at nine, giving the mourners ample time to chat, gossip, console Florence, and ogle Linda's too-youthful dress before the service began at ten on the dot. Imogene pulled in a representative from almost every family and organization in town. Oliver saw a couple of his old teachers from high school, now in their seventies or eighties and as spry as ever. The women's club showed up en masse, along with many of their husbands, and he realized that even at fifty-five he belonged to a different—not necessarily better—generation than his sister.

The only unpleasantness was caused by a young reporter from *The Asheville Citizen* who cornered Oliver in the hall. Dressed in a trench coat and dark glasses—apparently his idea of a cub reporter's garb—he thrust his tape recorder at Oliver's face.

"Got anything to add to the story, Swindler?"

"Not a thing. And it's 'Mr. Swindler' to you."

"How do ya feel about two bodies being found in your family home?"

"Better than finding three. I realize the importance of getting a good story, but isn't this a new low even for your group?"

"Hey, dude, don't get sore—I've got a job to do."

"Well bug off and do it somewhere else," Oliver snapped. He walked out to the hired limo where his two sisters waited in mourning.

As they drove the two miles to the cemetery, thick clouds

sent giant fingers of steam into the river valley, and for a moment the sun, as if through a scrim, brightened everything—but only for a moment.

The cemetery overlooked the river. Cars entered through wrought iron gates that spelled out "Fernglade Cemetery," each letter comprised of stylized fern fronds that dripped with rain. They followed the winding road to the upper left sector of the grounds.

The section was dominated by a ten-foot-high Egyptian temple, a marble cenotaph topped with Diana on the hunt. It was surrounded in all directions by smaller, less impressive obelisks and headstones. A number of hydrangeas, now leafing out but still with remnants of last year's bloom, dotted the browned lawn. With some thirty cars stretched out along the road it took some time for everyone to arrive at the graveside.

No pallbearers were needed. The coffin was already in place as the funeral party walked up to the open grave. At least a hundred people watched and listened as Reverend Willard—the young pastor of Imogene's church—conducted a short but dignified service. Oliver was surprised by a strange look that passed between Linda, who stood closest to the open grave, and Clark Wechsler, who hovered beside her holding a vast black golf umbrella over the two sisters. Lust is rare to see at funerals, especially between people on the downside of middle age, but if the look he spied passing between them wasn't lust, then those two needed lessons in unspoken communication.

He thought about it all the way back to town and the parking lot of the funeral home.

"I'll drive Linda back to my house," said Florence, and we'll have a late meal there. Will you call tonight?"

"Sure, when I finish at the paper. And don't say anything negative about working. It's easier to keep busy."

The raindrops were getting smaller as he walked back to

the *Republican* office, where he spent the next two hours writing a feature story on the two murders in Fernglade. He then reviewed the obituary his sister had written for herself; he tried to rewrite it with less modesty and more praise, but soon discovered that her own version was nearly perfect.

Around five o'clock the phone rang.

"Oliver? Clark Wechsler here. Wasn't the service nicely done?"

"Yes, it was. I'd forgotten what a beautiful spot the cemetery is in."

"I called to tell you I spoke with Linda and then went back to meet with my partners. We're prepared to raise our offer to $575,000, though that's absolutely as high as we can go. Now you do understand that's for the two lots and the land on the other side of Wechsler's Creek."

"I understand, Clark. If we sell, we sell it all."

"And we must have an answer soon. Can't dawdle over this particular deal."

"I'll discuss it with Florence once more tonight. Our lawyer is Albert Seller—and if Florence agrees, he can call you tomorrow."

"You're not making a mistake, Oliver. It's the best opportunity of your life." Wechsler's pomposity oozed over the over the phone. After a brief, but still too long, pause, he added, "Should I send the bill for the funeral to Seller?"

"Yes, if you would, Clark. Thank you. I need to get back to the paper now. We have our deadlines, too."

He was seized with the desire to scrub out his ear.

At six he drove to Florence's house. They talked at length, but Oliver soon began to feel he didn't care what they decided.

It was dark and chilly when he drove back to Fernglade. He parked his VW on the street and walked into the hotel.

"Any messages?" he asked Ackermann.

"No, nothing." Ackermann said without looking up, and

went back to reading a worn copy of *People*.

"How's the TV reception?"

Ackermann took his cigar out of his mouth. "The best. Clear as a bell. I'm a partner in the cable franchise. You should have been here when they trucked the dish up to the top of the hill. That was some job."

"Anything on at this time of night?"

"Try Channel Eight," he said, going back to his magazine.

In his room Oliver took off his shoes, spread out on the bed and turned on the old but serviceable television. Using the well-worn remote, he tuned to Channel Eight.

The picture had the look of a 1960s home movie. A young couple were having cocktails—for about two minutes—in what looked to be a hotel room with decidedly upbeat background music. The girl undressed the man, then herself, in less than thirty seconds and proceeded to attend to his needs in ways that had even Oliver confused. He'd been in the Army and considered himself to be fairly sophisticated, but obviously Fernglade had something to teach even him. He watched for a few minutes, but when the leather boots and Fu Manchu masks came out, he switched to the networks. Their programs were cleaner, though not half so imaginative. He turned off the television and picked up his book.

Ackermann, Black, and Wechsler, he told himself, were some trio. Not nearly as diverse—or evolved—as Galapagos finches. He happily went back to Darwin's *Voyage*.

Chapter Thirteen

One thing Oliver enjoyed about National Public Radio was waking up in the morning to the same stories of disaster that inflict the world every day—but instead of the commercial approach that highlights only death, destruction, or rampant greed, NPR's slower, methodical point of view leveled out the horror to a more acceptable level.

That morning, Oliver dressed while listening to stories that provided ever more evidence that the public sector remained in the hands of idiots and the insane, but as he laced his shoes he heard about the French concern with the death of wildlife on their highways where motor vehicles injure or kill 3,250 large mammals and countless amphibians in one year. So, they began building underpasses or "deer passes," called *cerviducs*, to enable these large mammals to cross in safety. They also were creating a series of special amphibian tunnels called *crapauducs* to help frogs and toads of France get to the other side. The world cannot be entirely bad, he thought.

Then he thought of the labyrinth beneath the streets of Fernglade and wondered what animals used those tunnels for escape routes. Oliver did not like dilemmas; he preferred simple constructs and clear answers. If he told the sheriff about the tunnels, Black and the others would either deny knowing about them or dismiss them as historical curiosities, useless remnants of the past. But anyone wanting to get around town without being observed—Wechsler's little cabal came to mind—could easily do so without ever having to come out into the open. The sheriff should be told, he thought. Just maybe not quite yet.

Breakfast at the diner was uneventful. It was clear that the same people were there at the same times, in the same spots, every weekday morning. He hoped he would not become one of them.

He arrived at the paper just before eight, gave Mary-Beth his social security number and received in return a newly-issued press card for the *Republican* and a deputy sheriff's card for the county. As he passed Adrian's desk he smiled warmly at her, and upon entering the workroom was surprised to see the presses and the paper folder busy at work, under the watchful eyes of an elderly gentleman with a stocking cap on his head and an unlit cigar in his mouth.

The man nodded at Oliver, removed the cigar, and introduced himself as "Old Warren."

"Is there a young Warren?" Oliver asked.

"Yep, my son—he's only sixty-eight. We got a big job yesterday afternoon from one of the real estate agents in town who's had—he calls it "an image change"—so he needed new stationery, new calling cards, and billheads. Wants them last week. So we try to oblige. And now the diner decided to improve its image for the Atlanta folks and wants new menus with a fancy new logo."

"Better feast than famine. How long have you been with the paper?"

"About forty years. I started with old Mullens when he took over. The shop did well over the years, enough to keep me in groceries and build up a pension. I've printed a lot of 'No Trespassing' posters in my day. Now Greig wants to build up the business again." He lowered his voice as if to share a secret, though all he added was, "Frankly I was getting tired of retirement." Without a pause, he asked, "What name do you want on your business cards? Oliver Swindler enough?"

"Fine. Middle initial is 'S' and means nothing, just like Harry Truman. Not even a period. I'd just as soon leave it out altogether. Happy to meet you, Warren." Oliver climbed up the spiral staircase to the round table and his desk.

Once again Scoop was propped up in a chair at an impossible angle, eating chocolate doughnuts and drinking a diet soda.

"Hemingway," Oliver said, "didn't drink that swill."

"Well, if you want me to drink the swill that he did drink, just let me know—glad to oblige. I meant to tell you that the paper—in your honor—is doing a special issue devoted to Gardening in the Mountains and we have to start planning soon—lot of writing assignments and photos to get."

"Could we get together with Adrian sometime next week?"

"Sure," he said before turning back to his keyboard.

Oliver went downstairs for a cup of coffee and came back to a ringing phone. It was the supervisor of one of the river towns asking that the paper print his Letter to the Editor uncut and uncensored.

"I haven't received it yet," he answered. "And I can't guarantee to print any letter without reading it first. But I'll be glad to give you a call when it arrives."

He hung up. Not the best way to approach the press, he thought.

"Who is this guy Dyson?"

"He's a dimwit," said Scoop. "There's no way you can please him, so don't even try."

The phone rang again. The mayor of Sylva wanted the paper to run a story on the town's refusal to accept flood plain maps prepared by the Federal Emergency Management Agency.

Moments later, a caller without a name demanded to know when trout fishing would open. Oliver told him to call the Chamber of Commerce, and suddenly remembered that needed to ask the DA's office what was happening about the porno ring. The secretary told him the grand jury wouldn't meet until Thursday and there would be nothing new until then. He noted down to save space for a follow-up story in next week's edition.

Scoop left for the supermarket, and Oliver pondered whether it would be a good time to call Clark Wechsler. But what tone should he adopt? Righteous indignation at the man's lying about Imogene's willingness to sell the family house and land; feigned acceptance of the lies, and the opportunity to find out how far Clark would go, wondering what might turn up; naïve gullibility coupled with a touch of incipient greed? As if in response, his phone rang.

"Wechsler's Funeral Services here," said an oily male voice. "Is Mr. Swindler available for a personal call?"

Quickly Oliver decided to play nice, and go along. "I'll be glad to," he said.

"Just a moment," said the man. With a click Oliver was on hold while the phone played pop-tune elevator music for the next three minutes. Oliver wondered why a small-town funeral parlor would need, or want, to put out such irritating noise. At last, without warning, it gave way to Wechsler's unctuous voice.

"Oliver! I know how busy you must be, having suffered such great travail, but I wondered if you would do The Leader and I the honor of visiting his Stalker Mountain Clinic and Guidance Center—you know that's the formal name for his worthy attempts at helping mankind—if you'd join us later this afternoon, say around one o'clock?"

"Well, Clark, I wish I could. But thanks to an old tradition, I'm supposed to drive the paper's photocopy to Asheville this afternoon." Why, he thought to himself, with instant communication on the worldwide web, should he do such a thing in this day and age? Oliver almost smirked as he imagined Wechsler struggling to find a way to sound oily, sincere, pushy, and angry all at once; an instant before the man erupted, he added, "On the other hand, though, Clark, I don't have to be there until later in the day, so I suppose I can find a little time right after lunch."

At 1:10—deliberately ten minutes later than promised—Oliver drove out to meet The Leader of Stalker Mountain Clinic overlooking the river from on high.

First it was necessary to negotiate the old Stalker Mountain Bridge, a narrow trestle of one wide lane supported by crisscrossing rusty steel girders with a "DANGER—NARROW BRIDGE" sign at either end. He followed the road for about half a mile until a large painted sign came into sight. It was wood cut in the shape of a pyramid, atop a short pillar of oddly-matched stones, and read: "The Stalker Mountain Clinic, Fernglade, North Carolina," and, below the address, "Hearts at Rest."

He turned onto a fairly wide paved road that wound between high trees, then passed an old barn on his right, where a man dressed in dungarees was patiently shepherding half a dozen goats toward the open barn door.

A few yards farther on his left was a large rebuilt farmhouse with parking spaces in front for several cars, marked by a small sign instructing "Head In." Oliver hadn't the foggiest notion of what that meant; however, the lot being empty he parked—of course—head in.

He approached the front door via a flagstone path bordered with daylilies. The door opened to rustic kitsch, a combination of the soft and cushiony textures found in 1960s-era big-eyed-child Margaret Keene paintings, with an overlay of snowy Bob Timberlake homesteads.

The woman at the desk looked up with a smile and said: "You must be Mr. Swindler. Welcome. Reverend Stalker is in the conference room, straight through that door to your left."

Oliver walked into a room dominated by a huge conference table, sixteen-foot ceilings of heavy-hewn oak beams that crossed wide expanses of white plaster, and a large, overly ornate chandelier hanging over the table. Floor-to-ceiling windows on the right opened out onto a vista of sumptuous early spring beauty.

Three men sat at the far end of the table, Stalker in the center, Simon Black on his right, who jumped up like a marionette.

"Oliver, welcome to our home. You have met the Reverend, of course. Let me introduce Martin Stein, the legal counsel for the Stalker Clinic. He's come to us from the island of Manhattan, via Atlanta, and now resides primarily in Fernglade."

With the self-conscious presence of a man who sees in himself someone of immense importance, and without rising from his seat, Stalker intoned, "Mr. Swindler, I'm delighted you could take time off from the responsibilities of that newspaper and join us here for an inside look at our mission and our deeds. Martin, why not pour some port wine for Oliver?" As he waved his hand the rays of the afternoon sun struck his diamond ring.

Tom Brown's doggerel rose unbidden to Oliver's mind as he stared at "the Leader."

> "I do not love thee, Dr. Fell,
> The reason why I cannot tell;
> But this I know, and know full well,
> I do not love thee, Dr. Fell."

The man's eyes were dark, almost black, and drew one in like swamp water attracts a snake.

He continued in his soothing pastor's voice. "Of course you know Simon as a friend and fellow toiler at the newspaper. As for

Martin, he is our legal brains and counsel, a dedicated man who left a thriving practice to guide our course through the muddy waters of redemption."

Stein handed Oliver a glass of very dark, richly flavored port in a small, cunningly cut crystal goblet, its edges sparkling in the sunlight shining through the window.

Though he maintained a pleasant and unaffected demeanor, Shakespeare's adjuration to "kill all the lawyers" flashed through Oliver's mind. After a slow, appreciative sip of his port, he asked, as cordially as he could, "How, and why, did a big-city lawyer leave the excitement of a large law practice to work in our small town?"

Stein said, with an almost unbidden glance toward Stalker— *As if for approval,* thought Oliver—"Well, my wife, who was also an attorney in the same firm, and I liked to come up here on weekends from time to time. Over the years I came to realize I was tired of traveling back and forth and, at the same time, we both wanted to taper off our work load. So I thought I'd try to find some legal work up here—not very likely for an outsider like myself. But, then, by chance, my wife needed some advice on a personal family matter, and our good friend Clark Wechsler mentioned the Stalker Clinic as a wonderful place she could go to for guidance. And before you know it, The Reverend asked me if I'd be willing to serve the clinic. It had been such a help to my wife, how could I say no? And a wonderful bonus is that we don't just ferret out small legal problems, or take people to court, institute lawsuits, all those things. Instead, just like the Clinic's practice, I've learned to mediate, and find common ground, and now we often, in essence, find solutions to problems without going to court."

Reverend Stalker smiled rather like a Cheshire cat.

At that moment—*Right on cue*—the receptionist slipped quietly into the room and, deeply apologetic, asked The Reverend if he might possibly be able to take an important phone call from a disciple in Atlanta, who desperately needed counsel.

"Of course," Stalker said with a frown of contrived concern. "Martin, I suspect your advice might be needed with this call as well. Simon, will you guide Oliver through the maze of our retreat?"

As the two men left the room, Black stood and came around the table. "Come along, Oliver, and let's look at the physical manifestation of our spiritual organization."

In the sunshine, they walked down a graveled path to a worn-shingled, one-story building that cried out with rusticity and country charm. The carved sign over the door consisted of old-style letters, washed with gold, and read "THE SHOPS AT STALKER MOUNTAIN: BAIT AND TACKLE."

A number of glass cases displayed every sort of high-end fishing gear; what looked to be very valuable antique bamboo fly-rods on the walls were interspersed with a variety of stuffed fish. A man in branded Orvis clothing was straightening out little boxes of flies, and straightened up with a smile that exposed two gleaming gold teeth, just left of center.

"Jonathan Wheatley," said Black, "allow me to introduce Oliver Swindler, our new editor, one of my colleagues at the paper."

"I went through school with your wife, Mr. Wheatley, and met her again at the bank last week. It's a pleasure to meet you."

"Mr. Swindler, Loretta spoke so highly of you that I feel as though I've known you for years. Welcome to my little bit of earth at the Stalker Retreat. Are you interested in fly-fishing at all?"

"In my youth," Oliver chuckled, "I often fished the Laurel and the Toe Rivers. A long while back. Then for some reason, my interest dissipated. Maybe it was city living. But I have to admit, I wouldn't mind trying it again one of these days now that I'm back here in the wild."

"I hope—and Loretta hopes—you'll come have dinner with us one night."

Their next visit was to the retreat's health food store, filled with loaves of freshly baked bread, full-grain rolls, cunningly packaged jars of jellies and jams, even little knitted tea cozies— all stamped or embroidered with "Stalker Mountain" in red letters across the bottom.

The girls who waited in the shop wore outfits reminiscent of Victorian maid's uniforms, with little doilies on their heads to keep stray hairs from polluting the baked goods. There were no customers in sight.

Oliver turned to Black after inspecting some of the appetizing treats. "Is this branch of the Stalker Mountain Clinic's commercial enterprises something new? There don't seem to be many customers."

Black's voice sounded as uncomfortable as his darting eyes looked. "We just finished most of the remodeling a few weeks ago in preparation for the coming summer season. And," he added, "all of the sales staff belong to the clinic or the church in one way or another."

The two men soon approached another low building that had clearly once been a small garage or livery stable. A subdued sign of silver letters incised on a black background read, "Eternal Rest and Pre-Need Planning." They waded through plush dark purple carpet into the state-of-the-art coffin selection salon, where a wide deal table held thick catalogs of coffins, hardware, coffin linings, and the other appurtenances of what might be considered a "high-class"—or at least a high-cost—funeral.

"The Reverend," said Black with the air of one imparting a profound, admirable truth, "belongs to a family long in the service of the funeral arts. In the Great Depression, his forbears would embalm family members in exchange for food—chickens, eggs, milk, vegetables—or for services around their homes—carpentry and such—or even, sometimes, gifts of land."

"Doesn't this conflict with Clark Wechsler's business?"

"Hardly," said Black, his voice dropping almost to a whisper. "There are always discriminating folks—there always will be, we hope—who appreciate the refined ... classy, if you will ... even profoundly spiritual burial provided by the Starker Clinic."

Oliver's eyebrows rose in a double arc, and Black couldn't quite decide whether his expression indicated skepticism or curiosity. He decided to assume the best, and he continued in a more businesslike, journalistic tone. "That's as opposed to those folks on the lookout for a more, um, affordable investment, not to mention ... well, a bit of that common touch that Clark provides."

"And," he added, with an implication that he was imparting insider trade secrets to a fellow scoop-seeking reporter, "both of them buy from the same suppliers, so together they're entitled to rather big volume discounts." He chuckled. "It's really no different than Wal-Mart or Winn-Dixie, if you know what I mean."

Oliver looked Black directly in the eyes. "I'm beginning to get a good idea," he said.

"Do you have time to visit the school?" Black asked.

"You have a school up here?"

"Yes, a private school, very small. And very select. In the last marking period, four students received A's, with two B's, and six C's—there were no failures."

"I'd like to, but as you know I have to take the paper to Asheville before four, and there are still things to be done."

"Of course," said Black.

Chapter Fourteen

Back at the paper, Oliver tried to hold his temper, reminding himself that when dealing with the Very Reverend Stalker and the Stalker Clinic, being quiet and careful might be the best path to walk. But each of the men—Stalker, Black, and especially Wechsler—had a personality that grated on him like sandpaper. After a few minutes of sitting at his desk fuming, discretion lost out to anger, and he dialed Wechsler's number with a sour look on his face. As soon as he was put through, he let fly.

"You can give up, Clark. You and your pals. Admit the goddamn truth," he said through clenched jaws and teeth. "My sister had no intention of selling her property to you or anyone."

"Now who told you that?"

"A good friend who knew Imogene well, and who can and will be believed over you."

"Oliver, calm down. It just isn't true. Imogene really did intend to sell. You have my word on this."

"Your word! I wouldn't believe you under any circumstances. You can forget the sale and don't try to convince my sister Linda; it will be two against one."

"I'd be very careful if I were you," said Wechsler in a voice now tinged with malice.

"That cuts two ways," Oliver replied and hung up the phone.

He called Albert Seller and instructed the lawyer not to agree to any business connected with Clark Wechsler under any circumstances, until he heard news to the contrary. Not even to pay the bill for Imogene's funeral.

Oliver tried to calm himself with deep breathing, followed by looking through the pile of papers on his desk, and finally by stretching his arms and pacing the office. At last he sat down and began to scribble on a clean notepad. Random words at first, then two columns, plus and minus, of options he might have to take if Clark persisted. He had just written "SBI?" when the phone rang.

"Mr. Black—"

"Mr. Black is no longer the editor. This is Oliver Swindler."

"I'll have to change our records here. Well, Mr. Swindler, did you say, this is George Peters from the NC Department of Transportation. I'd like you give you some information about replacing the viaduct over Wechsler's Creek. What they call the 'old bridge.' I'd like to give you an update so you can run a story in this week's paper, if you would."

"We're a newspaper, Mr. Peters, and we go to press tonight, so fire away. If it's newsworthy, I'll be glad to fit it in."

"Thanks. Well, in short, we sent engineers over there late last week to inspect the viaduct, and structurally it's in worse shape than we expected. Most of the guide rails have been severely corroded by salt. Most of the folks living up there know about that, so it'll be important to let them know that we plan to start maintenance and improvements the beginning of next week. That means the right or outside lane—the right lane heading out of town—is going to be closed for at least two weeks—right through Easter. Of course folks won't like that, but they'll be glad when it's fixed. We plan to start work next Monday, so we'll be closing off that lane and hopefully getting timed lights operating at either end before this weekend. I'll send you a map of the detours in today's mail. So, if you would warn your readers, I would appreciate it."

"Is it really that bad?"

"Could you think of another reason for a department like this to move as fast as we are?" he asked with a chuckle. "I know our reputation—as fast as a sleepy snail."

"Could you use the FAX setup to get that map to us right away? I can put the map in if you get it to me in the next half hour."

"Will do, Mr. Swindler. This number, or ...?"

Oliver gave Peters the downstairs phone line. "Thanks for letting us know, Mr. Peters. And don't forget to change your contact information. It's S-W-I-N-D-L-E-R, first name Oliver."

After writing up his notes and marking it for a boxed feature on the front page, he called down to Mary-Beth and asked her to bring the fax to Scoop or Jerry as soon as it arrived. Then he called Florence and told her about Imogene's visit with Harriet Talmage.

"Oliver, I never did believe that Imogene really wanted to sell," she said. Frankly, I'd never feel comfortable with all that money. If you're against selling, too, then we shouldn't sell. I'll happily go along with you."

"It's more than the money. And, Florence, I'm not sure we shouldn't eventually sell. It's just that I'm concerned about Clark Wechsler lying about Imogene's wishes. Until we find out who killed her, I think the whole deal should be on hold."

"I'll tell Linda but she won't be happy."

"Linda is never happy, Florence. Never was, never will be. But thank you for being the one to tell her. Bye for now."

Oliver sat silent for a few minutes, bothered, staring at the wall, just this side of depressed ... until Scoop bounded up the stairs, the whole floor shaking with his enthusiasm.

The two spent the next hour finalizing the paper, placing the bridge story on the front page. They discussed coming events, and took continual phone calls with "important" last-minute stories. The Social Security office wanted free space for its columns; Oliver said they could send a request in writing. The Senior Citizens of Fernglade wished their upcoming soirées would be covered, as did similar groups of three nearby towns. Oliver wondered if these groups really wanted to attract support for their cause; he suspected they simply liked seeing their names in print.

A cultured, plummy voice—Mr. J. B. McNamara—requested that the paper sponsor a charity's yearbook. Ads would be sold by an outside organization while the paper underwrote the printing cost.

"What's it called?" Oliver asked.

"Tools for Teachers. We support education for the poor."

"And you're a registered non-profit charity?"

"Oh, yes, of course. We have paperwork."

"What percentage of the take would go to the program?"

"A goodly proportion, of course."

"Exactly how much?"

"Well, I can't say right now."

"Call me back when you can." Oliver hung up.

At twelve o'clock Adrian asked if Scoop and Oliver wanted to go to lunch. "I thought it was about time you visited Clark Wechsler's lunchroom."

"Or," said Scoop, "the Boom-Boom Room."

The Big Toe Dip sat next to the building where Adrian lived. The front of the store was devoted to magazines (mostly smut and scandal sheets, along with three old issues of *Time*); on the opposite wall, a counter was piled high with candy and nonprescription drugs. Two narrow aisles of shelves filled with sweatshirts, rubber balls, and cheap toys led to the dining area. About fifteen by twenty feet, delineated by a low picket fence and an open gate guarded by a Styrofoam "wooden" Indian, the lunchroom held half a dozen tables with only a few chairs occupied.

Adrian chose a table some distance away from a closed door in the back wall, where an electronic bug zapper hung above the jamb, glowing blue and in full operation.

"That can get noisy," she said. "I'd rather stay away from it."

With forced cheer the waitress informed them that the Special of the Day was a tuna salad sandwich and Tomato Two Thirty soup.

After they all three ordered the special, Scoop said in a loud whisper, "They call it that because if you're too late for lunch, or hungover at five, it's still available later in the day, or even for dinner."

Adrian chuckled—*It's almost a giggle*, thought Oliver, warm feelings rolling over him— and said, "He makes a lot of money in the summer but things slow down for the fall and winter. Hunting season helps a little in November and early December, but ...."

"The diner's still better," said Scoop.

Even freshly prepared, the soup tasted stale and the tuna salad thrown together. The winner of the turkey-shooting contest was to be announced at two-thirty, so Oliver was glad of the excuse to leave the Boom-Boom Room as soon as they could.

Scoop ran upstairs for his camera while Mary-Beth handed Oliver the check so he could be photographed presenting it to Mr. Fred Grover of Tenafly, New Jersey. The procedure was straightforward, the posing easy, but Oliver's irritation grew steadily.

"Do I have to do this?" he murmured to Adrian after the fourth or fifth shot.

"It goes with the territory." She winked. "Think of it as a perk of being editor-in-chief."

Oliver was disproportionately relieved when Mary-Beth called him to the phone. He even took notes as Mrs. Phyllis Wiley, chairwoman of the Upper Toe River History Group, explained, as if to a wayward child, "The organization's Annual Dinner next month needs, indeed, requires" excellent press coverage both in advance ("to sell tickets, of course!") and after the fact. "Our archives contain the newspaper's reports going back to 1951!" she told him, the clear implication that any gap in coverage would be on his head.

Five minutes later Oliver politely interrupted to explain, "The paper needs, indeed requires, a typed news release with all pertinent information, double-spaced, in 12-point font. I'll do my best to find some space for it." He rang off.

"Mary-Beth, is it possible for you to take messages for me when we're getting ready to go to press? You know, names and numbers and what they want, since it's way too late for this week."

"Of course, Oliver. Simon always wanted to impress people with his 'accessibility'—and find some angle for himself. So I got in the habit of..." Her voice trailed off.

At three, Greig Davis wanted Oliver to meet his wife, finally back from the city. Alice was everything Adrian and Mary-Beth had warned him about. He maintained the proper reserve and reminded himself to always be exceedingly careful in interacting with her.

By three-thirty the paper was finished. He checked the front page once more, then Jerry counted pages and packed the finished flats in an old photo paper box.

"Now you know where it goes?" Jerry asked.

"Over to Asheville."

"Right. The paper is one block before you reach the bridge over the French Broad. Right now, it should take about an hour down and the same back. Don't drive too fast along the river since the deer are often out at this time of evening."

Oliver told Adrian he would call her in the morning and made arrangements to meet with Scoop Thursday morning to map out the next few weeks. He walked to the hotel and picked up his car, carefully setting the boxed newspaper flats in the back seat.

The drive to Asheville was about fifty miles. Unlike his evening trip to the mall the previous week, Oliver took time to observe the changes along the route. Some sections of the winding road were unchanged, just wide enough for two car to pass, but others were beginning to see new gas stations and convenience stores, and even a used-car dealership. He passed dozens of campgrounds and canoe rentals, some decent looking, others downscale, a few that were downright sleazy; thirty years before, there had been only one.

As the light began to soften, the sliver of a moon seemed to float from cloud to cloud until it eventually became a fuzzy haze. Oliver crossed the Toe River and noticed that some of the views were—or could have been—spectacular, if not for the billboards polluting the mountain vistas.

He was surprised to see and remember the old stocked fishing pond on his left, now with a flea market crowding against it. To the right the hill made an almost vertical climb, the bare rock relieved in places by stunted bushes clinging to a rather barren life. Then a two-foot shoulder became a three-foot wall of stone blocks and mortar, all that stood between the car and a wide drainage ditch. He passed a small overlook, just large enough for a couple of cars or a small RV to park and enjoy the views. Every inch of the barrier wall was graffitied with signatures and snappy sayings in Day-glo colors.

He stopped in Mars Hill for gas and a package of peanuts, and just before five-thirty he was delivering the flats to the Asheville pressroom. The night manager assured him they would be treated with care and the print run would be back in Fernglade by eight in the morning.

Oliver thanked the man for his diligence and the mutual support. "We couldn't afford any of this equipment on our own."

The man answered, "We're all in it together, aren't we. And of course it helps us, too, to run these presses as often as we can. It's a big investment, this new computerized equipment. Quick turnaround's the key, so we don't lose money on the whole deal."

He waved Oliver off. "Next time you'll just send it down over the computer, I suppose. It's good to meet you though. Drive safe up there. The roads aren't too easy at night unless you know 'em well."

Oliver didn't tell him he was a Fernglade native: he'd been away so long he scarcely felt like one anymore. He tuned in the radio to far-flung stations, finding little of interest, and finally reverted to Asheville's classical station and left it there. Traffic was light on the highway and even sparser on Route 19, but he wanted his eyes on the road. As he began the climb up the road leading back to Burnsville, throwing the gearshift into second, a car sped past him at well over the speed limit and was soon out of sight.

The night was now fully dark, the crescent moon completely hidden by cloud cover; the only light was reflected from small white signs that warned against parking along the route. Never a hot-shot driver, he was taking his time, enjoying the music and solitude, and looking forward to getting back home. He kept one eye on the bright white and yellow lines of the road to make sure he stayed in his lane as the road began to curve.

Suddenly, directly ahead of him, the night exploded into a brilliant flash of white light, as though a giant light bulb had turned on and then ruptured in silence.

Instantly his Army training snapped into play. He had been trained in night fighting, and he instinctively closed his eyes to mere slits. From memory he formed a mental image of the next curve and, using the picture in his mind of those winding painted lines as a guide, he stepped on the brake and steered himself into the opposite lane; unfortunately he overjudged the width and smashed the left side of the car hard against the stone retaining wall he had passed an hour or so before. If not for the wall, his car would have continued into the gully, wide enough to swallow a VW, where nobody would see it unless they already knew where to search.

His eyes were still slightly blinded. Flashes of luminescence pulsed both inside and outside his eyelids and he felt stunned, immobilized. There was a crack on his head where he'd hit the rearview mirror, and he could feel blood trickling down the bridge of his nose, then falling drop by drop onto his beard. He tried to move his arm, but his body wouldn't respond.

He was sure there was nothing broken, but he was still in a state of shock, so he sat quietly for a few minutes, the only sound Shubert's *Piano Sonata in A Minor* floating out on the night. Then he was aware of the bright lights of a car or truck some distance up the road.

A flashlight bounced up and down, and he sat as still as he could, willing every muscle to freeze into immobility. The light moved closer. It peered in the window and played up and down his body and the inside of the car.

"How is he?" a voice called from some distance.

"Looks dead to me," said the man outside the car.

"Don't touch anything. How much damage to the wall?" the question still came from a distance away.

"Not too much. It'd look like the car went over the edge of the ditch, if we can lift it up. Shit, the wall's only a few feet high and that's a thirty-foot drop. Can we stay around and watch it burn?" The speaker sounded like a man wrapped about as tight as ten gallons of water in loose wax paper.

"Shit, I'm glad it's a VW," said the other voice coming closer. "C'mon around to the back."

"Ouch! Shit, I bumped my knee."

"Crissake, just hurry up and help me lift this can."

"God damn, Harry, I just burned my fingers. This damn thing's hot."

"You'll get over it, asshole. Lift!"

This isn't real, Oliver thought to himself. He felt the car begin to rise. Once over the edge they would light the gasoline dripping from the engine and—

In the distance he heard a siren. It was coming closer.

"Shit man, here comes the cops."

The car fell back to earth.

"C'mon let's go. This guy's bought it anyway."

Oliver heard their footsteps as they ran back to their truck. He listened, motionless, as they started the engine and watched through still-slitted eyelids as it turned toward Burnsville. Relieved, suddenly in pain as well as fear, he fainted.

When he came to there was no sign of activity around the car, no ambulance or police. All was silent. Apparently the approaching siren had been sound randomly carried on the night air; probably a fire truck responding to a call down below the hill. At least it had scared off the two men.

He carefully turned around on the seat, slightly dizzy, and felt his temple; it had stopped bleeding. His driver's door was tightly wedged against the stone retaining wall, so he carefully clambered across the gear shift to the passenger seat. He had to rest for a few minutes while his head continued to pound. He jerked on the door handle, opened it, and fell out onto the roadway. He sat quietly for a few moments leaning against the car.

It was getting cold. Gripping the door handle, he pulled himself up and stood in the middle of the road. Except for a few twinkling lights in the distance, there was no sign of life—half an hour from Asheville and he could have been on Mars. And if those men had pushed the car over the edge and lit the gas, no one would have doubted that it was an accident. They'd think that he was driving so fast that he hit the wall and bounced over the edge.

He remembered seeing a restaurant just beyond the road began to twist into esses, so he slowly walked in that direction using the wall as a support. The Beetle left enough room for another car to pass, but he doubted if there would be much traffic before morning.

An owl hoo-hooed from somewhere above him, and his right foot kicked a bottle that proceeded to roll down the road.

Ten minutes later he reached the restaurant. The season was over; a handwritten sign on the door, visible when he lit a match, read "See You in April!" But it was also the country, and luckily the restaurant had an outside pay phone. He suddenly remembered that dialing 911 was the new way to call for emergencies, and he dug into his pockets for twenty cents to make the call; an operator quickly connected him to the police station. He reported the accident, warning them about the car in the road, and they agreed to meet him in front of the restaurant. Then, with his last two dimes, he called Adrian to ask her if she could come pick him up.

A pair of uniformed troopers, their car lights flashing, arrived soon after. They drove him back to his wrecked car, already being lifted onto a tow truck from a local garage they had called in. He gave the truck driver his name and asked him to check the damage and call him at the paper as soon as he had an estimate.

As the tow truck pulled out, Oliver handed his license, registration, and press card to the taller of the troopers.

"Are you okay? Want us to call an ambulance?" he asked, looking at Oliver's documents with a flashlight.

"No, I'm just a little woozy." He paused and added, almost with surprise, "I have a headache, but I'm pretty sure the only damage is this bump on my head. Well, and my back hurts a bit. I called a friend of mine to pick me up. She should be here in another twenty minutes."

"Any idea how this happened, Mr. Swindler?" asked the shorter of the two men.

"No. I was just driving along, not that fast, when suddenly a very bright light appeared in the road ahead of me. I tried to stop as soon as I could but I smashed into the retaining wall."

He told the troopers about the two men and their

conversation about tossing the car over the edge.

"Could you describe them?"

"No, I kept my eyes closed—to make them think I was dead, or unconscious. They didn't sound too bright. But I'd recognize their voices if I ever hear them again. Oh, and one of them called the other one 'Harry.'"

"Why would anyone want to do this to you?"

"I've no idea," said Oliver. "But I'd appreciate it if you could call Sheriff Phibert in Burnsville and report this accident to him. He knows me, but I want him to hear about this from an official source."

As the trooper took notes in a small notebook, his colleague called out.

"Hey, George," he said, pointing with a large flashlight, "there was a big truck parked here. You can see part of the tread in the dirt here where the paving stops. There's also some cigarette butts."

"Well, Mr. Swindler, there's nothing else we can do here," said George, "but we'll get hold of the sheriff and give him our report. In the meanwhile, why don't you sit in the cruiser 'til your ride gets here. I'll drive you back to the restaurant; it'll be easier for your friend to see us there. And by the way, now you're living here, you'd better get your license and registration changed. And sign this release, if you don't mind, sir. It's a waiver for us calling an ambulance."

They parked near the phone booth. When Adrian pulled up about twenty after nine, he walked carefully from the troopers' car to hers, still feeling light-headed. He thanked the troopers once more before Adrian turned back onto the road. He gave her a brief, but complete, description of his past ninety minutes.

"Any idea as to who was responsible?" she asked.

"Well, of course I do. Earlier today I turned down Clark Wechsler's offer to buy Imogene's house. Basically told him to stuff it, and called him a liar. The only mystery to me is how to prove that he was behind the attack."

After a silence, he added, "Thinking about it, I doubt Ackermann and Black have the cunning to come up with a scheme like this. Not that Clark does, either, but he's a genius by comparison. It clears Luther, at least: he's still in the county jail. Of course, whoever did this knew I'd be driving to Asheville and back tonight—which Clark knew. And besides him and his pals, there's no one else I know who could have a motive for trying to kill me."

He stretched and groaned. "God, does my back hurt. It feels like someone drove a rusty spike up my spine."

"Have you had back trouble before?" she asked.

"Yes, and this is right up there with the worst examples of past ten years."

"Anything I can do?"

"Don't hit any bumps or congratulate me for anything!"

"No, I mean when we get back," she said kindly.

"There is, if you don't mind," he said. "Get some ice and rub it on the small of my back."

"We'll go to my place," she said.

He didn't remember the rest of the ride, just the purr of the motor and the hum of the tires. He woke up with Adrian gently shaking his shoulder.

"What time is it?" he asked.

"Almost ten. Here, give me your hand. Okay. You up?"

"Barely."

"Use the stair rail."

"Don't fuss. I'll make it without breaking apart," he snapped.

Ten minutes later he was flat on Adrian's couch, his navel pressed uncomfortably against an upholstery button on the middle cushion. A stainless steel bowl of ice sat on the floor and Adrian was gently stroking his back, up and down, with a damp washcloth filled with ice.

"God, that's cold!" he shivered.

"Is this the right thing to do?" she asked.

"You bet it is," he answered. "Chiropractors found out from research on sport injuries that heat is the worst thing for a muscle injury. Short applications of cold are the ticket. Tomorrow I'll call Dr. Hill and get over there as soon as he opens in the morning."

"You just lie there and rest. I'll make a pot of herbal tea."

Her apartment was warm and comfortable, and he lay upon her couch without a shirt and a back that made him wince with pain. What a break, he thought, dozing intermittently to Adrian's kitchen sounds. The tap, filling the kettle. The lid snapped on. The hiss of the gas stove....

He snapped awake when she brought in a tray with two cups and a pot wafting the aroma of ... chamomile? hibiscus?

"Sage and lavender. With a touch of peppermint. Good for aches," she said, pouring him a cup. "You better stay here for the night. I can move you to the bed or—"

"No, this is fine. I really don't want to move right now." He took a sip and felt warmed and comforted. "You know, I suddenly thought, nobody will see me in the hotel tonight, and I'm sure nobody saw us come up here. Clark Wechsler will think I'm at the bottom of that ditch in the ashes of a burned-up VW. When he does see me he'll shit a brick. Can we get started early tomorrow?"

"I know Dr. Hill and his wife," said Adrian, "I'll call them first thing in the morning."

"And I'll call Phibert and ask him to be crafty when he talks to Clark Wechsler. He doesn't have to lie, but maybe he can just imply that I'm in the Burnsville morgue."

While his mind raced, he noticed that his body was relaxing, the pain in his back diminishing with ever sip. He scarcely noticed when Adrian gently took the empty teacup from his hand. Another thought tempted him, dissipated, and he was sound asleep.

Chapter Fifteen

I t was a little after dawn on Thursday when Oliver awoke on Adrian's floor. Sometime in the middle of the night he must have found it more comfortable to lie prone on the living room rug than to sink his sore back into the cushions of her couch.

With a great deal of effort he got to his feet and, like an orangutan, shuffled over to an upright chair to put on his shoes.

At seven-thirty, Adrian came out of the bedroom dressed in a housecoat that increased her girth twofold. She mumbled a greeting and made her way to the sink, where she filled a kettle with water and put it on the stove.

"What do you want for breakfast?" she asked.

"Moose steak?" he offered.

"Too early to be witty! Cereal? Eggs?"

"Just toast."

She set the table with a bowl for herself, a plate for him and two cups, no saucers, and popped two slices of whole wheat bread into her toaster. They were both silent as she put cereal in her bowl, set out butter and jam for him, and prepared a pot of tea. When she brought his toast he looked at her with a rueful smile.

"I'm just starting to recoil from last night's experience. For a few moments I felt like I might be Bridget Driscoll," he said.

"Who is Bridget Driscoll?"

"Was," he answered. "She was the world's first recorded automobile fatality, run over and killed outside the Crystal Palace in London, sometime in August 1876."

She poured two glasses of orange juice, and said, "Here's to the memory of Bridget." Silence reigned again.

At eight he tuned the radio to the local news. The lead story was about the county publicity department's continuing attempts to convince the Board of Supervisors to increase their budget. Then came a fist fight in a local bar that resulted in a man taking a chain saw to his friend's car, followed by odds and ends of business news. Not a word about a car crash along the old Asheville highway.

"I'll bet Clark is sitting back right now congratulating himself over a job well done," Oliver said to Adrian, his eyebrows raised in an implied question mark. She responded with a noncommittal shrug and went to call Dr. Hill, leaving Oliver shifting his weight left, right, forward, and back as he tried to find a comfortable position—or at least one that didn't hurt.

"He'll see you at nine. His wife won't be in the office until ten so he said go right in the front door and knock on his private office. Can you make it alone?"

"Sure. The ice really helped. If he's a good chiropractor, I'll be at the office by ten, maybe still uncomfortable but standing upright. And thanks for the breakfast and for picking me up last night. Now let me call the sheriff."

Phibert had already heard about the accident.

"It hasn't been reported to the papers or the radio. The troopers told me there were no witnesses, so I thought I'd just keep it quiet for now. It'll be interesting to see the reaction of folks in your town when you go to work this morning. You planning on going to work? You weren't hurt, were you?"

"No," said Oliver, "just a wrenched back that I'm taking care of this morning. But you will admit it was attempted murder?"

"No question about it, and I'll be on the lookout for those two men, but without a description it's pretty hopeless. The problem is that Clark Wechsler has an alibi for your sister's murder, and outside of him there are no suspects and no motive."

Black's face, and Stalker's, flashed into Oliver's mind, but all he said was, "How are things going with Luther?"

"I'm continuing to hold him until Friday. Then I'll let him go. There'll be something else to harp about by then."

Oliver assured the sheriff that he'd call him if he learned anything new. Then he called the paper and asked Mary-Beth if the new papers had arrived and if everything looked all right.

"Greig's delighted," she answered, "Alice felt that some of your page breaks were not too considered, but she agreed that you were the boss."

He left Adrian's apartment—taking the stairs with great care—in time to arrive at the doctor's office as the bank clock struck nine.

The chiropractor's office was in an old house on Main Street across from the bank and had once belonged to the Shattuck family. Despite his pain, Oliver's editor's eye saw that everything was in good repair: the clapboards were a spanking white, the windows sported black wood shutters, the gutters were new, and the knocker on the black-enameled front door was polished enough to reflect his face in the flat space that read "Dr. Henry Hill, Office of Chiropractic."

He walked into a long hall lit with a small brass ceiling fixture. Brass coat hooks lined the left wall with a brass umbrella stand just inside the door. A clear glass sliding panel opened to a bright but empty receptionist's office on the right.

Gray carpet led past the coat hooks to an open doorway into a waiting room; its counterpart, just past the receptionist's, was marked "Private." He knocked, entered, and was greeted by a heavyset man just under his own height, with curly gray hair and a Van Dyke beard. Bright blue eyes were magnified slightly by a pair of gold-rimmed glasses.

"So you're Oliver Swindler. A pleasure to meet you. Come in and—with care—sit down. You'll find this chair better for your back than most. It's from a set of old-fashioned dining chairs. Straight-backed, as you see." He chuckled, then added, "Our ancestors apparently had mixed feelings about food, but they dined well and most were uncomfortable at table.

"Let me get a form here. Never can find them. Thought they were here but Jane, that's my wife, is an excellent receptionist but compulsively neat, everything in its place—except she never tells me where its place is. Oh, I'll use this and fill one out later."

He then took a careful medical history on a lined notepad and asked about Oliver's family.

"Please accept my condolences about your sister, Mr. Swindler. I was proud to claim her as a patient. Not too often but every year about canning time she would have a tendency to overdo. Now, I understand your back went out late last night in an auto accident?"

"Yes. A friend helped me rub it with ice last night, and I slept on the floor. It was the only comfortable place."

"Well, follow me into the treatment room. Take everything off but your shorts."

He gestured to a small group of curtained dressing rooms and then toward the treatment room door. "I'll be in there when you're ready."

The room was like most in the chiropractic profession, including large black and white drawings of a full-figured male that portrayed the various nerve endings in the body, a plumb-line in one corner, comfortable soft carpet, and a large, automated treatment table in the center of the room, onto which Oliver carefully lowered himself.

As he began his manipulations, Hill said, "I had an old-fashioned table that my father used, but when you turned the handles the noise of the chain-link drive reminded a lot of patients of what I suppose was their concept of the torture chambers of old. Like the rack, you know? Some of them just couldn't tolerate the sound. So last year when the Chiropractic Convention was held in Atlanta, I bought one of these—all electric, smooth as silk. Now, I need you to relax, and then let's bend this leg to the right."

Hill was strong and muscular, and he moved Oliver about with ease. Fifteen minutes later, Oliver was standing again, still in some pain but walking upright.

"You'll probably need another treatment by Friday, and if it gets worse of course, feel free to call me at any time. I know what back pain is like."

Oliver dressed and returned to the office. His pain relieved, he once more became aware of his surroundings. Hill's desk was littered with two skulls in wooden mounts and a Seiko clock that imitated the movements of an acrobat. Oliver gazed in fascination at the shiny pieces moving about, amused both at its relevance to a chiropractor's practice and its old-fashioned style.

"So how's everything at the paper?" the doctor asked. "Lord knows it needed a new approach. Enjoying the job, right? Quite a difference from ... you moved from New York, I understand?" Before Oliver could answer, he continued, "Oh, I hear Jane in the front office. Here, take report out to her and I'll be there in a minute or so."

Behind the glass panels was, undoubtedly, the woman who had tripped over him in the hotel stairway three days before.

"You!" she said.

"Me."

"He can't find out," she whispered, imploring him with frightened eyes.

"Of course not." Still she gazed at him fearfully, and he smiled compassionately before adding, in his most reassuring tone, "Trust me."

"Who are you?"

"Oliver Swindler, the new editor at the paper. And according to your husband, my sister was a patient here."

"Of course, you're Imogene's brother. Silly of me. With that name you have to be in the family."

"And you're in trouble."

She paused to fiddle with the keyboard that dominated her desktop. After glancing at the door to her husband's office, she said quietly, "I just don't know where to turn."

"You're being threatened—or blackmailed?—by Black?"

"It's that obvious?"

"Well, when someone like you, who obviously cares for her husband's welfare, is as upset as you are over what could easily have been a harmless meeting, that's the only thing I can imagine. And I know Black … and his room number. Is there somewhere we can talk?"

"Not now. Please. Thursdays are horrendous in this office. We're booked up until at least three."

"Could you get away for lunch? What if I had Adrian Knapp call you with some problem, woman stuff you know, could you meet her?"

"I'll have to do something. Have her call before eleven."

She looked up with a professional yet motherly smile as her husband came down the hall. "Henry, I put a big pile of health forms on your desk yesterday." She turned back to Oliver. "He just can't keep track of anything."

"Thanks again, doctor. It was good to meet you, Mrs. Hill."

He left the office, crossed Bridge Street and walked down Main toward the newspaper, making sure that he took ample time to stroll by the windows of the funeral home.

Wechsler was just coming out the front door as Oliver approached. The mortician turned with an automatic smile that lasted no more than a millisecond as Oliver smiled at him with smug satisfaction. Wechsler's face reminded him of the same changes of expression he'd seen on so many actors' faces in the horror films he loved, as they recognized the Wolfman, the zombie, or the haunting spirit returned from the dead. From professional courtesy to terror and back to jaunty friendliness in two or three seconds.

"Good morning, Clark," he said.

"Oliver. How ... nice to see you ... out and about."

"It's ... nice to be here," he answered. "It promises to be a wonderful day."

"Will you be at the paper later?"

"Probably, although I hurt my back last night and may take most of the afternoon off."

"Your back?"

"Yes, I had a small accident last night outside Mars Hill. Fortunately nothing serious. You, too, have a great day."

Back at the paper he asked Adrian to call Jane Hill and set up a luncheon date at Ralph's for one this afternoon. He remembered that Thursdays were busy for the chiropractor, but Mrs. Hill's involvement with Wechsler was too important to wait.

"She'll be there," said Adrian.

Mary-Beth handed him a fresh copy of the paper, and he spent the next few minutes turning through page by page looking for mistakes.

"You missed a continued line for the carryover on the murder story, but that's the only thing I found," she said. "And here's some mail that came this morning."

He walked back to Davis's office.

"Congratulations, Oliver. It's a good job."

"Thank you. I'm sure I can get into full gear by next week."

"Don't worry about it. You're doing fine."

He went up to his office. Scoop generally took Thursdays off, and Oliver wished that he could, too. Instead he sat down, being careful of his back, and called the sheriff.

When Phibert was on the line, he said softly, "Sheriff, I just encountered Clark Wechsler outside his business. Any jury that saw the look on his face when he saw me would send him up. He's guilty as hell."

"Swindler, there's no use in questioning him right now. So far I don't have any leads on those men, and until I can trace them the best I can offer is a twenty-four hour watch on you. Or ..." his voice trailed off.

"Or what?"

"I could get you a carry permit—I assume you don't have a pistol permit. You don't seem the type, if you don't mind my saying so."

"No, I don't."

"How about it?"

He thought for a moment. "Okay. I'll come over this afternoon."

"Right. I have a Smith & Wesson—a personal weapon, not official—that I can lend you. That way you won't have to feel beholden to the idea of owning a gun."

The mail was mostly press releases. One, from the Planning Department, stood out. He read it through, then twice again, before carefully refolding it and slipping it into his breast pocket.

At one o'clock, he and Adrian drove to Ralph's tavern. They were just finishing their lunch when Jane Hill walked in.

"Adrian, Mr. Swindler, I really don't know why I'm here but

I've got to do something."

"Why not simply tell us about it?"

Oliver and Adrian waited patiently while she hemmed and hawed, settled and resettled herself in her chair, exchanged pleading glances with Adrian, and finally took a deep breath and, Oliver suspected, silently prayed for permission to speak. At last she did.

"You have to understand," she said. "My husband is a kind man and a good man. That's why I find myself in a terrible position. It's not easy to set up a practice in a town like Fernglade, unless you've lived here for three generations; it takes that time just to stop being called a newcomer. But this is the town that Henry wanted to come to. He's wanted to live here ever since he was a child and visited relatives in the area. It's been hard for us both but with a great deal of sacrifice on our part, he's built up a following. A pretty good one, in fact. You know how busy it is. Um, could I get a cup of coffee or something?"

"Sure," said Adrian, "I'll get it. Keep on with your story."

"There's a sense of responsibility that's part of living in a small town. And when one of the members of the town planning board retired, Mrs. Rawson asked me to join. We're in the garden club together, that's how she knows me. Then Mr. Ackermann and Mr. Black moved in—not to mention that.... Hmmph. 'The Very Reverend' Mr. Stalker. And things began to change."

Oliver nodded encouragingly.

"Not at first, but slowly, this, this sort of movement began to "bring the town up to date"—which really meant just to take advantage of the money that was coming in with the summer folks coming up from Atlanta, not to mention the National Park. Excuse me if I jump around a bit."

"That's okay, take your time."

"My family comes from Gwinnett County down in Georgia and Henry's originally from Asheville. My father was a doctor who specialized in internal medicine, but he was chief surgeon in the county hospital. He was involved in a terrible case of malpractice during the late forties. I was just a baby at the time.

"It was a big case: He was charged with killing the wife of a local politician and businessman. The charge turned to murder when a member of the husband's family said my father was having an affair with the woman and took the opportunity of killing her on the operating table when she refused to leave her husband.

"The trial was big news all over, even in parts of North Carolina. Father claimed his innocence right from the start but there were jealous men on the hospital board who didn't approve of his approach to medicine."

Adrian brought coffee and Jane paused for a moment.

"Where was I? Oh, Daddy was modern, he liked the new methods, and the board was all made up of old fogies. They wouldn't support him. Wouldn't even give him the time of day. And the end result was my father committed suicide. He left a letter proclaiming his innocence and a review board in the hospital later proved he was blameless. But the problem with accusations like this is once they get around it's difficult if not impossible to stop them. My mother left town for a while and we had enough money to start over, and of course Atlanta's a big place so eventually she was forgotten ... but she was so bitter. She died still hating every one of them.

"Then that cheeseburger deal came to town represented by Clark Wechsler. I won't dwell on this, but eventually that bastard Black called me at the office and demanded that I show up at his hotel room. I said go to hell until he mentioned my father's name. The end result was, either I vote on the planning board at its meeting tonight to allow Heavenly Cheeseburgers into the town, or he'll make sure that everyone knows about my father. That last threat came the night I stumbled over you in the hall. Now, you understand, of course Henry knew about my father because I told him years ago. And if I had told him about Black's threat, he would have called the police. But I know small towns, the damage would have been done, and Henry doesn't have the money needed to survive until it all blew over.. And I just don't know what to do, Mr. Swindler! I just...." Her voice trailed off.

"You're right, Mrs. Hill. I can't disagree," he said. "The very thing that makes small towns pleasant places to live can occasionally make them ugly. But I'm not convinced that the threats of exposure would ruin your husband. Tell me, were any of the other members of the planning board threatened?"

"I don't think so. But I've heard that two or three of them don't support it, and I'm expected to be the swing vote. Without me it might be a tie."

"Well don't you worry, just come to the meeting tonight. Remember, I'm 'the press.' I'll be there to cover it for the paper. But the fact of the matter is, I don't think it will even come to a vote."

"But Mr. Swindler—"

"Call me Oliver, and please trust me. I'll see you at the meeting."

Driving back to Fernglade, Oliver told Adrian what he had found out from the Planning Board flyer that morning.

"Years ago the state passed a law to control development. But it's a major piece of legislation, complex and very confusing—so confusing that many municipalities have never complied with it. And until recently there was little chance of a city or township being sued for failure to comply—or even being scrutinized. But with so much growth, more and more people are aware of it. The law, I mean. And believe me, any major fast-food chain with restaurants around Atlanta and places like Raleigh and Durham knows about the changing feelings concerning unbridled development.

"Now, it's possible our local planning board is ignorant, or that they've forgotten about the new rules—or maybe they don't really care—but I guarantee you Clark Wechsler knows."

"So what does the law do?"

"It can cost these developers money. Any delay for them is usually spelled out in tens or hundreds of thousands of dollars. There's a short form available that would take about an hour or two to fill out. But if a planning board is dissatisfied with their answers, or really feels that the project is not up to snuff, they can demand the lawyers fill out the long form, and that includes background information, impact studies, parking analysis, all sorts of paperwork that may take months to complete. Then if the planning board doesn't like it they're empowered to hire their own experts at the developer's expense to check the answers. Jane Hill doesn't have to worry about being blackmailed, and Clark Wechsler can be stopped in his tracks."

At the paper he left Adrian with a promise to call after the planning board meeting. He walked from the office to his sister's house and let himself in. As one of the heirs he figured he could use her car as long as his was out of commission.

After the simplicity of his old Bug, the automatic everything of Imogene's nearly new Pontiac took him a while to get used to. So did the comfort, which he appreciated more than the power. He was even grateful for the lumbar support in the six-way power seats; his back was feeling sore again.

The drive to Burnsville took about thirty-five minutes. Oliver pulled up to the sheriff's department building at three-thirty. Phibert's office was part modern and part country: while bland chrome-and-laminate furniture predominated, an eight-foot mounted sailfish hung on the wall above his desk.

"Do you ever worry about being stabbed if that thing should fall?" Oliver asked.

Phibert chuckled. "That wall's concrete, and my fish is bolted on. It won't fall." He shuffled through papers on his desk. "Here's a license for you to carry a weapon. And this gun is from my personal collection, and it's just a temporary loan, so it's covered by the license."

"You really think I'm still in danger?"

"Of course—they just tried to kill you last night, son! You don't think they're serious? Now I'm sure it's one of those Fernglade dips behind it—my money's on Clark Wechsler—but unfortunately," he said with a sigh, "in this country a man is innocent until proven guilty, and I can't prove any of them was involved. Not in your sister's murder or that man you found in her kitchen, or the attempt on your life last night. Not yet, anyway."

"So I have to wait until one of them tries something again. Well, after tonight I'm sure they will."

"What happens tonight?"

Oliver told him.

"Would Mrs. Hill swear out a complaint?"

"I'm not sure. Not if it would hurt her husband."

"I'll let it go for now so they can get in a little deeper."

"Can Luther still be freed?"

With the sheriff's assurance about Luther and the gun heavy in his jacket pocket, he drove back to Fernglade for supper, though he had no intention of eating at the hotel.

For generations, Fernglade's high school was a two-story, turn-of-the-century brick building with a magnificent cast iron fire escape hooked to its front facade, located just past Dr. Hill's house on Main Street. The keystone was inscribed with a somewhat grandiose "Public School No. 1." The building stood on solid rock, and following World War II, when central heating replaced pot-bellied stoves, a new school was needed—preferably in a building with a basement. The town bought property out on the County Road and joined the neighboring district of Hanford in building a new east county high school.

For years the old building stood empty, but as bureaucracy grew, boards and commissions and task forces proliferated, Fernglade raised taxes—despite intensive complaints—and adapted the old school as its Municipal Building, with an oil furnace in the first floor rear and an updated, upgraded electric system. For the past few years, it had even enjoyed air conditioning.

That night the parking area in the old school yard was filled early, forcing the majority of visitors to use the bank's lot across the street. Oliver was surprised that Clark Wechsler didn't charge a fee.

The pickup trucks all had local plates, many of them commercial, and most held rifles or fishing rods on their rear window brackets. Of the cars, at least half were Audis, BMWs, Saabs, or Volvos, representative of the summer people with their Georgia tags; the rest were local and ran the gamut from older Chevys to a brand-new Cadillac.

The auditorium was almost full. Locals were congregated on the right, city types on the left. After quick scrutiny Oliver was confident that he was the only member of the media present, and all the empty seats—just like when he was a student—were in the front row. Neither Ackermann nor Wechsler was in attendance, though Greig Davis, his wife Alice, and Mary-Beth invited him to join them on the right side of the room. He nodded to them but took the front-row seat on the aisle.

Old Glory was draped on a pole at the right of the stage; a state flag balanced it opposite. A faded proscenium mural showed the progress of man from the arrival of Columbus to the steamboat on the Mississippi River. Sitting behind a large deal table slightly to the left of center stage were the members of the Fernglade Planning Board: Jane Hill, Mrs. Rawson, and five men. A portly gentleman holding a pipe, the board's lawyer, sat at the left end of the table, nearly center stage; at a smaller table farther right were three men, clearly lawyers for Heavenly Cheeseburger or its franchise holders.

At precisely eight o'clock, the man in the center of the table gaveled the meeting to order. Immediately all the locals stood— the city people followed moments later, after realizing what was expected of them. Veterans, including two board members and one attorney, saluted; the rest placed their hands over their hearts as they intoned the Pledge of Allegiance. The crowd returned to their seats with a rustle and a round of coughs.

"Good evening, ladies and gentlemen. I have to say I'm surprised to see such a turnout at what we all thought was a relatively unimportant meeting. My name is Christian Silliman and I'm chairman of the Fernglade Planning Board. The gentlemen at the table to my left are attorneys representing the Heavenly Cheeseburger's Restaurant chain. Now, before we begin the hearing we have one or two other items of business to attend to. The secretary will read the minutes of the last meeting."

"Excuse me, Mr. Chairman," said one of the restaurant lawyers. "But would it be possible for the board to waive the reading of the minutes?"

There was a slight sigh, then stillness, from the audience.

"Hardly, Mr. Wolfert. I don't know how you folks from Atlanta run your business, but we read our minutes here. Mrs. Rawson, if you will?"

Mrs. Rawson adjusted her glasses and picked up a large black ledger, one of a high pile of books sitting directly in front of her. She turned on a well-cared-for Channel Master Tape Recorder, opened a plastic wrapper, and inserted a new tape. For five minutes she slowly turned page after page of the ledger, enunciating the events of the past two meetings with the enthusiasm of someone reading the death rolls from the last war.

At last she finished, and the chairman looked up from his stupor. "You have heard the minutes. Do I have a motion?"

One of the men at the table interjected, "Mrs. Rawson, we

heard about the Myer's subdivision at nine o'clock, not eight-fifty. Remember Alfred was late because of an ambulance call."

"You're absolutely right, Tom," said Mrs. Rawson, "I'll just make that change. You know I took my watch to the Brennan's Jewelers the next day and had it adjusted."

"Do I now have a motion?" asked the chairman.

"I make a motion," said Jane Hill.

"I'll second," said another man.

"All in favor say aye."

"Aye."

"So ordered."

"Now," asked the chair, "is there any correspondence?"

"Yes," answered Mrs. Rawson.

At that moment a sign some three feet high was hoisted up on the right side of the auditorium with bright red letters: *UP WITH HEAVERNLY CHEESBURGERS!*

It took a moment for the city people and the majority of the country folk to notice.

"Put down that sign," shouted someone on the left.

"Put it down, Barry," echoed a voice on the right.

"Put it down," said the chair. "You know the rules, Barry."

Thus ended the first and last "spontaneous" demonstration of the evening, wrote Oliver in his notebook.

The planning board lawyer tamped his pipe, searched his pockets for matches, then asked the man on his left if he had any. The audience was getting restless, chairs shifted as people turned to murmur to their neighbors.

"Excuse me," said Mr. Wolfert, after talking with the other two lawyers, "would it be possible to speed things along?"

The board lawyer lit his pipe. Silliman whispered to the man at his right. A message was passed along. The lawyer put down the pipe with a sigh. Silliman then conferred with the other members of the board.

"Mr. Wolfert, we're all for progress but there are set procedures. Before we open the meeting to your presentation, we have other responsibilities to perform." It was clear to Oliver that, whether or not Silliman supported the chain's coming to Fernglade, he was not happy with outsiders telling him how to run his board.

"Mrs. Rawson, has everyone seen the request for a hearing on the Westbrook family subdividing their lot into three divisions?"

"Yes, I mailed all the members copies last week."

"Is it agreed that we should schedule a public hearing for next month?"

The entire board shook their heads, yes. Their attorney made notes in a small spiral-bound notebook. Silliman invited a motion to hold a public hearing the third week in May. The motion was made, seconded, and approved.

"You see, gentlemen," said Mr. Silliman, gazing blandly at the reddening faces of the outside lawyers, "other people have rights beside you."

"You tell 'em, Silli," cried a voice.

"Order! Now, although it's somewhat irregular, we will set aside our other business and listen to your presentation."

The shortest of the Atlanta lawyers rose, set up a lightweight aluminum easel, and unfolded an architect's drawing of a Heavenly Cheeseburger restaurant. Fully displayed, the cardboard towered over the little man. There was audible laughter from the crowd.

"Mr. Chairperson—" he began.

"Chairman," said Silliman. "It may be 'chairperson' where you come from, but I know exactly what sex I am."

Laughter rolled through both sides of the audience.

"Very well, Mr. Chairman. My name is Nicholas Collins and I'm happy to be a representative of one of the finest restaurant chains in America. Heavenly Cheeseburgers is an example of the success of the American way. What began as a small hot dog stand outside of Sentinel Butte, North Dakota, is now a multi-million dollar franchise operation spanning the entire United States.

"Now here is an architect's rendering of what we propose for the corner of Main and Mill Streets. You will note that it's a brick facade with large windows, a charming tile roof, blacktopped parking lot, and of course beautifully landscaped."

His voice droned on as he turned one sheet after another on his easel, describing in endless, unwanted detail the materials to be used, the credentials of the corporate designer who "tailors all our outlets to fit the communities that welcome them in"; the colors and materials, the sourcing from verifiable American manufacturers....

Oliver took notes from time to time, but when he noticed that even the other two corporate lawyers were stifling yawns, he decided to save his ink for more interesting developments.

At 9:30 the second lawyer began, with a short speech about all the jobs for the town's unemployed teenagers and senior citizens and how everyone would benefit. This one, Oliver thought sounded like a benevolent overlord arriving to lift everyone in Fernglade out of a lifetime of impoverished serfdom. He sensed, from the restlessness and occasional murmurs behind him, that the audience did not appreciate his condescension.

The third man having nothing to say, Silliman threw the meeting open to the public.

By ten-forty they were still talking, and the city people were having none of it. They came to the mountains for rusticity, not the wind-blown hamburger wrappers and jammed parking lots they'd left behind in Atlanta. Most Ferngladers were not too happy either; they liked things just as they were. The local historical society called destroying the old Hanley House "an unforgivable sin," and a rather obese man in overalls complained, "They'll put the diner out of business."

A few neighbors suggested there might be increased business for local farmers—"They gotta get their beef and onions and maters from somewhere, don't they?" said one to loud cheers—"And the kids'll earn some spending money," added his wife—but they sat down deflated when informed that Heavenly Cheeseburgers bought all their supplies from a central warehouse in North Dakota—and that local workers would be paid the local minimum wage.

Finally Silliman had heard enough. At ten past eleven, to silence the last speaker, Niles Weed—whose three-minute allotment grew into a fifteen-minute diatribe—he banged the gavel with such force that the head flew off into Mrs. Rawson's lap.

"Order, Order!" he cried.

"Four burgers and four shakes, hold the fries," shouted someone to the guffaws of his friends.

"Mr. Weed, sit down!"

Oliver raised his hand to no avail until Jane Hill whispered into Silliman's ear.

"Who are you sir?"

Oliver stood up with a wince of pain. "My name is Oliver Swindler. I'm the editor of *The Republican*, and I have a question."

"We'll certainly accommodate the press, but please, Mr. Swindler, be brief."

"Chairman Silliman, does the board intend to ask the Heavenly Cheeseburgers Corporation to fill out the short form or the more comprehensive assessment form of the Environmental Quality Review Act?"

Only those people in the front could hear the town's lawyer say, "I told you so."

"I beg your pardon?" said Silliman, looking directly at Oliver.

"Here, I'll quote," and Oliver reached for his copy of the state Handbook for Local Officials: "Will the project have a major effect on the visual character of the community? Will the project adversely impact any site or structure of historic interest, and will the project result in major traffic problems or cause a major effect to existing transportation systems?"

Nearly all the city people began to applaud, as did many of the Fernglade crowd. Two of the company lawyers exchanged a resigned glance and closed their briefcases while the third went over to fold up their easel and flip charts.

"Order, please," shouted Silliman.

"Mr. Chairman," said the town attorney, pointing his pipe at the restaurant chain's men, "I suggest that board might need to table this decision until the lawyers for the corporation fill out and submit the long form required by this environmental law."

"Will someone make such a motion?"

"I will," said Jane Hill.

"I second," said Sidney Van Dozzer. Originally a supporter of the developer but quick to read an audience, he planned to run for the Board of Aldermen at the next election and knew when it was smart to switch horses.

"All in favor?"

Six "Ayes" echoed from the table.

"Mrs. Rawson, have you got that?" asked the chairman.

"Of course," she snapped.

With a rustle of shoes and chairs the crowd slowly filed out into the night air as the town attorney lit his pipe and winked at Jane Hill before following them out The eldest of the lawyers moved to the big table and shook hands with Silliman, then joined his colleagues for the long drive to Atlanta.

Oliver's back was aching. He called Adrian, who offered to have the ice pack ready when he arrived.

Chapter Sixteen

drian woke Oliver at eight o'clock. Another night on her floor had done his back a world of good, but another appointment with Dr. Hill would not be a bad idea.

They had a pleasant breakfast and by nine he left her apartment and walked over to the paper. Mary-Beth offered him a broad smile as he entered; he noticed that the white enamel scale had been replaced by a large potted philodendron twining up a plastic statue of Venus di Milo: turkey season was over for everyone. Mary-Beth was one sweet kid but someday, he vowed, he would re-pot that plant.

"Your sister Florence called. She was really very upset and asked that you call her as soon as you can. She wouldn't tell me a thing. Also—and I trust you're ready for this one—Clark Wechsler called for Greig. The phone rang the minute I opened the door this morning. He's called twice since. I already warned Greig; he's having a much longer breakfast than usual, so get ready for a major temper tantrum. Oh, and congratulations on giving the Planning Board an opportunity to turn themselves around. It was the only topic of conversation in the diner this morning."

"I'll go up to my desk, but let me know when Greig wants me. Adrian said she'd be in by ten."

He called Florence from his desk. She answered calmly, though her voice clearly showed she had been crying quite a bit.

"It's Linda. She stormed out of the house yesterday afternoon. Wouldn't even let me take her to the bus. She yelled and screamed, she threw things around the house, broke dishes, and even brought up the fact that I'm only your adopted sister. After fifty years that really hurt."

"What was it all about?"

"The money and the house, of course. Oh, Oliver, it was really a terrible scene. She said the land and the house were all hers until you came along to mess it up for everyone. She said nothing belonged to me. I told her it was only money and that she and her husband were in good health and lived well. Then she really began to rant and rave. Her husband was nothing, she cried, nothing. She hated him. She hated me. She hates you. Pretty soon I began to get a little more of the story. She's in love with Clark Wechsler and apparently they've been having an affair for over a year! And she hasn't been living with her husband for most of that time."

"That's too funny for words! I don't know if you noticed, but the looks they were exchanging at the cemetery—well, it doesn't surprise me."

"It isn't funny, Oliver. It isn't funny at all! She acted crazy. She was lasing out at you. My God—" she started to cry again—"she was terrible."

"Did she go back to Atlanta?"

"I have no idea. I waited a few minutes after she left and went over to the bus station but she wasn't there and a bus had just left for the city. She might have been on it. There was no way of finding out. I know she had a return ticket."

"Would you call her apartment later?"

"Sure, but I wonder how much of what she told me was the truth. I've only spoken to her husband Edward once. I was never invited to the wedding, just told about it."

"Call me if you hear anything."

As he hung up he heard loud voices from below and walked over to the stairs and listened.

"I'm fucking sick and tired of this goddamn paper. I won't be treated this way. I'm through with the whole mess."

"Please calm down, Clark, there's no sense in talking this way," said Davis.

"Look what I've done for this town: new businesses, a good place to eat, prosperity for everyone. Your fucking paper has gotten plenty of ads from me, plenty of ads. You just see how many more you get from me now."

"Please, calm down and remember your health. Here, let's go in my office and be comfortable."

"Calm down? CALM DOWN! You've ruined me. You fired Black and brought in this bastard. Look what he did...." The voices faded away to a distant roar as Davis took Wechsler into his office and closed the door. The best thing for me, thought Oliver, is to sit tight.

Scoop bounded up the stairs. "Boy, listen to that guy scream," he said and moved a pile of papers on his desk to add more. "Mary-Beth told me about the Planning Board last night. To think we're the only paper that has the story. I mean that's great, really great."

As if on cue, a reporter from the Middle Valley paper called, eager to learn what was the story behind Clark Wechsler's threat to sue the paper—and Oliver personally.

"I really don't know," Oliver said. "I think the best thing for you to do is to call the chairman of the Fernglade Planning Board and ask him. Then when you have pertinent questions of me, I'll be happy to answer."

He hung up and turned to Scoop. "What happened at your river meeting?"

"It was as exciting as yours. The feds have formed a committee to come up with a master plan for the river. Naturally most of the people appointed last night are for anything the government wants. So all the locals against the Park Service cried foul and started to wave freedom banners and sing protest songs. The end result was confusion and the Park Service gained another three squares on the game board."

"What ever happened to the good old days?"

"They never really happened," said Scoop.

Just then Davis came up the stairs.

"Oliver, that man is mad ... and I mean mentally. I always knew he was kind of strange, but now he's frankly demented. At first I thought I'd bring you into the discussion but then I realized that would be folly. He not only hates you but also blames you for causing your sister Linda a great deal of unhappiness and frustration. I finally calmed him down by merely listening but I really do believe he could use professional help. I would advise you to give him a wide berth for a few days."

"Just exactly what does he blame me for?"

"Botching up the sale of your sister's house and telling the Planning Board what to do with the cheeseburger place."

"You realize, Greig, that things like this restaurant won't go away. But at least when they come back again, the town can demand they give certain assurances—and although a battle might be lost the outcome of the war is still open. And thank you for quieting him down."

"You're welcome. And thank you, too."

"Oh, Greig. Could you call your broker this morning and find out just how big that restaurant chain is and what kind of holdings they have?"

"Sure."

"And Greig, to change the subject: when's the last time

you've been down in the basement?"

"The basement? Well, not for some time, if fact, not since we checked for flood damage, and that was some time ago."

"Thanks," said Oliver.

He watched Davis disappear down the spiral stairs, and spent an hour with Scoop planning the following week's stories. The county was holding a series of public hearings on the next year's taxes: the state was interested in land around the Hiwassee River Basin; over all hung the threat of many of the old local hotels turning into condominiums, elating realtors but angering local people who would lose jobs. The summer season was approaching, with its hordes of hikers and boat lovers, and Atlanta tourists would flock in to see nature for a day or two; he'd have to find some good features about and for those groups. And for local residents there would be Farmers Market reminders as produce became available. By August would come the opening of trout season, followed by the October leaf watchers, fall deer season, Department of Agriculture harvest reports, and, of course, at least one morning a month entertaining the ladies who wrote local columns on this, that, and the other.

"You'll love those ladies," said Scoop, grinning broadly from his tipped-over chair. "Home decor, gardening tips, how to get rid of mold and mildew, 'society' claptrap, a what's-the-world-coming-to-modern-house-design lament... They might even write about race relations in 'big cities' like Asheville. Hell, Oliver, if they could've been drafted, they'd've bored the North Vietnamese into submission."

"I'm glad they appeal to you, since I expect to see you there."

"No way."

"Sorry, Charlie, you protested too much."

After lunch Oliver walked back alone to pick up Imogene's car from Adrian's and move it to the hotel parking lot. He couldn't stay with her every night—as happy as he would have been to do so. He drove down Main Street, turned at the hotel and pulled into the lot. Two big provision trucks were once again parked in front of the service door, and Oliver wondered at the amount of food that Ackermann brought in through the parking lot, compared to the amount that was served in the dining room.

As he began to open the car door, Black came out of the hotel and walked over.

"Afternoon, Oliver," he smiled, the lines about his mouth and nose wrinkling up about the edges. "That was a clever bit of business at the Planning Board."

"Not that clever," Oliver answered, "I just asked them about a law that's been in existence for some time. That's what newspapermen do, after all: ask questions."

"I'm sure there will be other opportunities—for everyone." Black turned on his heel and went back inside.

In the afternoon Scoop drove Oliver to Monticello to exchange his New York license for a local one; on the way back they stopped at the courthouse to check the calendar for upcoming cases. Oliver felt he was settling nicely into the routine of an editor responsible for his own time and not answering to someone else. Coupled with a touch of pride in "educating the public," it was an altogether pleasant feeling.

Inside the courthouse the gold-lettered door of the County Clerk's office caught his eye, and he walked in and asked to see the deed on the Hanley place. Following the instructions of the assistant clerk, he filled out the proper request form, and within ten minutes he had learned that Clark Wechsler was not the sole owner: he and Linda held the property in partnership. Moreover, the property line extended all the way down to the edge of Wechsler's Creek, totaling almost three acres.

As he was leaving the office, deep in thought, a man with a high shock of white hair over a receding brow called after him from an inner office. "Oliver, Oliver Swindler. Wait up there!"

Oliver recognized one of Imogene's long-ago flames, now the County Clerk.

"Jack Putnam. It's been years and years. Hello and how are you, my friend?"

"I'm fine, Oliver. Just fine, thank you. I missed seeing you at Imogene's funeral. Well, I saw you, but didn't have a chance to say hello, and tell you how sorry I was. And am."

"It was a gray day, Jack," Oliver said, "for all of us."

"I liked your sister. Hell, I was in love with her for the longest time. Sometimes even now I wish it had all worked out. But, alas, you can't redo your life, can you."

"Well, sometimes you can make a fresh start, but no, you can't go back and do it differently. What about you, Jack? What are you up to these days?"

"Oh, I'm still buried in the tedium of public office: wills, estates, contracts, deeds. The same as always, in fact: keeping track of everyone else's business for them. Rather like you, I imagine. Congratulations on the new job."

Oliver chuckled. "We just have different ways of making sure public information really is public."

"Is that what you're doing here? Digging up some dirt?" He laughed conspiratorially.

"As a matter of fact, yes, in a way. Not so much dirt as just public record. Did you know that the old Hanley house in Fernglade now belongs to Clark Wechsler?"

"Oh, yes. I sure do. And he's bound to make a pile on that development deal, Oliver. Everyone's been whispering about it."

"How big a deal is it?"

"Restaurants, canoe landing, a hotel, you name it. It's a big piece of land for right in town. He'll make a great deal of money … if it all goes according to his plans." He paused, with a twinkle in his eye—the very quality that had kept Imogene from considering him a serious enough man for her to marry. "I hear that it didn't all go according to plan last night at the Planning Board meeting." He smiled, inviting Oliver's confidence. "Something you brought up, I believe I heard. Well, as the poet wrote, 'the best-laid schemes ...?'"

"... gang aft agley," finished Oliver with a smile, thinking to himself that Clark Wechsler was more a rat than a mouse or a man. Miss MacKenzie had taught English to generations of Fernglade students, and as the daughter of immigrants loved reading Burns in a proper Scots accent.

"Just doing my job, Jack. Speaking of which, I'm due back at the paper, but I do hope we'll get together soon."

"Oliver, you need anything, just call, okay?"

"Right, Jack. I'll do that."

Oliver walked down the preformed concrete stairs of the new county building; he missed the old classical style. At least this shoebox still had a newsstand, he thought with relief.

As Scoop backed out of the parking lot, Oliver asked him what possible use the burger proposition might have for three acres of Hanley land plus at least two acres of Swindler property, all abutting the creek.

"Easy," the young man answered. "Canoe access. Boating—'river adventures' is the new catch phrase—is big money, and the National Park Service is bound to control future businesses, so everyone's rushing to get a foot in the door. That creek is deep and wide enough to carry canoes and rafts, right down to the river."

"That's what the County Clerk said—and everyone knows about it too. And the burger joint is more than a chain of restaurants. They're into time-share properties, recreation and theme parks, and general real estate development."

"How did you find that out?" asked Scoop.

"I called Greig. His broker looked it up. Oh, would you

mind stopping at the antique shop just up the road? There, the one with the big 'open' sign."

"Sure thing, Oliver," and he pulled into Harriet's driveway.

While Scoop looked at the postcard collection Oliver drew Harriet aside. "Do you have a ring I could look at? Not too expensive, and not too gaudy. Something that Adrian would like and could be used as an engagement ring for older folks."

"I've got just the thing. Give me a sec." She left the room for a minute and came back with sparkling red fire held between her fingers.

"This is a large garnet," she said, "beautiful but only a semi-precious stone so it's more affordable than rubies. And I think they are more beautiful. Those are seed pearls around the edge and the mounting is gold. And it's her size."

"It really is beautiful."

"I think your sister was hoping something like this might happen."

"It's not for sure, you know, I haven't even asked. In fact, we haven't really even had a 'date.'"

"Trust me," she said," I think you'll get a yes."

"I'll have to owe you."

"No problem. If you welsh out, I'll send my killer chicken after you."

Dinner at Adrian's was pleasant, though hardly intimate with Scoop as a third wheel. She baked her own delicious bread, and dessert was a fresh-baked blueberry pie topped with ice cream. The three talked companionably for hours until Scoop thought he should be starting for home.

Oliver stayed for another cup of coffee, toying with the idea of giving her the ring, before deciding to wait until the outcome of the next few days was clearer.

At her front door he asked, "Do you have a flashlight?"

"Yes, I'll get it. Oliver, what are you up to?"

"Nothing," he lied. "I want to get something out of Imogene's car and the convenience lights aren't working. I have to have Frank Wallace take a look at it one of these days."

He kissed her good night—lingering, but not too long—and went down the stairs to the street. The bank clock chimed eleven.

It was cold with a light wind, and Oliver could smell the river. A flock of birds of flew across the face of the full moon. Way upriver Oliver heard the whistle of a train. It could have been a hundred years ago as he walked along, but for the lurid glare of the orange streetlights.

No lights were on in the funeral parlor except for a pink glow behind the potted palms in the front window, but the supermarket had every fluorescent lit as a number of clerks stocked the shelves for the weekend.

The hotel lobby was, as usual, empty. Oliver heard voices in the bar but had no desire to see whose they were. He went quietly up the stairs to his room and turned on the television set.

The weather report warned of gathering clouds with rain starting early in the morning and continuing on into Sunday. *Hawaii Five-0*, in reruns, soon had him speculating on how Honolulu would compare with Fernglade—and whether Adrian would like living there. Before the show ended he turned off the television, and soon enough he was dozing in the chair.

At twelve-twenty he suddenly awoke to a sound in the hallway. He sat still, barely hearing the soft footsteps. They had stopped right outside the door, then continued down the hall. He decided to wait until two o'clock before starting out.

With his duffle bag and some spare towels he made a form in the bed that, he hoped, would resemble a sleeping person, then threw the blanket casually over the "head."

Taking the flashlight and donning a light jacket, he stepped out into the hall. The sheriff's gun was in his pocket. Except for the light at the top of the stairs everything was dark. Oliver wanted to know what those trucks were doing every day at the hotel and just what Black and Ackermann were up to, and he was pretty sure the basement held some of the answers.

He had no idea where the hotel's basement door was, and the last thing he wanted was to be caught walking stealthily through the halls. He went downstairs, quietly passed the dining room, and cautiously opened the front door.

Staying close to the storefronts, he retraced his steps toward Adrian's apartment, then crossed the street. Main Street's windows were dark, and no one was about as he walked quickly to the newspaper offices. Once inside, he sat in Mary-Beth's chair in the dark and watched for anyone who might have followed him. There was no sign of movement.

Satisfied, he opened the basement door, pulled the light string, and tiptoed down into the tomb of paper, heading straight to the 1920s. The kerosene lamp hung as he had left it by the old wooden door, and he was sure nobody had been down there since his previous visit. He pressed the thumb latch and, his caution tensing every muscle, walked through, leaving the door open. The light was very dim, 10- or 15-watt bulbs at most, so he turned on the flashlight and walked through the tunnel to the main chamber.

There he stopped to listen. Nothing. He turned into the hotel tunnel; it was short, less than twenty feet. In the flashlight's beam he saw another door, tightly closed but with a knob and a keyhole instead of the old-fashioned thumb latch. He put his ear against the wood and thought he could hear faint traces of music, like a cheap, tinny radio, but nothing else. He switched off the light and as quietly as possible turned the knob.

The door was well maintained; it opened easily on well-oiled hinges. After gazing unfocused into the blackness, his eyes adjusted, and straight ahead he caught a faint glow that outlined another door. He took a chance and turned on the flashlight.

The room was at most ten by ten feet, boxes of liquor along both side walls; from the careful way they were stacked, they surely contained full bottles. He walked softly across to the other door; it, too, had a keyhole. Still careful of his back, Oliver crouched down and peeked through.

He saw a long, dark, narrow hall; halfway down a single utility light hung, unlit, from a cord. Light spilled from an open door at the far end and revealed a flight of stairs. Stealthily he opened the door and stepped into the hall. Now the music was louder. The static made the country sound even twangier than normal.

Flanking the dim light were two more doors, the one on the right resembling the heavy, insulated doors he'd seen on meat lockers, very thick with a small window in the middle and a heavy handle designed to lock the cold air inside. The left door was ajar, made of planks painted white. He opened it cautiously; the music was coming from close by.

Suddenly he heard noises from the stairway. He quickly shut the side door and retraced his steps. His eyes were adjusted to the light now, and as he peered through the keyhole he saw a thin man in jeans and an old woolen shirt take the last step down to the hard floor.

The man flipped the light switch and sang to himself as he pushed a two-wheeled dolly down the hall. A voice from the stairs above, just loud enough for Oliver to hear, called out: "Harry, goddammit, hurry it up." He knew the voice: it was Black. And this, then, was Harry, who had wanted to push Oliver's car into the ditch and set it afire.

Harry opened the locker room and pushed his dolly inside, leaving the door ajar; a cold mist wafted out into the warm hall. Over Harry's croaky singing Oliver could hear the sound of boxes being shifted around.

A few minutes later Harry reappeared, the dolly now stacked with five crates marked "Perishable" and "Keep Refrigerated." He grumbled to himself as he struggled to turn the dolly toward the stairs. A voice came from above:

"Harry, you got five boxes?"

"Right, I've got five boxes. I counted 'em. I counted five fucking boxes, okay? That's all there is."

"Okay. That completes this order. You can shut everything off down there."

"Sure, sure," said Harry in the kind of voice that comes from smoking three packs a day. "Orders, always orders. Someday—"

He shut the refrigerator door, pushed the dolly to the stairway, and turned off the light. The radio stopped. Oliver was almost amused watching Harry realize—as Oliver could have warned him—that the dolly was facing in the wrong direction, and then struggle to turn it around in the narrow space. The thought crossed his mind that if not for Harry's stupidity and Black's impatience he probably would have been burned alive.

Oliver didn't stir while he listened to Harry struggle up the stairs. At last he came back down, closed the stairway door with a sharp bang, and the hall was pitch dark. Even then Oliver waited another fifteen minutes, his heart beating double time, before he turned on the flashlight and returned to the hall.

He opened the refrigerator door and went in.

The room, thirty by thirty with ten-foot ceilings, was so cold he could see his breath. Two refrigeration units hung down on iron straps, pouring out cold air from high-speed fans. The lights along the walls were enclosed in glass jars and the concrete floor was marked with the rubber treads of Harry's dolly.

Oliver swung his flashlight toward the back and stood frozen to the spot staring at what looked like butchered bodies.

With a start he realized they were animal carcasses, neatly skinned, hooked on a series of metal trolleys attached to the ceiling that wound their way around the perimeter of the room. He counted sixteen deer, all safe in cold storage. With them was a black bear, un-skinned, and smelling slightly gamey even in this cold. A number of boxes were piled up around the outer walls, each neatly labeled: turkey, rabbit, grouse, bear, pheasant, trout, and various cuts of venison. To his left, startling in its proximity, hung the curved beak and talons of a Golden Eagle.

"So that's it," he said softly. He followed his train of thought silently as he began to shiver. Ackermann was supplying a few trendy restaurants from New York to Atlanta with fresh but illegal game out of season. Wealthy city people would pay anything to have fresh venison, in season or not, as well as brook trout, pheasant, and whatever else caught their fancy. What a deal, he thought. You rape the mountains of wild game, cut it up and package it, and make another illicit fortune. And what kind of goon would buy an eagle? Even as he asked, he knew.

Walking back to the darkened hall, Oliver quietly shut the locker room door and stepped across the hall.

He knew what this room would be. It was the same size as the locker but much warmer. At least six utility lights hung down over a slaughterhouse completely outfitted with grinders, saws, butcher blocks, and wrapping tables. Lines of skinning and boning knives hung on magnetic strips along the walls.

On the edge of one of the tables the flashlight's beam fell on a jacket, a pack of cigarettes, and a large brass ring with keys. At the same moment a light went on and he heard someone coming down the stairs.

"Oh, shit," he intoned. Turning out his flashlight he crawled on hands and knees to the far corner of the room where he crouched down behind a butcher-style band saw.

Harry walked into the room, still mumbling to himself.

"God damn," he muttered, "I'd forget my dick if I could."

He picked up the jacket and looked down at the floor.

"Huh, wonder where the fucking hell this came from. Pretty, ain't it. Sure as hell it ain't mine," he said to himself as he reached down and picked up something shiny and sparkling from the floor.

Oliver reached into his pocket for the almost perfectly round stone, studded with mica chips, that he had picked up on the path to Luther's the other morning—a world ago. It was gone.

"Must be Mr. Black's," he said. "Well, maybe it's mine now," he snorted. "Finders keepers!" and a dim chuckle were the last things Oliver heard as Harry closed the door.

Once again Oliver sat motionless for several minutes before he had the courage to get up. He put his hands on the edge of the band saw and pulled, his back beginning to ache now. Once upright, he turned around and there on the edge of the butcher block was the key ring. Harry would be back.

Oliver almost ran to the door and into the hall. This time the footsteps coming down the stairs spoke of more authority. "God damn you, Harry, you really are dumb as shit!" said Black.

There was only one place to go: the meat locker. Oliver moved fast. He prayed that Black wouldn't notice the little pool of cold mist in the hall as he went into the other room. Once inside he felt his way, carcass after carcass until he reached the back wall. There he crouched down and shivered, from fear as much as the cold. He knew that people say that your life passes before your eyes as you sink down in the water and drown. The same thing happens, he thought, when you're freezing.

Two minutes later the light over the little window went out and he knew that Black had recovered Harry's keys. He shivered his way back to the door.

Everything was quiet. He stepped out into the dim light

from the open stairway. He lit the flashlight and at the same moment heard the switch as the hall light came on.

"Hey, who the creeping hell are you?" said Harry, who stood a foot away and had obviously been ruminating in the dark about the key ring. Oliver had a suspicion that his nerve endings went on and off without warning; he prayed Harry had not seen his face in the dark car and wouldn't remember him.

"I'm Bob," he answered, a lump welling up in his throat, "I'm the new guy, from Asheville," and thinking of Harry's character, continued, "I had a smoke, then sat down and fuck me if I didn't fall asleep! Oh, you picked up my lucky stone. Can I have it back?"

"Hey, man," Harry said. "Done the same thing myself, I reckon." He held the mica stone out to the light, then gave it back to Oliver.

"Here you go. Glad you didn't lose it. I'll tell Mr. Black I met you."

"No, Harry. Don't mention it to Mr. Black, all right? He'll just get angry at me for sitting here instead of working and then he'll hit me," and Oliver cringed. "You know how he is. I'm not even supposed to be here taking a nap. I'm supposed to be working for him up at the funeral parlor."

"Well, I don't know—"

"HARRY!" came Black's voice down the stairs. "Where the fuck are you. If you don't get your ass up here I'll beat you within an inch of death!"

"I gotta go," said Harry.

"Please, Harry, let me be a secret—our little secret."

"Okay, Bob," said Harry with a smile, "mum's the word."

He walked back to the stairs with his finger on his lips. "Coming, Mr. Black." He turned off the light and shut the door. Still catching his breath, Oliver retraced his steps to the main chamber.

For a crazy reason he would never understand, he decided to trust to luck once more, and instead of returning to the newspaper office he followed the tunnel that led to the river. It was about three hundred feet long and ended at a very old wooden door, only five feet high and three feet wide. He opened it with great difficulty and looked out to the river through a crisscrossed maze of shrubbery and vines. It would take a machete to get out of this door. It was so overgrown that it would look like a hobbit hole to anyone looking up from the river or the opposite shore.

He had half a mind to take the tunnel to the funeral home in hopes of scaring the hell out of Clark Wechsler, but decided against it. Luck can run out. And Harry might not be quite as stupid as he seemed.

The trip back through the tunnels was uneventful, though when he reached the newspaper basement he had a nervous moment: two of the hanging lights were moving slightly, causing eerie shadows on the piled edges of the stacked old papers. But he soon realized it was only a breeze that had probably started with his opening of the river door.

Back upstairs at last, he saw, spotlighted in the glow of a streetlight, a big meat truck parked in front of the hotel. Harry— with grudging help from a man Oliver assumed to be Lou—was changing a tire.

The back door to the newspaper led out to the lawn and the big sycamore tree. From there he followed a worn path that paralleled the buildings on Main Street. Still chilly, he stepped through a hedge behind the canoe rental store and came out on Bridge Street.

He couldn't go back to the hotel. Nothing would let him lie down in peace, much less sleep, knowing that Black might be across the hall. He walked across to Adrian's building and climbed the stairs, then knocked on her door.

"Oliver, what's wrong?"

"Let me in and I'll tell you."

He sat on her couch, shivering deeply, while she poured him a scotch and water, no ice.

The drink warmed him, and his back relaxed. Finally feeling safe and blessedly unemotional, he told her the whole story, as clearly and with as many details as he could muster—like a newspaper man, he told himself. When he was done at last, and she returned to her bed, he again lay down on the cushions on the floor. He felt truly comfortable for the first time in a week.

Saturday

Chapter Seventeen

Waking up at Adrian's was getting to be a habit—and a nice one. The ambience was far superior to the hotel's; it felt especially refreshing, and safe, after wandering the catacombs and encountering Harry. He rolled off the cushions with care as his back was starting to hurt again. He would call Dr. Hill this morning, but breakfast with Adrian came first.

The curtains on her front windows were wide open but the sky was so leaden that it looked more like an early winter evening. Rain streaked across the glass.

She had a great many stops to make today; Saturdays, she found, were good for meeting her clients without weekday pressures. "I've got to go to Asheville, Trust, Burnsville, Micaville, and Mars Hill, then wind up back in Fernglade, hopefully by five."

"Whoever said that being in sales is easy?"

"Nobody who ever worked for a newspaper. Listen, one of these nights we need to just go out, away from here. There's a wonderful restaurant over in Weaverville, just north of Asheville, that would be three stars if it were in Manhattan. Called La Cucina Milana."

"Dress up?"

"No, it's still casual, but believe me, the food is superb. They know me, so I can usually get a table. What about tonight?"

"Let's play it by ear," he said. "We've both got a lot to do today, but it does sound good."

"I'll meet you back here at six."

He picked up his jacket—making sure the gun was still in the pocket—then quickly kissed her goodbye.

He returned to room 10 only to collect his duffel bag. It was nine o'clock when he opened the front door of the paper to meet the smiling face of Mary-Beth. "No calls, yet," she said, "But just wait."

He went up to the editorial office with a cup of hot coffee in hand, balancing it carefully as he negotiated the spiral stairs. As soon as he was settled at his desk he made an appointment to see Dr. Hill. Jane penciled him in for three.

Then she said: "Mr. Swindler—"

"Oliver, please."

"Oliver, I've thought it over and I ... well, I've decided I will press charges against Simon Black."

"I'm calling the sheriff this morning about him and Ackermann; shall I mention it to him?"

"If you would, I'd be so grateful, Mr.—Oliver. We'll see you at three o'clock."

After a heavy swig of coffee, Oliver suddenly wished, for the first time in years, that he had a cigarette; he was even tempted to look for a small bottle in any desk drawer. With a surge of fortitude, he conquered the urge and dialed the sheriff.

He told Phibert about the tunnels, Harry and Lou, the specter of Black always hovering in the background, and what must be a very lucrative business in illegal wild game.

"I know that Clark Wechsler is also involved. And I'll bet that the dead body you found in my sister's kitchen is a pal of Harry and Lou. Believe me, those two guys are an example of evolution in reverse. I shudder to think of the methods that Black must use to keep them under control."

"If you don't mind my saying this, Mr. Swindler," said Phibert, "that was a stupid thing for you to do. If they'd caught you we would never have found out until your body washed ashore anywhere between here and the French Broad River."

"I know, Sheriff, but it's done now. But look, the other thing I wanted to tell you is that Jane Hill says she's willing to press charges on Black's threat to blackmail her. Or extortion, or whatever the charge would be. You just need to call her and tell her who to talk to—the DA, or a lawyer, or whoever."

"That'll have to wait. Based on your tip, I'll send a squad out this morning to raid that tunnel, but I have to try to reach somebody in Raleigh for advice on the charges. The deer and bear fall under state regulations, but killing an eagle sounds like a federal crime. Fortunately, Judge Morgan always is in his chambers on Saturday mornings—he likes to catch up on his paperwork—so I can get a warrant without any problem. Meantime if you come over to Burnsville, Luther can be released into your custody."

"If you don't mind, Sheriff, I'd rather stay in town for the arrests. It's a big story for Fernglade. And Luther'll understand."

"Suit yourself," said the sheriff, not unkindly, and hung up.

The next few hours were difficult. Oliver was tempted to take a folding chair out on the sidewalk and watch as the police cars drove up, but discretion won out. To keep his "idle hands from doing the devil's work," as his grandmother had always said, he sorted through the mail to see what might need editing down the line. He wrote an editorial on Easter and the religious proclivities of Americans, checked Scoop's story on the river meeting that he found on his desk, and blue-penciled his interview with the county Director of the Budget concerning rising property tax rates.

Scoop came in about ten-thirty and Oliver told him of the morning's developments.

"Hey, I can't wait. This I've got to see."

"Now, are you going to Burnsville today?"

"Yep, right after we finish lining up next week's schedule. Well, and after we watch the circus across the street. Why?"

"Phibert's letting Luther out today. I wanted to pick him up but I left Imogene's car keys somewhere. If they're in my hotel room I'd rather wait 'til those guys are put away before I look for them."

"Okay, I'll drive you over and back—but I'm going to put in for mileage." He lit a cigarette. "Why do you care so much about Luther? You haven't seen him for, what, twenty-five years? I don't want to be mean, but what is he except a nutty old hermit? What's he ever done?"

After a moment Oliver spoke softly. "No. I hadn't seen him for a long, long time, and I guess he hasn't done very much in his life. Nothing you'd have noticed. But however little and unimportant it was, he always did it with a pure heart. I guess he's just probably the most decent fellow I've ever known. If that's not enough for you, then just take me over there so we can bring him back home."

Scoop turned away and booted up his computer. Oliver couldn't tell if the boy was chastened, or simply indifferent; it didn't matter, and he didn't care. He, too, went back to his desk.

Some twenty minutes later Scoop looked out the window to the street below.

"Here they are," he cried.

Three cars from the Sheriff's Department, all with flashing lights on top, were parked on the diagonal in front of the hotel. The street was blocked from either direction.

Scoop picked up his old camera from the desk, making sure it was loaded with film, then said: "One just went up the side street. C'mon Oliver, let's go."

"Just let me sit up here for a moment. I'll be right down."

"Right." Scoop lumbered down the spiral stairs, every step

vibrating. Oliver sat for a few minutes, then slowly went down to the front sidewalk where Mary-Beth, Davis, and Jerry stood and watched. Davis held a large umbrella; the flashing lights of deputies cars filled the street and parking lot and reflected off nearby windows, but there was no noise or movement visible from their vantage point.

"Anything happen?" he asked. "Did they get 'em?"

"Are you kidding?" said Mary-Beth. "For a minute it sounded like a gang war in there. Didn't you hear the shots?"

"Not a sound," he answered. "Fill me in."

Just then four deputies emerged from the hotel, escorting Black and Ackermann, both handcuffed with their jackets over their heads, to one of the patrol cars. Scoop immediately began snapping pictures again.

Sheriff Phibert crossed the street. "Well, Swindler, we got 'em. Literally caught 'em in the act. There was a truck in the rear being loaded with a shipment of wild turkeys. The bill of lading was for an Atlanta restaurant that I couldn't begin to pronounce. And the amount of game in those lockers, well, it should put them all away for a good long time.

"Harry and Lou are brothers, by the way. Come from way back in the woods of Graham County—I don't think they even have electricity at their cabin. They—well, drinking moonshine from the age of nine or ten, probably poisoned with old lead pipe ... they're just not right in their minds. Not just not smart; they're kind of barely this side of crazy. And it was their other brother, that was Wilfred, who was the second body in your sister's kitchen."

"Why? What was he doing there?"

The sheriff looked at Davis and Mary-Beth and lowered his voice.

"This is not an official statement," he said. "It's off the record, and confidential. All right?"

They nodded in agreement; Scoop had drifted up the block to get better angles for his pictures.

"Ackerman pretty much lost it; I suppose he's the weak link. He couldn't keep from talking no matter how much Black tried to shut him up. And he—Ackermann—claims Black strangled Wilfred in a fit of temper," the sheriff said. "He says Black also thought of using the straw cord to put the blame on Luther. And that Wechsler killed your sister."

"Clark? Killed Imogene?" Oliver's shock was apparent; Mary-Beth took his arm and tried to comfort him, but he shrugged her off.

"Black denies everything, of course. Says he didn't even know about the illegal game. He says Ackermann sold the meat and Wechsler masterminded the whole thing."

"Do you believe it? About Clark killing Imogene, I mean?"

"I don't know, but one of them did it."

"How long can you keep them in jail?"

"By the time I get back it'll be too late to find a judge for arraignment. Morgan usually goes to visit his grandchildren in Hickory Saturday nights. So I can keep them twenty-four hours, maybe even 'til Monday morning. By-the-by, shooting a Golden Eagle is a federal offense—up to two years. A grand jury can be convened on about a moment's notice with something this big, but I won't kid you, they can probably get out on bail. You know they have some hotshot lawyers, and you have to remember, I have no proof of Black's involvement other than what you saw in the tunnels, and, well, it's not eyewitness, just ear-witness, if you know what I mean. And, of course, Ackermann's accusations. Maybe Jane Hill's statement will help, but that won't be in the record until she swears out her complaint, and that might not be 'til Monday."

"What about the bills of sale for the Atlanta restaurant?" Oliver asked.

"Well, just like the general records in the hotel, all of them had Ackermann's signature, not Black's."

"Any sign of Wechsler?" asked Davis. "He made some outlandish accusations in my office yesterday and I'd like to see him in court."

"No, he seems to have skipped." He turned back to Oliver. "We're not likely to get statements from those two brothers any time soon. They're so scared of Black they won't open their mouths. But once I get them separated they'll come around."

"What about when they ran me off the road?" said Oliver. "Lou called Harry by his name, and I'll swear to both their voices. You can't miss that country accent." He grinned. "I wonder if I could get him to talk if I pretend to be his new friend Bob, the way I did in the tunnel."

"I don't think you need to go that far, Swindler. Let us do what we need to do. You're a reporter, not an undercover agent."

Oliver was persistent. "That reminds me, Sheriff. Remember I told you Trooper Hindshaw who stopped me for a license check said they were looking for illegal drugs? Did you find any sign of that?"

"Not yet, but we're still searching. I wouldn't be surprised if that's part of their scheme." The sheriff began to sound exasperated. "Don't worry, we'll get enough to put them all away. Right now I want to find Clark Wechsler."

"There's one last thing, Sheriff." Oliver said. "It's about my sister, Linda." He glanced at the others, who reluctantly slipped back through the door into the *Republican* offices.

"Florence said Linda's having an affair with Clark Wechsler. Well, I just remembered something Linda said last Sunday after we left the funeral home. I guess I didn't notice it at the time, but it must have stuck with me. She was talking about selling the house and everything in it, said that even the china would bring a lot of money. She mentioned that the only piece of china that was broken was the Chinese Willow-Ware. How could she have known that? She was supposed to be in Atlanta."

"I appreciate your telling me that, Mr. Swindler. That's very interesting. Don't worry, we'll look into it."

They both noticed the deputies' cars ready to head back to the county jail. "One last question!" Oliver called out as the sheriff crossed the street. "What's the connection with Reverend Stalker?"

"That's something we still have to find out about, Mr. Swindler. For now, I need to get these gentlemen safely tucked away."

As the police cars left the square, Oliver climbed back to his office and took notes for the story for next week's paper. Scoop soon joined him and said he'd like to start for Burnsville.

They stopped at a diner for lunch and reached the sheriff's office about one-thirty. They were back in Fernglade by two; the heavy rain had now turned to a light mist.

Oliver walked Luther up to his house just to get away from the town for a little while. Although everything in the woods was soaked, the temperature had risen slightly; with the humidity it felt like a tepid steam bath. As they passed a grove of blooming red maples, Luther stopped to check the bees.

"They look all right," he said. "They'll be out hitting all the wildflowers the next few months so's to store up enough honey for the winter. I'll come down tomorrow and take the ribbons away."

They climbed the hill through the gathering mists. Here in the clearing an unexpected chill was in the air. Luther went straight to his garden and, assured that everything was in good shape, opened the front door and entered his house. "You want a glass of wine, Oliver?" he called from the window.

"Sure, Luther," Oliver replied.

They sat on the small hewn bench next to the front door and sipped and listened to the water dripping from the branches in the woods, resplendent with their promising salute to spring. Three crows flew overhead and cawed at something only they could see. The freight train whistled as it passed through town.

"Thank you, Oliver," said Luther. "You, and your sister, you've always been good friends to me, and gettin' me out an' all ..."

"It works both ways, Luther. Nobody else ever saved me from drowning, my friend." He stood and shook the older man's hand. "I need to be getting back now. Thanks for the wine. It's good to have you back home."

Oliver walked back through the woods, past wet and shining rocks covered with lichens, the ground littered with last winter's leaves, and early spring flowers poking through.

It started to rain heavily as he passed the beehives and reached the old iron bridge over Wechsler's Creek. By the time he crossed Mill Road and stopped next to the Hanley house, his shoes were squishing with every step. Wallace's garage was dark; even the antifreeze sign was gone. The newspaper was dark. A few people were shopping in Shields.

Suddenly he remembered where he'd left Imogene's car key: in the ignition. He had been so flustered by Black's sudden appearance in the parking lot that he forgot to remove it. He decided to drive to Adrian's building and wait there. The car radio and heater would keep him comfortable.

He wondered what would happen to the hotel with Ackermann gone. With morbid curiosity he walked through the open front door: the building was utterly silent. In the dining room the ceiling lights shone down on overturned chairs and tables, each surrounded by piles of broken crockery and drifts of sugar.

The colored lights in front of the bar were still in place, but only a few were glowing, the rest smashed in their sockets. But it was the mirror that held his eyes. Bullets had apparently hit it in two places, and a crack now extended from one end to the other. It was no longer a mysterious window to another world, but broken debris, ready to be pulled off the wall and thrown out.

He went out to the parking lot, picked up the Oldsmobile, drove out to the side street and turned left onto Main.

Adrian's car was not in front of her apartment and the Olds hadn't yet warmed up, so he cruised down to the bank parking lot and back, turning left when he reached the old road that wound up the hill and came out on the other side of the river. Mist continued to drift in and partially hide the trees that lined the road.

When he reached the viaduct he found trucks unloading equipment and putting up danger signs. The special signal to control one-lane traffic was already in use. He turned right and drove to Bridge Street. The backwoodsman sign was dripping beads of water from its oar.

Back to Main and still no sign of Adrian's car. The street was quiet, with only the supermarket showing signs of activity. As he passed the funeral parlor he glanced inside. A woman's face was looking out between the potted palms. It was Linda.

Immediately he made a turn into the side street by the hotel and backed out onto Main. He left the car running in front of the funeral parlor and ran up to the front door. It was open. He walked into the main showroom.

"Linda," he called, "it's Oliver."

"Swindler, you bastard," said Clark Wechsler. He was partially hidden by the palms, standing next to an open coffin of beige enameled metal, lined with pink silk. Linda stood at his right. "I never thought I'd see you again. Now," he said, motioning with a gun, "get to the back of the storeroom."

"Do as he says, Oliver," said Linda. "I don't feel very close to you anymore."

Oliver walked to the rear of the showroom.

"Through the door," she said.

They walked into a large room. Uncrated coffins lay on the floor in disarray and smaller boxes of chemicals were scattered about. Clark pushed Oliver to the center of the room. Linda stood just behind and to his right. She opened her purse and took out a compact to check her makeup.

"I should kill you on the spot, Swindler, for everything you've done. You were always a rotten little bastard. You were always laughing at me. I should shoot you and leave you to rot."

"No, Clark," said Linda, "He's still my brother."

"You didn't care too much about your sister."

"I never liked her that much," said Linda, screwing up her face in thought. She put back her compact. "But she was my sister."

"You killed Imogene," said Oliver with a cold fury that surprised even himself.

Wechsler stared at him as if he were stupid. "Of course I did! She refused to sell the land, and without the land there's no deal with the restaurant. We had plans, Oliver, big plans. There would have been a big, lucrative complex on both sides of the Creek. But no, Imogene was too good for that. She was willing to put up with the noise and everything else and then call me twice a day to tell me what an idiot I was to think she'd ever relent. That bitch!"

"So that's why you—you killed her so brutally?"

"It wasn't brutal." His eyes narrowed as he described the scene, and Oliver could tell that he was enjoying the memory. "I used a kitchen knife, and she died instantly. It was as neat and clean as could be. But that was the problem, you see. Anyone examining the body would have known it was done by someone who knew anatomy, like a doctor ... or a mortician."

"Clark, honey," said Linda, "We've got to go."

"Where did you get Luther's knife?"

"Wallace had it. He asked me what it was and of course being from around here, I knew. I suddenly thought what a great idea it would be to pin it on Luther. Dumb, crazy hermit. What a sap. I left the body on the floor and went over to the garage. Wallace had left the knife there, so I took it. Nobody saw me. I came back and slashed her up, bashed the back door, broke some china, made a mess...."

"And Linda came back with you—stood there while you—"

"Why not? She'd been living with me for weeks. And Imogene was already dead."

Oliver looked at his sister with scarcely disguised loathing. "Who killed Wilfred?"

Wechsler laughed. "That was Black. He lost his temper and choked the guy. He didn't mean to, but," he paused for a moment, "Simon's not an easy man to handle. He flies off the handle, does stuff you didn't plan for—he's a real pain in the ass. But he's useful. I realized we could get rid of the body by making it look like Luther choked him with the straw he made the hives with."

He turned to Linda. "And you've been here all this time?"

"Of course. I never married Edward, you know. I saw no reason to waste my life with him. I came up here last year when Imogene asked me to attend a funeral with her. I met Clark and we fell in love, so I started coming up on my own. Nobody knew."

"Linda helped me all through the negotiations with Heavenly Cheeseburgers," said Wechsler.

Oliver had a sudden realization. "You told Clark all about Luther, didn't you. You never liked him."

"I certainly never approved of him being a friend of yours, Oliver. A lowlife with no family, living the way he did, taking advantage of Imogene.... Just knowing him lowered us all." With an impatient look she pulled at Clark's sleeve, "Hurry up. And don't forget to take some of those drugs, they're too valuable to leave."

"You're behind the drugs?" Oliver asked.

"Certainly," Wechsler replied, "why not? Only fools use

them, but fools pay good money. We've been bringing them in for months in caskets from a warehouse in Florida."

"You creep," Oliver said. "And my sister thinks Luther's a lowlife. Just where do you think you can hide?"

"That's easy. When you have enough money you can do just about anything. I also know a whole lot about makeup; morticians have to make people look much better than they ... did, so it won't be hard to change our appearance." He chuckled. "I think we'll go south to Mexico first. How about somewhere warm for next winter, Linda?"

He turned to look at her. It gave Oliver just enough time to pull out Phibert's gun. "I don't think so, Clark. Drop your gun."

"Oh, come now, Oliver." Wechsler was smoothness personified once again. "You won't shoot your sister. In fact I doubt if you've got the guts to shoot me."

"Clark, honey, Oliver left Imogene's car out front. It's still running. We could get away. They know your car, but this one would give us extra time. Just leave him. Go get the money from the safe."

"Should I, Oliver? It sounds like a good idea to me. I'll make a deal with you: give us fifteen minutes to get out of here. If you try to come after us, I'll shoot you down ... and I won't miss. And don't bother trying to call the sheriff. The line'll be cut. Deal?"

The men held their guns on each other, neither moving.

"Sure," Oliver said at last. "Get out. Both of you. You've got your fifteen-minute lead. After that all bets are off."

Wechsler went into his private office and in less than a minute returned with a briefcase in one hand, the gun in the other.

"Let's go, Linda."

"Goodbye, Oliver," she said. They walked out without looking back.

As soon as the car pulled away, Oliver went out to the

sidewalk. He didn't know what prompted him to walk back toward Mill Street. The rain had stopped, but a heavy mist carried sounds down from the hill overlooking the town. He heard tires squeal from the end of Bridge Street heading toward the viaduct.

He ran along Main Street to the sound of the bank chimes ringing the quarter hour. Then he heard the horn. It kept on and on, blaring in a monotone. Another joined it at a higher pitch.

The viaduct, he thought. *They don't know about the roadwork.*

There came a fierce shriek of skidding tires followed by the shrill cacophony of shattered glass. As he reached the Hanley house he looked up and saw headlights shining straight ahead into nothing; he watched as the Oldsmobile climbed the railing in a shower of sparks, taking with it rusted pieces of guard rail and shards of glass that sparkled like jewels.

For a moment it hung, balanced over the riverbed. A tongue of flame appeared and quickly grew. The headlights slowly tipped toward the water below while the flame shot out the back like a roman candle; both lighted the way as the car plunged toward Wechsler's Creek, not far from Clark's dreamed-of campground. The Olds exploded just before it hit the surface.

Phibert later reconstructed the accident for Oliver. A large truck had turned in front of them, blocking the side road; they had no choice but to go straight. Wechsler either didn't see or didn't care about the new signal; he went right through the red light. But traffic was coming from the other side of the valley, coming directly toward him on the single lane. He must have turned to the left, trying for the closed lane, but instead hit a pyramid of rebar that lifted the car right through the guard rails and over the edge.

It took almost an hour to pull the car from the creek.

When she finally returned from her sales calls, Adrian found Oliver sitting on her stoop, a few tears falling down his cheeks. They cancelled their plans for dinner.

Chapter Eighteen

Sunday was a bust. The weather continued to be gloomy and Oliver wasn't in the best of moods. He breakfasted on buttered toast and three cups of coffee, and it seemed that the tongues of fog that joined the sky with the distant river, momentarily visible through the front window, were soon going to invade the apartment.

He moped around for a while in a desultory way, flipping through the *Times*, drinking more coffee—Adrian was now making it decaffeinated—and still putting off calling Florence.

At noon Oliver made tuna sandwiches, feeling useful for a change. They avoided talk of "the situation," as he had come to think of the unexpected mayhem in his old home town. To fill the silence Adrian told him she had to drive over to Asheville; did he want to come along?

"No," he answered. "The reason I can't get started is the thought of making all these phone calls ... but I'd rather talk to Florence on the phone than meet her in person. You go ahead and I'll wait here for you to get back."

He waited until she was well on her way, and then a while longer while he gathered his thoughts. It was past one o'clock when he finally called his sister.

Florence had heard on the radio about the arrests of Ackermann and Black and their "henchmen," and of course about "the shootout at the hotel," but there had been nothing in the news about the events on the bridge. Nor did Scoop or anyone else have pictures of that scene. Telling her was difficult, and took a while, but as shocked as she sounded, her voice took on a rather indifferent tone when she asked about funeral plans for Linda.

"There are still three places left in the family plot at the Fernglade Cemetery. I guess she can have one of those ... if you still consider her family, Oliver."

They agreed to meet the next morning to discuss arrangements. When they hung up, he was surprised that they'd spoken for more than an hour; they hadn't had such a long conversation in years.

He wanted to stretch his legs, so he left the apartment and strolled down to the bridge, pleasantly surprised at how easy it was to walk; Saturday's follow-up session with Dr. Hill had done wonders. He sat and watched the river flow for half an hour or so, his grief over losing Imogene interspersed with a mixture of sadness and relief over Linda's death. Both feelings easily dissipated whenever Adrian came into his mind; it suddenly came to him that he was being self-indulgent—youthful—with his fickle moods. He walked back to Adrian's with what felt like new purpose ... and a spring in his step.

He called Sheriff Phibert and asked for Linda's body to be released to the funeral home in Burnsville. He also told the sheriff about the drugs hidden in Wechsler's caskets. Then he got the bad news: Black was out on bail.

"Sorry, Swindler, even though there's going to be a murder charge lodged against him, he's out. Ackermann wasn't as lucky; that dead eagle in cold storage seems to mean more than a human death. He's locked up. But Black's out."

"Even with my testimony on what Clark Wechsler said?"

"Even with that."

"How did he get out on a Sunday?" Oliver almost shouted.

"I told you, he's got hot-shot lawyers. One of them goes to the same church as the magistrate, and after the service he set up a special hearing, and Black posted bail about an hour ago. You know how it is in a place like this.

"Lou and Harry and a couple of other guys—the ones that shot the game—have a pile of warrants against them, so they're being held over until we can formally charge them, along with Ackermann. The grand jury meets on Monday; I'll call you then. Want me to send a few men over?"

"No, thanks," he answered. "I'll be fine. But I appreciate the offer ... and all your help, Sheriff."

In fact he was worried about Black. The man had one hell of a temper and nobody and nothing to take it out on. Yet maybe he understood that he couldn't dare any more trouble.

He called Greig Davis at his house and explained they'd have to have another short paper the following week. "Although," he said, "the front page will have a story like no other paper, at least for a week or so."

Davis laughed and told him not to worry.

Scoop's answering service told him that Scoop was out for the day.

Adrian arrived home just before five.

"I realize there's nothing to be happy about, but why don't we get cleaned up and go to dinner. That place in Weaverville— La Cucina Milana. I'm sure I can get reservations if I call now. It's usually not terribly busy on a Sunday—just pastors and their families, birthday groups, that sort of thing. I know they'll have a table for two."

"Okay," he sighed, "might as well, but my heart's not in it."

The viaduct was closed to all traffic. A detour had been set up that led to the old country road along the banks of Wechsler's Creek. It twisted and turned, and Adrian drove slowly. It was already starting to get dark.

"You have to watch it along here," she said, "the deer are apt to jump out without warning, especially at this time of day."

It took them half an hour to reach the restaurant, which, he was glad to discover, exceeded her description. The only other patrons were two large groups and two other couples. They had a good wine served beside a crackling fire; dinner was prepared from scratch. Machine-made Oriental carpets covered the wooden floor, high-backed chairs surrounded old oak tables, and the walls were devoted to French and Italian movie posters of films that all featured—for reasons unexplained—gorillas. A scale model of the Empire State Building whose King Kong climbed up and down at the touch of a switch stood in the corner by the men's room door. There was no wild game on the menu.

After excellent panna cotta and cannoli served with coffee, they sipped brandy and talked quietly about the last week.

"Oliver, there's one thing I never understood. What was the light that was supposed to drive you out of control on the road to Mars Hill?"

"I realized what it was when you mentioned the full-page ad for the new mini-mall in Burnsville. It was a big searchlight mounted on a truck bed. They're easy to rent, and remember, Black used to be a press agent so he's probably familiar with them. If they search the records they'll probably find his fine hand somewhere. What I assume is that he leased the searchlight, and then had the brothers load it into the truck and park up there on the ledge right after dark. Then they simply waited for me to return home. I suspect that Black followed me and then raced ahead of me after I finished dinner. There aren't many vintage Beetles like mine on the road—it would have been easy to identify mine. I even remember a car passing me going like hell just before the car went out of control; that was probably him—he probably signaled them with his headlights."

As they rose to leave a blast of thunder and the sound of pouring rain on the roof filled the restaurant. A brilliant flash of lightning crackled by the front window, aiming for the nearest power line, and almost immediately every light went out. Moments later the manager appeared with candles for each table; the waiters distributed complimentary glasses of brandy.

Oliver toasted Adrian's charm and saluted her health. As they touched glasses, he reached into his pocket, took out the ring, and set it on the table in front of her. To his relief, but as expected, the lack of ceremony seemed not to bother her at all. She picked it up with a smile, and without a word, slipped it onto her fourth finger. The "ring finger."

It was almost ten o'clock, and except for them the restaurant was empty; it was clearly long past Sunday closing time. They thanked their host and walked out to the car.

Adrian drove back from the restaurant to the bridge. The rain had stopped, the air was clean and refreshed, and everything was sharper and clearer in their headlights than on the trip over. The roads and trees glistened with dripping remnants of the storm, and no lights glowed from houses or streetlamps. The downed power lines had served a wide area.

With a flash of white and brown, a deer darted out from the woods on Oliver's right and crossed the road, missing the front fender by a hair. Adrian braked and pulled over to the side. "Every time that happens I get scared out of my wits," she said.

As she slowly pulled back on the road, the car was blindingly lit with the high beams of an approaching car. Its horn blew and the car passed them with such speed that their car shook in the windstream.

"Good lord," Oliver said, his voice trembling. "That's a crazy way to drive on these roads."

"At least I wasn't farther out on the road."

She drove even slower than before.

Oliver turned on the radio, tuned it to a pop station, and began to relax to the silky smooth voice of Mel Tormé. A mist rose from the river; it felt like a perfect evening. There were no other cars on the road.

About five miles from Fernglade a faint white light became visible on the overhead visors folded against the car roof.

Adrian adjusted the rearview mirror to cut the glare and took her foot off the accelerator. The light from behind faded. As they crossed a low bridge that spanned a creek, she slowed, then sped up again. She was silent as they began the two-mile-long descent of Mesmer Hill—so named because of the number of people who had fallen asleep at the wheel and gone off the road. At the bottom of the hill, the road curved left following Wechsler's Creek. She glanced into the rearview mirror and said, "There are some bright headlights coming up fast and I think, from their height, it's a truck. A big one. And he's driving way too fast for this road."

Oliver twisted around to look out the window. She wasn't kidding. The headlights were high off the ground, and getting brighter.

Adrian pumped the brakes to signal with her rear lights.

"He's getting closer," he said, "and I don't think he planning to slow down. Either his brakes are out, or it's deliberate." He thought about the previous "accident" and wondered: Could Black be trying again? Still?

Adrian pushed the accelerator. She was an excellent driver and knew this road well. Their tail picked up speed at the same rate, coming closer every second.

"He must be crazy, Oliver," she said. "He'll run us off the

road, and around here that's not a good idea. The creek bank on the left is really steep, and there's nothing on the right except a cliff."

She hunched over the wheel, knuckles greenish-white in the dashboard's glow. Their headlights were on high beam, and every tree trunk and blade of roadside grass stood out in sharp detail, the weeds bending to the shoulder as they roared past.

The road narrowed ahead where the creek turned away. "Oliver, hold tight. Up ahead the road goes through a rock canyon—it's called the Devil's Grotto—should've been widened years ago—don't talk. I need to concentrate."

Oliver saw that there was no more than two feet of clearance on the right side, and nothing—not even a guard rail—on the left.

"We have to get through there before he reaches us," Adrian said, as much to herself as to Oliver. She knew that at the end of the grotto, where the road turned sharply again, the truck would have to slow down to make the curve.

Still twisted around in his seat, staring like a gopher hypnotized by a cobra, Oliver said, far too loudly, "He's coming up really fast!"

The inside of the car was bright with the truck's headlights; every imperfection in the roof's upholstery was backlit. Adrian hit a bump and an old pile of newspapers fell off the seat and spread across the floor.

"Hang on," she said and pushed the accelerator to the floor. With a burst of speed the car leapt ahead and the rocks of the grotto flew past.

They were through the gap. With the panache and intense calm of a race-car driver, Adrian skewed the wheel and followed the road where it veered to the right. Oliver felt like an extra in *Thunder Road*; he later swore they were on two wheels for a second or two. Only a top-notch driver, and one who knew the road, could have gotten away with such a maneuver.

The other driver wasn't as good. Instead of righting the top-heavy truck at the end of the turn, he kept too far to the right; the truck veered off the road, and the front wheels drove directly up the wall of rock. Within seconds, the ten-wheeler dumptruck was rolling topsy turvy, end over end and side over side, until with a blast of sound it landed upside down at the edge of the creek bank. There, in a silence broken only by the sound of falling shards of rock, it hung as if on an invisible thread, teetering above the steep bank of the creek..

Adrian quickly came to a stop, then backed up fifty yards or so and cut the engine. She grabbed a flashlight from the glove compartment and the two of them walked cautiously toward the truck. It was still balanced on the precipice between the road and the drop-off, its wheels spinning over their heads. Its headlights were smashed to smithereens and twisted metal littered the road. As they watched, it began to slide down the bank, and in the gleam of Adrian's flashlight they saw the driver inside the cab, banging frantically on the glass. It was Simon Black; they could see his terrified face and hear his muffled cries for help. But the truck was starting to slide down to the water, slipping in agonizing slow motion but as relentlessly as flower petals opening in a nature film.

For a moment the truck stopped, caught on an outcropping. Grabbing the flashlight from Adrian's hand, he clambered down the grassy verge to the water's edge. The bank was steep, and his back and neck hurt from his contortions in the car, but he continued toward the water, as Black continued to scream.

Oliver picked up a heavyish rock and threw it at the windshield, but it didn't even crack the glass, just bounced off into the river as the truck began to slide again. The dead headlights and the front of the hood were already under water, and he could see Black's nose distorted against the glass as he struggled with the power window switch—useless, of course—and the locked door.

Water leaked from the engine compartment through the heating vents and every other opening, slowly filling the cab. Starlight reflected on the ripples as they swelled up about his neck.

Oliver pulled the borrowed pistol from his pocket and aimed for the spot between Black's eyes. He couldn't tell if the man's wide-open eyes were gazing at him with terror or with a plea to shoot. In the end it didn't matter: Oliver slowly lowered the pistol and put it back in his pocket. *I would have done it for a dying animal,* he thought, *but not for him.*

At that moment, the truck was pulled into the river's flow and soon everything was gone, the water eddying swiftly where the truck had disappeared. Oliver climbed slowly back up to the road. Adrian was crying softly, leaning against the car. He gently took the keys from her and drove the rest of the way back to Fernglade; they encountered no other traffic.

They parked in front of the newspaper office, in what was fast becoming his new home away from home, and he opened the front door with his bright new key.

With the flashlight to guide him, he reached Mary-Beth's phone and, for what he hoped was the last time in the foreseeable future, called Sheriff Phibert's office. The 24-hour answering service picked up, and after a moment, after ascertaining it was a true emergency, switched him through to the sheriff's house.

"Sheriff, this is Oliver Swindler," he said. "I'm calling from the newspaper. Adrian Knapp and I just witnessed an accident along County Road 32. Simon Black tried to force us off the road into the creek just beyond the Devil's Grotto. You know the spot, right? Well, he misjudged the road and hit that rock retaining wall, and the truck went into the river—Black was trapped in the cab. I tried to break the window and windshield but couldn't do it."

As an afterthought, he added: "We thought you'd want to know."

"Swindler, stay where you are," the sheriff said with a hint of a sigh. "I'll be there shortly."

From behind Davis's closed door a miniature desk clock chimed the hour. It was midnight.

They stepped outside, sat quietly on the steps leading to the office door, and listened to the soft rush of the waters of Wechsler's Creek and, from the top of a nearby tree, a screech owl asking:

"Who! Who!"

About the Author

Peter Loewer is a writer, graphic artist, photographer, and botanical illustrator who has written more than 30 books on natural history, gardening, great gardeners, and science for children.

He graduated from the Albright Art School of the University of Buffalo with a degree in graphics and a minor in art history, and upon graduation was awarded the Max Beckmann Fellowship to the Brooklyn Museum Art.

Among his groundbreaking works are the first book on ornamental grasses, *Growing and Decorating with Ornamental Grasses* (1973); the first book on nocturnal flowers for bloom and fragrance, *The Evening Garden* (1994); and *Thoreau's Garden* and *Jefferson's Garden*. His eponymous book, *The Wild Gardener*, was named one of the best 75 garden books of the 20th century by the American Horticultural Society.

For many years he hosted a monthly call-in garden show on public radio in Asheville, NC, where he lives with his wife, illustrator Jean Jenkins (who also designed the cover of this book). Peter has taught at the North Carolina Arboretum, UNC Asheville's OLLI Center, Montreat Elderhostel, Asheville-Buncombe Technical Community College, and at Penland School in Spruce Pine. He also practices printmaking and works on pen and colored-pencil renderings of native plants and their pollinating insects.

Peter worked for a time as a small-town newspaper editor, out of which experience came the inspiration for *The Last of the Swindlers*, his first murder mystery.

Also available from Pisgah Press

Mombie: The Zombie Mom	**Barry Burgess**	$16.95
Letting Go: Poems 1983-2003	**Donna Lisle Burton**	$14.95
Way Past Time for Reflecting		$17.95
From Roots … to Wings		$14.95
Gabriel's Songbook	**Michael Amos Cody**	$17.95
A Twilight Reel		$17.95

Robin Russell Gaiser

Musical Morphine: Transforming Pain One Note at a Time	$17.95

Finalist, USA Book Awards—Health: Alternative Medicine, 2017

Open for Lunch	$17.95

rhythms on a flaming drum	**Michael Hopping**	$16.95

C. Robert Jones

I Like It Here! Adventures in the Wild & Wonderful World of Theatre	$30.00

LANKY TALES

Lanky Tales, Vol. I: The Bird Man & other stories	$9.00
Lanky Tales, Vol. II: Billy Red Wing & other stories	$9.00
Lanky Tales, Vol. III: A Good and Faithful Friend & other stories	$9.00
The Mystery at Claggett Cove	$9.00

Homo Sapiens: A Violent Gene?	**Mort Malkin**	$22.95

A.D. Reed

Reed's Homophones: A Comprehensive Book of Sound-alike Words	$14.95

Dave Richards

Swords in their Hands: George Washington and the Newburgh Conspiracy	$24.95

Finalist, USA Book Award—History 2014

Trang Sen: A Novel of Vietnam	**Sarah-Ann Smith**	$19.50

Nan Socolow

Invasive Procedures: Earthquakes, Calamities, & poems from the midst of life	$17.95

RF Wilson

Deadly Dancing	THE RICK RYDER MYSTERY SERIES	$15.95
Killer Weed		$14.95
The Pot Professor		$17.95

Pisgah Press, LLC
PO Box 9663, Asheville, NC 28815-0663
www.pisgahpress.com